Hunted in the Valley

C.R. PUGH

ISBN-13: 978-1981777600
ISBN-10: 1981777601

TO MOM

You never pushed me to banish my dreams…
Instead you taught me to harness them,
and give them a happy ending.

1
Ravyn

The house was finally silent for the night; everyone asleep in their beds. All except me.

Just five more minutes, I thought as I lay there, staring at the ceiling. It was starting to sink in, what I must do tonight, the eve of my ninth birthday.

I was running away; making the long walk into the Old Sequoia Valley.

I'd thought of that ancient forest many times. The thought of actually journeying into it had my teeth nearly chattering from fear. A young girl like me had little chance of surviving out there.

Dinner earlier this evening was more subdued than usual. Everyone stared into their soup, trying to ignore the uncomfortable silence and the fact that I was supposed to be banished by the Elders tomorrow evening. Of course, they weren't aware I knew this information.

Pretending that everything was normal at that last evening meal was one of the most difficult things I'd ever done, but I was accustomed to lying. Though I'd wanted to scream at them, at the unfairness of it all, I kept my silence. It would do me no good. I was different, and I had secrets that would never be accepted here.

As I looked around the table, studying each of them, I wondered what they were thinking or if they had any feelings at all concerning my fate. Every so often, Father's spoon paused halfway to his mouth and his jaw clenched. Then his shoulders would slump in a deep sigh of resignation before continuing to eat again. Mother looked up only once. Her eyes lingered on my face but for a moment. That was all I'd needed to see; the unshed tears glistening in her eyes. When Father cleared his throat, she'd quickly ducked her head again as if she'd been caught doing something illegal. Perhaps she wasn't as indifferent to me as I'd always thought.

My sister, Camellia, seemed to be playing with her soup rather than eating it and refused to make eye contact with me. Though we were twins, Camellia and I were not identical. She was the spitting image of our mother, with hair the color of wheat and a perfect, porcelain complexion. Everyone in Terran loved her; her obvious beauty and gentle nature. Camellia was content to stay indoors, sew pretty dresses, and help Mother manage the household. The Elders had deemed her the perfect example of what a young lady ought to be. She would undoubtedly have suitors lining up for her when she turned sixteen.

Then there was me, the total opposite. My hair was pitch-black like my father's with skin that freckled from the sunshine. Keeping a home, cooking, and sewing didn't interest me at all, even though I'd learned how to. My amusement came from playing outside, climbing trees, and running amuck, as the neighbors so plainly put it. The only thing Camellia and I shared was the color of our eyes: a vivid turquoise we inherited from our father.

It's true that I didn't set much store by the rules. Father was constantly scolding me for saying the wrong thing and inadvertently insulting someone. I asked questions about what lay beyond the fields and forests of Terran, beyond the electric fence that had been built around our quiet city. No one in Terran seemed curious about the Valley like I was. My teachers dealt out punishments for questions and said I was being impertinent.

"The fences were built by our ancestors to keep us safe from what lies within the Old Sequoia Valley," my teacher had informed me. But this only led to more questions.

What was out in the Valley that was so dangerous?

The adults looked down their noses at me or ignored me, and the other parents had forbidden their children from playing with me from an early age. They claimed that my behavior was peculiar and worried that it would rub off on their children, even though I was not the only overactive child in Terran. If anyone in the clan knew about my *real* peculiarity, I would have been banished long ago.

Surely there were people in the world beyond the fence that had strange abilities like mine? Or at least people who wouldn't condemn them? There had to be some place out there where I didn't have to hide who I was or what I could do.

It was a secret I had never let a soul know about. But that wasn't the only reason I was running away from home.

There was a law in Terran that prevented overpopulation within our isolated city. Each family was allowed only two children: one boy and one girl. If a family already had a son, and ended up giving birth to another son, the second boy was to be given over to the Elders. It was the same for girls. No one knew what the Elders did with the infants, and if they knew they wouldn't say.

I believed it was cruel. Infants should stay with their mothers, no matter what. Where did they take the babies? Did they die? I'd probably never know.

But this law had been broken for Camellia and me. One of us should have been taken when we were born. I finally found out the reason why four days ago.

Sliding out from under the covers and placing my socked feet on the floor, I stared across the room at my sister. The rise and fall of her shoulders held me mesmerized for a moment. She was sound asleep, unaware of what I was about to do.

I removed the nightgown I had donned that evening to hide the shirt and trousers I wore underneath, then reached under the bed and pulled out my hidden rucksack. I'd been stealing food and supplies over the last four days; anything that might be of use to me in the forest. My stomach clenched with dread and hunger. I needed to eat but I feared that anything I consumed would come right back up.

Careful not to wake Camellia, I grabbed my bag and boots and padded softly to the door. A sense of familiarity washed over me. Was it just four days ago that I'd been doing this very same thing? I had only been heading to the kitchen, but it was the night that had changed everything for me.

Four days ago, I'd been sent to my room without supper, so I had gone to bed hungry. When I was certain it was late enough, I had decided to sneak down to the kitchen and steal something out of the pantry. I felt sure mother and father had gone to bed as well, so I slipped out of bed and tiptoed to the door. Careful not to make even the smallest sound, I turned the knob. The door groaned as I inched it open.

I froze and pinched my eyes shut, straining my ears for any sign that someone had heard me. Over my shoulder, Camellia slept soundly. My stomach churned as I waited for father to barrel out of his room, which was next to ours. If he caught me, I wasn't sure what he would do, and I didn't want to find out.

Once I was certain no one was coming, I let out the breath I'd been holding and crept down the hall. As I neared the kitchen, I heard voices. Mother and father were still up, talking. I held my breath again, sure that I was about to be discovered. Anxiously gritting my teeth together, I took a tiny step back, preparing to make a silent escape, when I heard father mention my name.

"Sona, it won't be much longer until Ravyn is gone and things can … go back to normal."

Curiosity getting the better of me, I peered around the corner to see father pacing back and forth across the kitchen floor. Mother sat at our dining table, hands gripping a cup of tea.

"Perry, she is still just a child." Mother set down her tea and rested her weary head in her hands. "This isn't right."

"We've been over this before. You know why Elder Dagan insisted we wait. A case of twins had never been seen before and the Elders told us we couldn't keep them both – not forever." Father sighed and ran his hands through his hair. "This is the only way. We must be strong."

"Yes, I know you're right." Mother paused to take another sip of tea. Her shoulders sagged and there were shadows beneath her eyes, as if she hadn't been sleeping. "When is he coming for her? Did you talk to Dagan about the details?"

"He told me to expect him on the evening before their birthday …"

I heard no more. A loud rushing sound had filled my ears and my heart had shattered into a million pieces. The Elders were going to take me away, even after all this time. I'd assumed, since we'd grown older, we were exempt from their awful rules.

After the initial shock had subsided, I began making my plans. Elder Dagan would come, but I wouldn't be here. I wouldn't let them throw me away like those other children.

My heart began racing again as I looked back at Camellia's still form on the bed. It was better this way. If I didn't go now, I never would. Just as I had done four days ago, I crept down the hall, avoiding the floorboards that creaked. I took one last glance into my mother's well-kept kitchen. Everything was just as it should be. The counters were cleared. The pots and pans hung neatly above the stove. Dainty little flowers lined the window sill and the entire house smelled of the rose-scented candles she'd made earlier this week. My eyes pricked with unshed tears. I blinked them back and took a deep breath, resigned to my fate.

With a quiet sigh, I turned on my heel and stepped into the foyer. After pulling on my boots, I stood frozen for several minutes, just staring at the doorknob. There was a tight feeling in my chest now and a lump in my throat that I couldn't seem to swallow. I wouldn't know what to expect beyond the fence, but I didn't have any other choice.

With that thought, I turned the knob and walked out the door, vowing never again to return.

2
Thorne

8 years later

"For the last time, Tallon, you cannot go with us on the hunt."

She had found me before dawn and had been badgering me relentlessly. Now inside the village's large stable, Tallon continued to plead her case. Her efforts were futile. I continued to saddle my stallion while she paced back and forth in front of the stall.

"But I'm ready, Thorne. It's not fair! You went on your first hunt with Commander Hawke when you turned fifteen."

"At fifteen, I had completed five years of training, not two. And if Commander Hawke had declared me unfit or unqualified, I would not have argued."

I clenched my jaw at her impertinence. Being her big brother *and* her commander had become complicated. She could not continue to think of me as family when we were training with the Warriors. As a Warrior she must respect my command. When we returned to Peton, perhaps I would place her under another Warrior. Surely that would temper her childish ways.

"You're pouting like a little girl. For that reason, and many others, you will not be going."

Grabbing the reins, I led my horse out of the stall. Tallon had folded her arms across her chest and was leaning against the stall door. Ignoring her sullen expression, I strode past and exited the stables. She followed in hot pursuit.

It was just a short walk through the pine trees to the main road of Peton. The other five Warriors who made up the hunting party were already there. The main road was basically a clearing that meandered through the trees. It ran from the front gates of Peton all the way to the Council Building, the epicenter of our great village. Peton had been constructed around this wide pathway long ago, just on the foothills of Mount Asa. Homes and shops had been built within the thin wooded area all along the road.

Just ahead, the road came into view. Villagers were milling about, doing business or simply wishing the Warriors a safe journey. Two horse-drawn wagons were already lined up on the road. Archer and Max, the Warriors assigned to drive them, circled around them to make certain they were fully stocked and ready to go. Gunter, Pierce, and Brock stood close by, preparing their own mounts.

"You think we won't find any exiles on the first day, huh?" I overheard Gunter ask Brock. "I think you underestimate Thorne's tenacity. I'm betting we'll reach our quota by lunchtime tomorrow," he chuckled.

"That's a foolish expectation," Archer chimed in. "The Valley is much too large an area to search in such a short time."

"What's your wager then?" Brock challenged.

Archer paused in his task and replied, "Day three." Then he smirked at Gunter. "I'll also wager that Gunter will be complaining about sleeping on the ground before breakfast tomorrow." Brock and Max guffawed even as Gunter snorted and muttered something indecipherable.

If I had not been irritated with Tallon I would have laughed out loud. He had definitely pegged Gunter correctly.

"And *I'm* betting that we won't make it into the Valley before dark if you don't finish packing," growled Pierce.

They continued muttering amongst themselves even as Tallon and I approached them. I continued to quietly lecture her. "Tallon, you have three more years of training to complete. Until then, you'll stay behind."

"But, Thorne …"

Halting at once, I loomed over her, narrowing my eyes at her second attempt to argue. "If you want to be treated like a Warrior, then you must start acting like one. A Warrior would not question their commander's orders. The Valley is no place for one who has not completed their training. I suggest you get back to it immediately."

Color rushed to Tallon's cheeks as she received her set-down. Pressing her lips together for a moment, she nodded and replied, "Yes, sir … *Commander*."

She turned on her heel and stomped away, back down the road toward the Council Building and the Warriors' training center like a spoiled brat. I gritted my teeth to keep from shouting at her. I hated to rebuke her all the time, but how else was she going to learn? If she were any other Warrior in our clan, there would have been severe consequences for her constant arguments and sarcasm.

I suppose there was no one else to blame. We didn't have a mother and our father, an Elder, was too wrapped up in Peton's politics to raise his own family. It had been left up to me and my older sister to see to my family's discipline.

"Big brother strikes again, huh?" Gunter, having snuck up behind me, pounded my shoulder in brotherly affection and grinned like a fool.

"I was just thinking how I've been too easy on Tallon all these years. She does not see that she is unfit to join us. Were we as quick to rush into the dangers of battle at that age?"

Gunter laughed outright at my question. "Of course we were. We were foolish boys then, and many would say we are still foolhardy. The Valley isn't called the Warrior's Playground for nothing. We wanted to play with the big boys at her age, too."

"Was that only four years ago?" I murmured, fingering the vicious scars on my right cheek. "She will never be ready to ride off to battle in my eyes."

"That is only because she's your little sister. It's normal to feel protective. And it's not exactly a battle we're heading off to, you know," he pointed out.

"Each time we leave the safety of Peton, there's a chance of meeting danger."

Gunter nodded. "True. I know you don't want to hear it, but she is much like you."

Crossing my arms over my chest, I peered over my shoulder at Tallon, who was still angrily marching down the road through the village. A moment later she was swallowed up by the crowd. "I do not see that."

"She is petite, like her mother, but strong and cunning like you. That's your stubbornness you see walking away from you." Gunter laughed a bit too much at that last remark. "Look, she came to you as family, but you were expecting her to act like one of the male Warriors. They never question orders because they know their place."

"Humph. Like you?"

Gunter chuckled. "Why don't you just marry her off? Then you wouldn't have to be the bad guy anymore. Some other man will have the privilege … uh, I mean *duty* to yell at her."

Placing my fists on my hips, I glared at him. "And who do you suggest I give her to when she comes of age? I doubt anyone would take her off my hands with that attitude. Anyone stronger than her would get fed up with her sharp tongue and send her back to me. Anyone weaker than her would be dead in a week."

Gunter threw back his head and bellowed with laughter. "Thorne, you always take life too seriously. I have taken it upon myself to try to loosen you up! And speaking of suitors, my friend -"

"We are not having this conversation again," I interrupted instantly, turning my attention back to my stallion and supplies.

"- I think it's about time you started thinking about a potential suitor. There are many fine women who have had their eye on you. Some have even approached me about it."

"I don't have the time or temperament for a life-mate," I muttered, mostly to myself.

"Your sister, Kemena, certainly enjoys being married. I don't believe her husband thinks she is the burden you believe a wife would be."

"Well, Kemena was always meant to be a wife, and Aaron is not a Warrior," I pointed out. "It's only a burden when your woman sits at home and frets about you all the time." Not only that, but I did not want to constantly worry that I would die out in the Valley and leave a family behind.

Gunter rubbed his smooth chin with his hand while he speculated. "You need a woman who would fight alongside you. There are many females who are training to be Warriors."

It *would* be better to have a woman who understood the life I had chosen. But I knew every female Warrior, and none of them had ever sparked my interest. They acted more like brothers-in-arms, which was the way it should be.

“You know they don’t suit me.”

“Well, you, my friend, are not getting any younger. You’ll need someone to take care of you as you get into your old age.”

“Don’t make me knock that grin off your face, Gunter.”

Before he could make another witty comeback, the other Warriors approached. “What is it?” My words were sharp, but I did not think I could tolerate any more badgering.

“There’s a new bet this coming hunt, Commander,” Archer said with a smirk, ignoring my obvious foul humor.

I narrowed my eyes suspiciously at the redhead. “It had better not include blowing up our supply wagon or any of the Warriors.”

The men snickered. Archer was well-known for tinkering with explosives, one of the reasons I liked bringing him on the hunt.

Max, a younger member of the team, chimed in, his eyes bright with enthusiasm. “There’s been talk amongst the trade-runners of a new beast in the wilderness.”

“The trade-runners are full of gossip.” I rolled my eyes at his superstitious nature.

“They say it’s deadlier than a Night Howler,” Max continued, refusing to be put off. “The trade-runners said they happened upon the dark beast a few weeks ago. It was standing over four dead men.”

I nearly scoffed, but his ominous words silenced my retort.

“They said it was injured badly,” Max continued. “Apparently it had been stabbed and shot multiple times, but it didn’t die. When the beast spotted them, blood dripped from its fangs. Its eyes were so terrifying they fled before it could suck out their souls. Long black hairs were all that was found on the victims. They said it must have been some sort of demon."

The men exchanged skeptical glances and then broke out into gales of laughter. I grinned and slapped Max on the back so he would not feel humiliated in front of the older Warriors.

I knew I was going to regret asking, but I did so anyway. "What is this bet then? Which Warrior will be the first to find this demon and kill it?"

"If anyone could kill a demon it would be you," Gunter declared with a wry smile. "With one glare, you would have that demon begging you for mercy, Thorne!"

All but Max snickered again as I shoved Gunter toward his horse and then mounted my own. "If you are all finished with your foolish talk then I'd like to get this hunt started."

Gunter kicked his mount into position behind mine, as was his rightful place. There was no one in Peton I trusted more than him. We had known each other all our lives which was why I had chosen him as my second-in-command when I had earned the title of commander a year ago.

Pierce and Brock followed Gunter on horseback while Archer and Max each drove their own horse-drawn carts. Archer's cart was filled with the food, supplies, and weapons we would need for seven days. A week was generous for a hunt, but former Commander Hawke had trained me to always be prepared for the unexpected.

Max's cart would hold new captives that we would bring home to Peton from the Old Sequoia Valley. This was our sole purpose for the hunt. These men and women were not meant to be slaves, though there were always some who saw it that way. Peton's forefathers had wanted to rescue any who had been banished into the forest. It had saved many people from certain death or starvation out on their own.

Warriors went out three times a year to retrieve exiles from the forest. Once in spring after the snows melted, once in summer, and once in the early fall before winter set in again. It had been a tradition for as long as I could remember. The number of exiles we needed each season varied depending on Peton's needs. Over the last few months, two of those captives had died of sickness. Our head blacksmith had retired recently and the captive that had worked as his assistant was promoted to head blacksmith. He now needed his own assistant. One of Kemena's healing apprentices married and decided to remain home to be a housewife. Four new exiles would be needed to fill those open positions.

There were some seasons when we did not manage to fill the quota. If that happened, then we all took a share of the extra workload. Other seasons we brought home more than enough. Regardless of what kind of luck we had in the Valley, we never left an exile behind if they needed help. Besides, there were always many jobs inside the city that needed tending to.

I whistled loudly to alert my Warriors that we were on the move. At the signal, many more citizens of Peton came out of their homes and shops to line the main road. They waved and cheered us off. This was one of the many traditions of Peton that I had always treasured. Even as a boy, I remembered watching the Warriors and hoping for the chance to join them. Upon returning from the hunt in a few days' time, I knew that our people would welcome us back in the same manner.

We rode through the city gates and out onto the beautiful meadow that separated our city from the edges of the Valley. Our borders were protected by a stone wall about twenty feet high that stretched around the western half of Peton, while Mount Asa served as a protective barrier on the eastern side. The Fairuza Sea was just beyond the mountain range.

Gunter quickened his horse's gait through the lush grass and joined me at the front of the line as we left the city walls behind. It irritated me that I envied his boyish face, free from the remnants of battles that we had fought together. The women all flocked to him with his green eyes and shaggy, brown hair that seemed to lie perfectly in place. I liked my own hair cropped shorter than most. It was easier to manage, but it tended to curl up and out in every direction.

"If you are thinking to continue badgering me about finding a life-mate, Gunter, your time is wasted."

"Actually, I was just going to let you know that I have found someone suitable for *myself*," Gunter answered back thoughtfully. "Now you don't have to fight so hard against finding one for yourself."

“I’m not fighting it! When I find a female that pleases me and does not cringe at the sight of me, then I will say the Binding Words. I have too many responsibilities to even consider it, anyway. And just who are you pursuing?”

“I haven’t spoken to her or her family yet, so I don’t feel I should divulge that information.”

I rolled my eyes as he fell back in line with the others, declaring the conversation over. We moved further and further away from our strong city, and I let my mind reflect on what Gunter had been trying to tell me. I was of a marriageable age, but none of the women appealed to me. The ones that might have been suitable shuddered at the scars on my face. The title of ‘Commander’ had drawn some interest, but I saw through their false flattery immediately. I was only eighteen when I had been declared commander of Peton, the youngest in history. Having held the position for just one year, I could not lose focus.

We finally reached the edge of the Valley and entered without hesitation. The trees in this outer edge were small, mostly fruit trees. The forest was thin here and the sun shone brightly through the foliage. The sounds of birds and other small animals rustling around could be heard, signaling that we were still in a safe zone.

As we moved deeper into the forest, the noise of the animals diminished. The sequoias were taller and grew much closer together, blocking out more and more of the sunlight. What was a happy meadow was now a dark and threatening forest, full of dangers that lurked in its shadows. Barbarians – men, and sometimes women, who had been born in the wilderness – lived like wild things. They were uncivilized, uneducated, and all-too-often starving, which made them do unspeakable things for survival. Cannibalism was not unheard of amongst the barbarians. These were not the kind that did well as captives in Peton, as Commander Hawke had learned from experience.

There were several other predators that lived and prowled in the Valley. Yellow-eyed Sabers grew up to four feet tall at the shoulder, ran on four paws, and had black and gray striped fur that blended easily with the shadows of the forest. They were named for their yellow eyes that glowed as they hunted their prey in the dark, and they attacked with long, sharp canines that extended from their jaws like curved blades.

The Night Howlers were even larger, at around five feet tall. This particular beast was nocturnal, had a large body covered in a black, silky mixture of fur and feathers, and its head looked much like a large bird with a sharp hooked beak. The four paws it walked on were built with claws like sharp daggers, and its wings spanned over twenty feet in length. The beasts enjoyed howling through the night; a signal to us that they were nearby.

I had been on every hunt for the last five years, with the exception of one, thanks to one of these flying harpies. Two summers past, the village was set upon by a Night Howler and I had been injured fighting the beast. It took three of us to finally bring it down and we each bore scars on our bodies from the battle. None were as prominent as mine. Three vicious looking claw marks ran down the right side of my face, from my temple down across my cheek where the Howler had taken a swipe at me. One of them ran through the corner of my eye, having nearly taken it out. Kemena, who was a healer, had been beside herself for days until she was certain that I would not lose the sight in that eye. It would have made no difference to me, except that I would never have made commander with partial blindness. They may not have balked at me for being a Warrior, but I would never have been allowed to lead with such a weakness.

I turned in my saddle to check on my Warriors. It was unnecessary, but I did so anyway. Every Warrior was trained to be vigilant in all situations. Hawke had trained most of us, and he had been an excellent teacher.

Just behind Gunter was Pierce, who was just a year younger than Gunter and me. The three of us were the strongest fighters in the group. Pierce was nearly as tall as me, standing around six feet, but with broader shoulders. His brooding demeanor kept people away, except for Archer, who seemed to be his only companion. Archer was the most intelligent Warrior of Peton by far. He was an average fighter with a smaller build, but he excelled in weapons and explosives. Every hunt he produced newer and more effective ways to set protective perimeters around the camp. They were full of nasty surprises for anyone or anything that tried to attack. Then there was Max who was excellent with horses and seemed to have a knack for cooking anything he could get his hands on. Of all the men, Brock was the only new Warrior to the hunt, but a promising recruit at the young age of sixteen. We called him a chameleon because his brown hair and skin seemed to blend in to the forest. The six of us were definitely an odd group, but I only chose the most skilled to be out in the Valley with me.

We were all silent, listening for any noise that would alert us to the possibility of an attack from man or beast. The talk of a demon in the forest had me feeling edgy. It was surely just a fable told to frighten children and keep them from running headlong into danger. Still, I felt a jolt of adrenaline shoot through my blood at the coming hunt. My gut was telling me that this one was not going to be the same dull experience it had been the past few times, and I was eagerly looking forward to the challenge.

The little light that was coming through the trees was fading fast, so I stopped the Warriors behind me with a raised fist.

"Let's make camp here for the night. We'll start the hunt at sunrise."

3
Ravyn

It had been nearly eight years exactly from the night I escaped Terran, and I was on the run again. Once again, I was fighting for my life inside the Old Sequoia Valley. This time I was older, smarter, and better prepared for what I would face.

"She has to be around here somewhere," said a familiar male voice.

Shifting just a bit to the right, I was able to make out the shadows of six soldiers standing beneath the tree in which I was perched. The sun had set hours ago, and the clouds formed a dark blanket to cover the moon. If it wasn't so dark, I'm certain I would know every soldier that prowled beneath me. They had been my comrades once. Now they were my enemies.

I was perfectly hidden within the darkness and the leaves that rustled quietly. My clothes, boots, and hair were pitch-black against the night sky, so they'd have to be looking closely to see the paleness of my skin in the dark. Even if it were daytime, they would still have trouble seeing me through the extensive foliage. The forest in this part of the Valley was extremely thick. The trees grew so close together and the branches were so tangled that, from the ground, it looked much like a basket that had been loosely woven together. Leaning forward carefully, I strained my ears to hear the conversation between the soldiers that were hunting me.

"Her tracks stop right back there. She can't have just disappeared," said a different soldier – this one a female.

They marched in noisy circles beneath the tree, eager to find a trace of my footprints, and they weren't even trying to be quiet about it. That kind of arrogance was going to get them killed out here. I wasn't the only dangerous creature roaming these woods.

"Turn on your spotlights. Search the trees," commanded the first soldier in his deep monotone voice.

Immediately, the forest lit up with thin, powerful beams of light. Their efforts were futile though. The foliage was so dense, they could shine a light right at me and still never see me. Even so, I settled back and drew my knees up to my chest to cover the white of my skin and stayed perfectly still. I didn't want to give them even a hint of a shadow to find.

"There's no sign of her over here," yelled the female from some distance away.

"General Wolfe gave orders for us to locate TS1 and bring her back, so that is what we must do," the first soldier replied.

TS1 – that was me. I was Test Subject One: the highest ranking soldier among them. At least I *was*.

I wasn't always a fighter. The soldiers had found me just a week after leaving Terran. Back then I'd been grateful. They had saved me from starving or being eaten by the Sabers that had been stalking me. I was only nine years old. How was I to know what would happen to me inside the compound? My training to become a soldier began at the age of ten and I never looked back. I was happy and thriving. For seven years I had a purpose. I wanted to be like those soldiers who had saved me.

When I was nearly sixteen, things drastically changed.

It was too dark to tell which of the six soldiers was speaking, but I knew they must be the higher-ranking ones. I thought I recognized the deep voice of Six, or TS6, as General Wolfe liked to call him. I wasn't sure about the female. Maybe it was TS12. They all started to sound the same after a while with their flat, lifeless voices.

General Wolfe only thought of us as numbers. We were expendable. He'd etched those numbers into the backs of our necks, making us his property. TS1 would forever be tattooed on my skin.

I rubbed the back of my neck. The General and his scientists had put me to sleep to mark me so I couldn't stop them. At least I'd been able to resist his brainwashing.

This group had to be close to giving up the chase tonight. The General's soldiers may be decent trackers, but they were terrible at hunting game for food. They would have to return to the compound to restock their supplies soon.

"It's time to go, Six," said the female. "We're not going to find her trail in this darkness."

The sound of approaching boots had me perking up my ears again.

"What are you fools doing?"

A shudder ran through me when I heard a sinister voice that belonged to the most sadistic soldier I knew. It was Two. I was still confident that I was hidden well enough to escape his notice, but I could never be too careful with him. He was a fierce fighter, intelligent, and more powerful than me. I was quick but even my own skill would be no match for him. None of the other soldiers understood why he was ranked lower than me.

"We tracked One to this area but …"

"I know perfectly well what you are doing, Six," he scolded. "What I want to know is why you are shouting so loud that anyone within a square mile could hear you? She's not stupid."

Two's voice was just as menacing as his looks. He was not that much taller than me, not quite six feet tall, but what he lacked in height, he made up for in brute strength. Two was built like a bull, with the darkest skin and eyes I had ever seen; a walking shadow.

Six answered, "We need more food and supplies. We're moving out and heading back to the compound."

"Yes, you do that," Two snarled. "I'll bet the General will be so pleased with your progress. Now get moving!"

The soldiers traipsed back into the forest toward the General's territory, leaving me alone in the dark. Once I was certain they were gone, I settled myself more comfortably on the tree limb and breathed a sigh of relief. I'd had to learn quickly to hide my trail and set false ones to confuse them, but there was always a small part of me that worried about making a mistake.

Reaching for my small rucksack, I pulled out some rope and lashed myself to the branch. This was going to be my bed for the night just in case they decided to come back while I slept. If my count was correct, there were still four search parties out hunting for me, six soldiers in each group. One group almost had me about two weeks ago, but I had managed to overcome them. These weren't just ordinary soldiers. They were more like robots, brainwashed to their master's will. They would keep coming until they'd fulfilled the General's wishes or I was dead. I was going to have to come up with a better plan than just running and hiding forever.

The Old Sequoia Valley was an ancient forest, an enormous buffer that separated all the clans on our tiny continent. According to the General's extensive map, there were five that were close: Terran, Peton, Murray, Ahern, and of course the compound, which was more of a military bunker than an actual clan. There were some who lived in the Valley, but it was foolish to try and do so. When I ran away from Terran eight years ago, I was unfortunate enough to run into a few of the deadly creatures that haunted these regions. I'd sworn that I would never set foot in this forest again, but I was so wrong. I would rather take my chances with a Saber or a Night Howler than be in the hands of the General again. I'd been on the run from him for four weeks now. That was a long time for even the most skilled person, so I knew my luck was going to run out soon. Winter was coming in less than two months, bringing with it a whole new set of obstacles.

Leaning my head back against the tree trunk, I took a deep breath and tried to relax my body. All I needed now was to rest up for a bit and then put more distance between the soldiers and me. With a little skill and a lot of luck, I could shake these soldiers off my trail and finally head east, toward the coast, as I'd always longed to do. For eight long years, I had dreamed of my oceanfront home and the peace I hoped would be found there.

I had only ever told one soul of my dream. Kieron. I'd met him not long after I started living at the compound. We had trained together to be soldiers. He'd been my best friend; my confidante; the one person on this earth that I loved. He knew all my secrets. And then he betrayed me. There was a gaping hole still left in me from the damage he and the General had done. That dream was the one thing that had kept me alive.

As my body drifted off into sleep, I earnestly prayed that my nightmares would leave me alone.

***

Lifting my head off my knees, I opened my eyes. I had been in isolation now for five weeks. At least, I thought it'd been five weeks. It was hard to tell with no windows and no clock. General Wolfe couldn't understand why it wasn't driving me mad to remain alone for this length of time. I wasn't going to clue him in.

The plain white gown I was wearing scratched my skin as I shifted positions in my cot. They had taken my clothes when they began their experiments on me. It was all part of the process of slowly breaking me, but they'd been unsuccessful so far.

It had *been five weeks. I was almost positive.*

The cameras watched me from the corners of the ceiling. They always watched. I didn't look at them anymore, knowing that I would just be giving them something else to document. I stayed still and waited; waited and planned, just like every other day I sat in isolation. I waited for the opportunity to break out of this horrible place and find the freedom I had been longing for.

Maybe it'd been six weeks. Yes, it felt more like six weeks.

The tattoo on the back of my neck began to tingle. It tingled whenever danger was near. They were coming for me again, like they did every week. I could sense the gasses slowly seeping into the room from the vents in the ceiling. I continued to stay still, knowing that panicking and losing control did me no good. I would not *give them anything more to document.*

The gray smoke filled the room quickly. I fought hard against my natural instincts. In the beginning, I had tried to escape the gasses, pounding and clawing at the door, but it was only a waste of my precious energy. I had even tried to hold my breath a few times, but my starving lungs wouldn't hold out for long.

Stretching out on the cot, I breathed evenly. I breathed in and then breathed out. I would not think about being strapped down to that table. I would not think about how he would cut me open for more of my blood. I breathed in and then breathed out.

It had definitely been longer than six weeks. It felt like forever.

The smoke filled my lungs. I clasped my chest to stop the burning, and then my eyes widened in a silent panic. I fought to remain in control, but tears filled my eyes against my will. I didn't try to hide them anymore. They wouldn't be able to see them through the smoke, anyway. My breath came in short gasps through my teeth as I forced my body to lie still on the cot. I wished they would just let me die this time. Just let me die, just let me die, just let me die ...

***

I awoke from my slumber clutching my chest and gasping for breath. There was no burn. No smoke. My tattoo wasn't tingling either. There was only a trace of the tears I'd been crying as I slept. I didn't have an explanation for why my tattoo often tingled when danger was approaching. Perhaps it had been something in the ink the General had used or that the tattoo was directly on my spine. Maybe it only happened to the soldiers that had been marked. Did the others get that sensation when I was in close proximity to them? Regardless, it was my sixth sense and it had been effective.

Wiping my face with my sleeve, I took a deep, cleansing breath to shake off the nightmare. I'd probably slept for a couple of hours, at best. Thankfully, I was still lashed to the tree and my weapons were all accounted for. Daggers were hidden in each of my boots and a pistol was tucked into my belt at the small of my back.

Once my heart rate had slowed, I stuffed the rope back into my rucksack, double-checked my supplies, and climbed down to the ground.

My stomach clenched, needing nourishment, but I had to move on while it was still dark. I wanted to be long gone with no trail to follow. Slinging my bag over my shoulders, I started jogging east again, further away from the General. I was careful not to leave any tracks as I weaved in and out of the trees, avoiding the large roots jutting out of the ground. I stopped only once to lay down a false trail, hoping to merely keep the soldiers running in circles, if they happened to find it at all. I hoped they wouldn't. I really did need a break from the running.

After an hour of hiking through the forest, my stomach's painful groaning convinced me to stop. I'd reached a different part of the Valley. Even in the dark I could see that the trees were different. Before, the trees had been smaller and easy to climb with their many branches intertwined. In this part of the forest, there were no branches close to the ground at all. Sequoias. The Old Sequoia Valley was named for these giants. They seemed to grow a mile high and some of their trunks were three times as wide as I was tall. Climbing these trees was going to be nearly impossible.

I looked around for adequate cover. The overhead canopy blocked out most of the sunlight during the daylight hours, but there were still ferns and other shrubs on the ground where one could easily hide. A person could never be too careful in the Valley. Aside from beasts and soldiers, there were plenty of other dangerous people roaming around. I hadn't quite figured out where they all came from. Were they children like me who had been kicked out of their clan and left to fend for themselves? Were they criminals that had been outlawed? Were they born out here? I hadn't crossed paths with anyone that felt like chatting, so avoiding them ranked high on my list of priorities.

I pulled out the squirrel I had snared and roasted yesterday and devoured it. Once the sun came up I would need to hunt again, but for now, I ate what I had available. It was times like these I was thankful I had come from a clan like Terran. They had their faults, but every person in the clan learned how to recognize and gather nuts, berries, and other plants that were safe for eating. I had become an accomplished hunter of small game out of necessity, but I would have starved long ago if it hadn't been for those plants.

The sound of water gurgling through the brush caught my attention. Once I gathered up my supplies and cleaned up all traces of my presence, I made my way toward the stream.

My eyes were constantly alert and aware of my surroundings as I cupped water into my mouth with my hand. Since I seemed to have lost the soldiers for the time being, I stripped off my clothing and quickly bathed.

I really tried not to complain too much about having to live in the great outdoors but, oh, how I missed being able to bathe on a regular basis – in warm water! I was constantly reminding myself that I would rather freeze to death in a river of ice-cold water than go back to my life with General Wolfe. I was dirty, but I was free, and I wouldn't trade that for anything.

The stream was so refreshing I wanted to stay submerged in it the rest of the morning, but I didn't have any time to waste. I dressed quickly in my black, long-sleeved shirt and black pants, pulled on my boots, and started hiking again.

Just before dawn, I was about to stop for another sleep when I heard a blood-curdling scream. The sound resonated deep in my gut and had me clutching at my chest for breath again, just like in my nightmares. I whipped my head this way and that, once again scoping the dark woods for enemies.

"Just breathe, Ravyn," I whispered to myself, trying to calm my racing heart again.

Crouching down, I took a few deep breaths and wiped my clammy hands on my trousers. Once the initial panic subsided, I stood up and instinctively started walking toward that scream. My feet skidded to a halt.

What are you doing? I thought. *This is no time to play the hero.*

I turned and marched in the opposite direction. Then I froze again. I looked back over my shoulder. Should I risk my life for someone that wouldn't help *me*?

This was just curiosity, plain and simple. Whoever had screamed was probably dead by now.

I pursed my lips together, frustrated that I couldn't just walk away. No one else would think twice about saving themselves. It could be a group of rabid barbarians or even some Howlers out for an early morning meal. Who would want to face that?

Just walk away, Ravyn, I told myself, and took another tentative step away.

My heart started racing again and my palms began to sweat. The sound of that cry couldn't have been more than fifty yards away. What would it hurt to find out what was happening? I wouldn't have to engage. I'd just peek through the bushes.

You're so stupid, I mentally scolded myself. *This is not your problem. Stop feeling so guilty!*

I knew if it were me screaming like that, no one would be there to help me or even be strong enough to save me … but I would still hope.

Muttering a curse under my breath, I turned on my heel again and slid my gun out of my waistband. It wasn't in me to abandon someone and walk away. But if I was going to attempt to save the poor soul, I would not blunder in like an idiot.

Creeping between the brush and the towering trees, I spotted two shadows standing in a clearing. From the looks of their broad shoulders and thick muscles, they both appeared to be men. It was difficult to see much more than that in the dark.

One of the men was looming over someone lying on the ground – possibly a girl or a small boy. I wasn't too late. The person was still alive and struggling against his bonds. The other man was crouched down, digging through the victim's things, searching for anything of value.

Wretched barbarians. They couldn't leave anyone be. They didn't appear to be armed – barbarians generally didn't have access to weapons in the Valley – so I tucked my gun back into my belt and pulled out my dagger. There was no point in drawing the General's soldiers down on my position with gunfire. I moved like a ghost, just as the General had trained me to do, prowling through the shadows until I was right behind the thief. Striking quickly, I used just enough force on the back of his head to knock him out, but not enough to kill him.

The other man heard his partner hit the ground with a thud and turned to see me standing over the unconscious body. Before he had a chance to react, I was striding toward him, dagger in hand. He swung his fist but I avoided it easily and smashed the pommel of my blade into his temple. He went down like a stone. There was no point in checking for his pulse. I knew he was dead.

Still gripping my blade, I stood over the two lifeless bodies on the grass. Now that I was closer, I could see that these men were not barbarians after all. They were too clean and their clothes too new. True barbarians didn't wear much more than tattered rags.

Even my own shirt and trousers were not as pristine as the garments these two men wore and I worked hard to keep myself clean. I supposed it was possible for barbarians to steal brand new clothes and shoes, but their bodies would still be caked in layers of grime. Barbarians completely lost their sense of self in the wilderness and became more like animals. These men looked fresh out of the bath.

Their shoes caught my attention as well. I knelt down and examined them more closely. They looked similar to my own, except they were almost brand new with barely any scuffs on them.

Both men had dark hair cut close to the scalp and no facial hair at all. Barbarians were not clean-cut like this. They had no tools to groom themselves or shave in the Valley so their hair tended to be long, tangled, and matted with dirt. Terran was the closest clan to this part of the Valley, just two or three days' hike from here, but Terran men would not be dressed in these clothes and boots. To be honest, these men reminded me of the male soldiers from the compound. Could they have lived inside the compound? Maybe I had never crossed paths with them.

I studied their faces again. There was nothing familiar about them. They weren't wearing the uniforms that General Wolfe issued to his soldiers, but that meant nothing. There were plenty of people inside the compound that were not soldiers, but still, it was strange …

A rustling in the brush broke my train of thought. Gripping my dagger a little tighter, I rose up into a defensive crouch and scanned the clearing once more. A young woman about my age stared up at me with wide, frightened eyes. This female was not a barbarian either. In the morning light I could see that her chestnut brown hair was somewhat tousled, but still clean and recently brushed. It fell straight to her shoulders, parted down the middle, and was tucked behind her ears. Her dark green shirt and brown pants were slightly frayed along the edges from wear, but still relatively clean, much like mine. The dirt on the palms of her hands suggested she might have been digging up edible plants that grew wild in the forest. She was a bit shorter than me and looked far too delicate to survive long in the Valley. There was no way she would have been able to defend herself against these sorts of men.

I relaxed my stance and bit back a foul curse when I saw that she'd been bound and gagged. General Wolfe had done this to me far too many times to count in the last year that I lived in the compound. No one deserved to feel that vulnerable.

She continued to struggle against the ropes, probably terrified she was about to be my next victim, so I slipped my blade back into my boot and approached her slowly with my hands stretched out in a peaceful gesture.

"I don't mean you any harm."

The woman nodded, but her eyes were still wide with fear. I understood. I wouldn't be trusting of strangers either, especially after watching me murder someone.

"I can't just leave you like this. Let me cut you free and then I'll be on my way."

Thankfully, she nodded her consent, so I inched closer and took the rag from her mouth.

"Thank you." She glanced at the men on the ground nervously, then back at me. "Are they …? I mean, did you …?"

"This one is dead." I nodded toward the man lying closest to us. "The other one will be out for hours."

After cutting her bonds I backed away from her. I wasn't a fool. This woman could be just as dangerous as the two thieves I had just taken down.

"Did they hurt you?" I asked.

"No, they didn't get the chance, thanks to you."

After glancing around to see that there was no sign of anyone having been here with her, I pointed out, "You know it's not safe for you to be out here alone."

She cocked her head to the side and smirked. "You're out here alone."

She was right, but I was a disturbingly excellent fighter. "I'm not safe either. I just get lucky a lot."

"I'm not really alone," she admitted, gathering her scattered possessions. "There's a village not too far from here. I live there."

My eyebrows furrowed in confusion. I didn't remember there being a village in this area on the General's maps. "Which clan is it?"

"Oh, it's not a clan. Not yet, anyway." She smiled again. Her eyes were a gentle brown that matched her hair. "There aren't that many of us. We made our own clan, I guess. Most of us were banished from our previous clans."

I bit my lip to keep from asking why she had been banished from her home. Many people had been taken in by the General because they'd been banished from their clans as well. It was nothing new. People grew tired of abiding by strict rules or silly superstitions. Some clans banished folks as a seasonal sacrifice to appease their gods. For some, it was done out of necessity, like in Terran. Of course, I was curious about her particular reasons, but if I inquired, then she would expect me to reciprocate in kind. Kieron always teased me about polite social protocol in the compound. He told me it was what *normal* people did. I wasn't exactly normal. There were some secrets I didn't want to share.

"And you've survived out here?" I asked instead. "It must be a large group."

"We aren't that large yet. Maybe forty people now?" she speculated.

I gaped at her. "Forty? That many were banished from your clan all at once?"

She giggled. "No, of course not. We collect strays – others who've been banished. My brothers have had their work cut out for them."

"Brothers? As in ... more than one?"

She gave me a quizzical look. "Yes. They can be a trial sometimes, but -"

"That's not what I meant," I said, interrupting her. "I'm glad for you … that you have people, I mean. Family."

Her eyebrows knit together. I could sense she was puzzled by my comment. How could I explain my complicated family history? I pinched my lips together and shifted my weight from one foot to the other.

Please don't ask me about it, I thought, mentally scolding myself for bringing it up.

She cleared her throat and changed the subject. "My name's Laelynn, by the way."

"I'm Ravyn."

The woman smiled as she picked up her bag and slung it over her shoulder. "You should come back with me, Ravyn."

"I …" It was on the tip of my tongue to accept. My curiosity was getting the better of me. I bit my lip again and glanced around the clearing.

"Look, I can see that you want to," Laelynn said with a grin.

I took a step back and crossed my arms over my chest defensively. "I don't think so."

"Where else is there to go? You've been banished too, haven't you?"

Shrugging my shoulders, I replied, "I'm heading to the coast."

"Sounds lonely."

That comment nearly had me changing my mind. Then I remembered how she had mentioned collecting strays. Laelynn had probably had this conversation a hundred times, talking people into joining their village. How could she trust that they were good people and not murderers or something? How did she know they weren't one of the General's mindless soldiers?

The thought of those soldiers had me taking another step back. If I were to stay, I could put Laelynn and her people in danger.

"Ravyn …"

"It's tempting," I confessed. "But … I can't."

"Have it your way. But you could at least come back and have some breakfast before you go. Our village is just down -"

"Don't say another word, Laelynn!"

It wasn't until I heard the deep voice that I realized we were surrounded by five strong men, all pointing crossbows at me.

4
Thorne

I was the first one awake in the camp, which was typical. I could never sleep longer than a few hours at a time anyway, so even before dawn I was out of my tent and making my usual morning coffee. It was my one indulgence on trips like these. My tent barely blocked out the night's wind, I had slept on the hard ground instead of a bed, and I had to bathe in the river. I was *going to* have my coffee.

Sipping the warm drink by the fire, I watched the light peek through the thick trees. This was one benefit of not being able to sleep: watching the sun rise in the mornings. My Warriors were just now starting to stir in their own tents, making their way out to wash the sleep off their faces. I snorted in amusement because I knew they could not sleep well on the hard ground either. Had we gone soft? Surely not. What would they do if I suggested we all sleep on the hard ground all the time, even in Peton? I'd have a mutiny on my hands! The thought made me chuckle.

"What is so funny this early in the morning?" Gunter staggered over to the fire, still wiping his bleary eyes. He sat down next to me and poured his own cup of coffee, muttering about an aching back.

"I was just thinking that you all look like a bunch of old ladies after sleeping on the ground."

"That's about right. You were probably up for hours getting the aches worked out of you while the rest of us got our beauty sleep." Gunter choked down a sip of the coffee and then gave me a disgusted look. "How can you drink this sludge? It tastes like dirt."

I shrugged. Hardly anyone in Peton enjoyed coffee like I did.

"We will leave Archer and Brock here with the horses and supplies today," I said.

"Do you have a good feeling about this hunt?"

I shrugged again and downed the last of my coffee in one gulp. No need to worry him about the feeling I had yesterday. We would deal with whatever challenges we had to face as they came.

"Let's get moving, my friend."

And with that, it was all business. We strapped on our weapons and stuffed our small packs with adequate supplies. If luck was with us, we could find one or two captives before lunch.

A few hours later, Gunter, Pierce, Max, and I were standing in the middle of a small clearing looking down at the bodies of two men. One of them was clearly dead, the other unconscious. Pierce and Gunter scanned the area for any signs of a struggle. No amateur fighter or barbarian could have done this.

"What do you make of it, Thorne?" Gunter inquired.

"The job was done neatly. The men were taken down by someone who knew what they were doing."

"I agree," said Gunter. "There's no sign of a struggle here and not much of one over by the dead guy."

I knelt down and examined the unconscious man's hands. "Take a look. No dirt under his fingernails."

"That's odd," Gunter remarked, looking over my shoulder.

"He hasn't been out in the Valley long," Pierce muttered.

"No," I agreed. "And his clothes. They are too clean. It is possible these two have only seen a few days in the wild."

Pierce snorted. "I'll bet it's less than that."

He glared at me briefly and then walked away again.

Gunter rubbed his hand over his face, thinking things over. "You know, it doesn't matter. Whoever did this left us with a new captive."

"Humph." It did matter, though. This man was clearly not starving and had not known the dangers of the Valley. In the five years I had been coming on the hunt, it was always the exiles who had experienced true hardship that were most grateful to be rescued. They made better captives – better citizens. They appreciated being a part of a clan again and made more effort to acclimate themselves to our ways. This man, having only recently been banished, might only feel resentment toward us.

Just as I was about to rise to my feet again, something on the back of the unconscious exile's shirt caught my eye. I had to look closely to see it. Carefully grasping it between my fingers, I brought it to my face to inspect it.

"What is that, Thorne?" Gunter knelt down beside me to take a look at what I was studying.

It was a strand of hair. A long, black strand of hair.

"I told you," Max muttered, crouching next to me, looking a bit pale. "It's the dark-haired demon."

5
Ravyn

The damp cell was almost completely dark. In fact, I was certain I'd been thrown into a hole in the ground. I couldn't be sure because one of Laelynn's burly brothers had knocked me out back in the clearing. I imagined they had carried me here. Wherever 'here' was.

How stupid could I be, getting myself captured like this? I should have bolted as soon as I had her ropes cut. A part of me was even sorry I had saved her.

Okay, so I wasn't that cruel. I would never have left her to those thieves. Regardless of my circumstances now, she didn't deserve what those brutes were probably planning for her after they'd robbed her.

The only light I could see was shining down through tiny cracks in the roof; some sort of door they'd constructed out of logs. There were no rodents or insects in here with me. For that, I was thankful. But they had taken all of my weapons and my bag, so even if I found a way to climb fifteen feet up these dirt walls and somehow managed to lift what looked like the heaviest door in the Valley, I would still have to find my belongings. The only thing keeping me calm was the fact that I was well-hidden from the soldiers hunting me. There was no chance of them finding me in this hole.

Why hadn't my neck given me a tickle of warning this time? Was it because I hadn't been paying attention? That couldn't be it. It had signaled that danger was closing in more times than I could count.

That was with the soldiers though, I thought. Maybe it only tingled when the soldiers were near. Or maybe I wasn't in real danger. That was something to consider.

I couldn't tell what time of day it was. My body would literally be aching with hunger if I'd been down here longer than a few hours. Then I wondered how long they might keep me here. Was I their prisoner now? I never agreed to come to their village in the first place!

My hands began to shake and my heart started racing again thinking about being trapped with no way out. I didn't know Laelynn at all. This could have been some elaborate trap set up by the General or Two. Maybe they *did* know I was here and they were coming to take me back.

"Stop panicking," I whispered to myself. "This isn't the compound. The General isn't here."

I clenched my fingers into fists and gazed up at the trapdoor again, thankful there was light coming through. Taking a few deep breaths, I pulled my knees to my chest, just as I'd done in the General's isolation chamber. It helped me remain calm and kept me from expending so much energy. I needed to think. There didn't seem to be a way out, but if I was patient and clever, I would find a way. I hoped that my trust in Laelynn wasn't misplaced and that she would argue for my release. After all, she had kept her brothers from shooting me.

The sound of footsteps approaching had me on my feet in an instant. This was the moment of truth. Was it the soldiers or Laelynn and her brothers?

I listened closely. Laelynn's voice was loudest amidst an argument with several male voices. I couldn't make out what they were saying, but Laelynn sounded furious.

Suddenly, light flooded the hole and I was forced to shield my eyes with my hands. Once I'd adjusted, I looked up to see Laelynn's smiling face and, of course, her five irritable brothers.

"Ravyn!" she said brightly. "How's your head?"

I let out the breath I'd been holding. "Fine. I'm just hungry, that's all."

"Good news! My brothers have relented." She looked at each of them in turn. "Well, mostly, but don't worry. I'm throwing you a rope."

She disappeared from view for a moment and then a rope was tossed over the edge. My hands were still a bit shaky, so I shook them a few times and wiped my palms on my trousers.

"I can do this," I said, placing my hands on the rope. The truth was, I was weak from hunger. I'd never be able to make it to the top on my own.

"Everything okay?" Laelynn called down to me.

I squinted up at her again. "I might need a little help climbing."

Laelynn muttered something to her brothers and then peered down over the edge. "Just hold on to the rope. My brothers will do the rest."

I gave her a quick nod and tightened my grip on the line. The brothers began to pull me up. My mind was prepared for it, but my body wasn't. My arms trembled and my feet were clumsy, trying to find footholds in the walls. It only took a few seconds to get to the top but it felt like an eternity. Once I reached the surface, I stretched out my arms and dug my fingers into the dirt to keep from slipping back. My upper body was about to give out. Laelynn and one of her siblings came to my rescue, grabbing hold of my arms and hauling me out the rest of the way.

Resting back on my haunches, I quickly surveyed my surroundings. Sequoias still dominated the landscape, so we couldn't have travelled very far from the clearing. Laelynn probably wasn't so foolish as to walk more than a mile from her village to scavenge for food. It wouldn't take much skill to retrace the brothers' steps and find my way back to the clearing where I'd knocked out those two men. From there I could continue on east to the coast. All that would have to come later. It was obvious I needed nourishment and rest.

Stumbling to my feet with Laelynn's help, I looked up to see five crossbows honed in on me.

I gave Laelynn a wary look. "I feel like I'm about to be executed."

"Nonsense," she replied, scowling at them. "They would never shoot a guest. That would be rude."

Now that it was daylight, I could see the resemblance between the six siblings. Like Laelynn, they each had brown hair of various shades and lengths. A few of them were lean while some were broader in build, but they all looked to be strong and decent fighters. They'd have to be, living out here in the Valley. One thing they all had in common at that moment was accusing brown eyes and frowns, all directed at me.

"This is not a good idea," one of them said. "We do not know her. She could bring trouble down upon our village."

Laelynn crossed her arms over her chest and gave each of her brothers a glare that could set their hair on fire. "She. Saved. My. Life. You know how things are in the Valley. Every man for himself, right? That's what you all agreed happened out here. And she risked her life for me. That tells me all I need to know about her."

Another brother spoke up. "I agree that saving Laelynn puts us in her debt, but I also agree with Hagan. I don't think she should wander alone in the village." He turned his eyes in my direction. "While she's here, she will be guarded by one of us until she is proven to be a friend." He signaled the other men to leave with a nod of his head. "I'll take the first watch."

"I told you, it's not necessary," she barked at them.

"It's fine," I reassured her. "In fact, I would do the same. I don't want to cause trouble." Little did they know, if I'd felt like hurting any of them, their crossbows would not stop me.

I glanced back at my guard, who didn't appear to be much older than Laelynn or me. Out of all the brothers, his hair was the darkest, almost like chocolate, and it fell to his shoulders in waves. He kept the top pulled back out of his eyes with a cord, much like mine.

Laelynn relaxed and smiled at me again. "Come. Let's get you into a bath and then we'll have a bite to eat."

Following her through the forest, I wasn't sure what to expect of their village. Crossbows were primitive weapons according to General Wolfe, who had all the latest in technology and firearms. That didn't mean they were any less deadly. The brother who followed us a few paces behind had his crossbow slung over his shoulder, but it was obvious from his posture that he was capable of using it in a matter of seconds. He made me nervous, the way he watched me; it was not like a man who simply watched a prisoner.

It was as if he saw inside me and knew my secrets. It was a foolish thought. Being amongst strangers was making me edgy.

Laelynn gave me a warm smile. "Well, Ravyn, if I didn't say it before, I'm very glad to meet you! My brothers are too, they're just not good at showing it. They *are* glad you were there to save me. That one's name is Kaelem," she said, pointing her thumb back over her shoulder. "You'll meet my other brothers, officially, at dinner tonight."

"I really shouldn't stay that long," I insisted. "I've caused you all enough trouble already."

"Nonsense!" Laelynn took my arm and pulled me along. "It's no trouble to feed one more person. It's the least we can do after throwing you in that awful pit. You look like you could use a good meal. The Valley isn't kind to wanderers."

I wasn't going to argue. It was true that I hadn't had a decent meal in weeks. Since I'd been on the run, I'd been eating only enough to get by each day. I felt certain I'd lost weight.

"All right, if you insist," I said with a nervous giggle. She laughed along with me, and it was music to my heart. There was something about her that I felt I could trust. Somehow I knew that she would never betray me. I couldn't even say that about my own family.

"So, you and your brothers are the leaders of this new clan?"

"My brothers were the ones that brought us here to build the life we wanted. I was younger when we left home, so they looked after me. And the people that have joined us look to them for leadership."

"That's what families should do."

Laelynn placed a hand on my shoulder. The simple gesture staggered me. What could I possibly bring to a friendship besides danger? Was there any hope that I might have companions or a permanent clan to call my own in the future? I had longed to see the ocean all my life, but I couldn't guarantee there would be others to share it with.

Climbing up the next rise, I started to hear the sounds of chatter and, as we reached the peak, I saw their village. Children were laughing and playing between the trees that camouflaged the community.

Laelynn stopped and we both admired the view.

"This is our village. We call it Linwood."

6
Thorne

Standing in the center of the clearing, I twirled the black hair on my fingers and stared down at the ground. Something was odd about the indentations in the grass and dirt. The grass was clearly matted down where the unconscious man had lain. We had not bothered moving the dead exile, but there was more to the story here. The grass was bent and twisted, and the dirt kicked up in patterns that suggested more than one person had walked away alive from this place.

"Are you coming, Thorne?" Gunter called out, interrupting my thoughts.

Still fixated on the ground, I waved him off. "Go on without me." I was not going to be satisfied until I figured out exactly what had happened in this clearing.

"Why?" he asked. "What are you doing?"

I glanced up at Gunter out of the corner of my eye. He stood at the edge of the clearing, ready to head back to our camp. Pierce was already marching through the sequoias with the still-unconscious man thrown over his shoulder. Max followed closely behind him.

"Just being thorough," I answered vaguely.

"Do you need me to stay?"

"I don't need a nursemaid," I muttered, flicking the black hair to the ground. "You three take a short rest and then head out again after lunch. Take Brock with you."

Gunter shrugged his shoulders. "You got it."

I watched him join the other Warriors in the trek back to camp with the exile. Once my comrades were gone, I turned my attention back to the markings on the ground. Max was convinced that this was the work of the demon he had mentioned back in Peton, but there had to be a better explanation. I did not believe in killer demons. Someone had knocked down two large men without shedding a drop of blood, and that someone was highly skilled. They just happened to have black hair. I wanted to know who that person was.

Even more mysterious was the second indentation in the grass. Another body, markedly smaller, had lain close by the two men. There were boot prints all along the edges of the clearing. I circled the area two or three times before deciding that at least four or five people had left this clearing alive. It was difficult to count since they had walked away in single file.

I folded my arms across my chest and stared off into the forest. The trail led west, away from our camp. It would be foolish to follow it alone. Four or five exiles in the Valley could be a sign of some sort of tribe or a group of dangerous barbarians. A wise commander would go back to camp and be thankful we were able to rescue another exile.

"Humph," I grunted, peering over my shoulder where Gunter, Pierce, and Max had disappeared through the trees. They would all think I was crazy for this.

I ran my fingers through my hair and set out after the group of exiles and the black-haired assassin.

I had travelled just a mile when I finally found them. Crouched down within the brush, I watched men come and go every thirty minutes, trading places with each other. There were five males in total, all armed with crossbows, guarding something I could not see from this distance.

I observed them for hours. None of these men had long black hair, so they could not be the assassin I was looking for. Did they know the person with black hair? Maybe these five men with crossbows were the ones who had incapacitated the two exiles. But that did not make sense. If these men felt threatened they would not go to the trouble of knocking a man out with a fist or some other blunt object. That was too risky. These boys would shoot to kill with those crossbows.

No. My mind was still set on that mysterious black-haired person.

Just when I was ready to move on, maybe find out if they had a camp nearby, all five men and one woman gathered together at the location they had been guarding so closely. They were arguing loudly, the woman's voice loudest of all. They lifted up a large trapdoor made out of thick logs that covered some sort of hole in the ground. I watched, completely entranced, as a female with long raven hair was pulled up from a pit in the ground. The hair was the same length and color as I had pulled from the clothing of that exile. But surely, she was not the one who had brought down those two men? Could this be the demon that those trade-runners had seen? I scoffed at the idea immediately.

From my hiding place, I judged the men to be comparable in size to many Warriors of Peton. They all had their crossbows aimed at this woman. Did they believe her to be a threat to them, a group of fighting men? How could she be mistaken for a demon?

One thing was certain; these men were not barbarians. They were too civilized. Organized. If they were exiles or deserters, then they could be fair game to be taken as captives. It was too soon to tell. I would wait and watch before deciding.

When they finally walked away from the pit, I followed. Keeping my distance, I trailed them back to their small village. The two women seemed friendly, so why had they kept the black-haired woman prisoner in a deep pit? Then I saw them link elbows. The black-haired woman visibly stiffened. She was clearly uncomfortable with the friendly gesture. Perhaps they were not companions after all.

The other female shared similar physical traits with the five men: that brown hair and tan skin. I suspected they were related in some way. The male who followed closely behind them kept his crossbow shouldered and ready the entire time. He acted as protectively as I did with my sisters. His gaze never strayed from the two females. The one with black hair still did not seem dangerous to me, but looks could be deceiving.

What was the connection between this family and the black-haired female? It did not matter. I needed to forget the woman and focus on the hunt.

I continued through the shadows of the trees until the village came into view. Men and women were striding purposefully through the village, hauling water from the stream or delivering goods. Everyone was working hard and taking care of their chores while children played nearby.

Their community was incredible. They had strategically built all their shops and homes up in the safety of the sequoia trees. The lack of low-lying branches would make it impossible to reach them without some sort of rope or ladder. They had developed a pulley system that carried their goods from the ground up into their tree-houses. It was extraordinary.

These were intelligent and resourceful people … definitely not what I had expected. These people had probably all been exiles at one time, but this was the makings of a new clan. I would not take any of them captive. These people had made this place their home.

Well, that was that. There was nothing to be done here. There were no exiles to rescue.

Then why am I still following them? I thought, rubbing my chin.

I crouched down under a large fern as I watched them escort the black-haired woman to one of the many rope ladders that hung down from the trees. They climbed up into the tree-house and disappeared.

That was my cue. Time to head back to camp and check in with the Warriors, but I could not make myself leave. Several hours later, I was *still* hunkered down in shrubs.

Evening came early in the Old Sequoia Valley. The shadows grew long, providing plenty of places for me to hide and observe the comings and goings of these people. Both women had stayed inside the tree-house but the brothers came and went, probably taking turns guarding the mysterious woman while she stayed with them. As the sun began to set, they all gathered for dinner, the aroma filling the air around me. It reminded me that it was long past time to be heading back to my own camp. The Warriors had surely eaten their meal and were turning in for the evening; all but Gunter. He would stay up until I returned.

Everyone in the village had returned to their tree-houses and most of the ladders were pulled up. All was quiet on the ground. There was only a quiet murmur of dinnertime conversation inside the home I was still spying on.

I was beginning to think that my time here had been wasted when movement above me caught my attention. Through one of the windows of the tree-house, I could see a few of the men standing and leaving the table. Two of the brothers climbed down the ladder and started marching straight toward me. I slipped deeper into the shadows, avoiding them easily.

"I know what you're thinking," I heard one of them say, "and it's not a good idea."

"Hagan, you know it's the right thing to do," the other brother replied in a hushed voice.

"Kaelem …" The brother started to protest, but he didn't get a chance to finish.

"I know what I'm doing!"

The brief exchange had me puzzled, but it was none of my concern. Once they were gone and all was quiet again, I stepped out of the shadows.

This little excursion was pointless. There was nothing for me to do here; no captives to take. I was preparing to retreat when something else caught my eye.

7
Ravyn

I leaned my head back against the end of the tub, breathing a deep sigh of delight. My bath was small; not even long enough for my legs to stretch out. But after all the freezing cold baths I'd been taking in the forest streams, I wasn't going to complain. My hair was freshly washed and my body was the cleanest it had been in a month.

It was too much trouble to draw me a bath, and I told Laelynn so, but she wouldn't hear it. She'd ordered each of her brothers to pull up a bucket of water to their tree-house and heated it rather quickly. She made the process seem so easy it made me think she bathed *every* evening. I scrunched up my nose, a tad envious of this luxury.

Regardless of their unexpected hospitality, I still had some reservations about Laelynn and her family. Laelynn's acceptance of me made me uneasy. Rescuing her from those two men in the clearing must have made us instant friends in her mind. Her brothers acted more like I'd expect. They were suspicious of me just as I was wary of them. All of this could have been avoided if they'd just let me go from the clearing. I had never accepted her invitation to come to Linwood. They'd brought me against my will. I decided I would be cautious until I was more certain of their intentions toward me.

I cupped water in my hands, lifted it to eye level, then let the water spill through my fingers back into the tub. My fingers had shriveled up into prunes and the water was beginning to lose its warmth. I didn't care. Content for the moment, I closed my eyes and savored this short time.

A sudden knocking at the door had me jerking upright and drawing my knees closer to my chest. Water splashed over the side of the tub to the floor in my haste to cover myself.

"Is everything okay in there?" Laelynn asked from outside the door.

"Sure. Why wouldn't it be?"

There were a few seconds of silence, as if she were trying to come up with an answer. Then she hesitantly replied, "I - I washed your clothes and they're hanging out to dry, so I'm setting these new ones right outside the door for you. They belonged to Kaelem … when he was younger. You know … since you're taller than me."

Guilt coursed through me. *She's just trying to be nice*, I thought.

Several seconds of silence passed before Laelynn called out again. "Anyway … here they are. Take your time!" she added. Then she left me alone, her footsteps fading away.

I leaned back against the back of the tub again but I couldn't take my eyes off the door. They were most likely waiting for me to come out to dinner. I could smell the sweet aroma of roasted rabbit. They had fed me earlier, but my stomach was rumbling again. With a sigh of regret, I stepped out of the tub, wrapped up in a towel, and padded to the door.

Cracking the door a few inches, I grabbed the stack of clothing Laelynn had left behind and took a quick peek down the short hallway. I couldn't see them, but I could hear the soft murmuring of her brothers' deep voices. They must have all gathered for the evening meal. It seemed reasonable for everyone to retreat to the trees once the sun began to go down. It was too dark to continue with chores or play and there was a risk of being attacked by a Yellow-eyed Saber after sunset.

I was still a little amazed that this home was a good twenty or thirty feet off the ground. The entire village of Linwood had built their homes high up in the trees and bridges dangled between each of the dwellings. Ropes and ladders had been constructed to travel up and down from the ground easily. They could also be drawn up when danger threatened on the ground.

A water-wheel had also been built down on the river that flowed through the village. "My brothers built it to grind corn and other grains for us and the village," Laelynn had explained. "But just recently they engineered it to lift buckets of water and other supplies up to the trees." She winked and smiled at me. "I enjoy my baths, too!" I had smiled politely at her enthusiasm. The piece of machinery *was* incredible. I was in awe of these villagers and how they'd thrived with their limited resources.

Once I had dressed and combed my hair, I left the bathing room. I walked down the hallway and into the main living area. All five of Laelynn's brothers were sitting at their dining table, talking quietly amongst themselves. Laelynn was standing over their old fashioned wood-burning stove, much like the ones we used in Terran. It most likely doubled as a fireplace during the winter.

"There you are!" Laelynn exclaimed, startling me and the brothers. They grew silent immediately. "Come in and sit down. My brothers don't bite … often." She waved me to an open seat at the table, and once again I was feeling awkward. Laelynn was back to being her hospitable self while the brothers clearly did not trust me. I supposed it was only fair since I didn't trust them either.

Kaelem was watching me again but I tried to ignore it. His intent gaze drifted from my turquoise eyes, over my wet hair, all the way down to my bare feet. I felt my face go up in flames, but I didn't give in to the urge to lower my eyes.

"What are you looking at?" I demanded, pointing out his rude behavior as I dropped into the seat Laelynn had offered.

"Kaelem, stop it!" Laelynn scolded, pointing her wooden spoon at him. Then she turned to grab some plates of food. "Here's some dinner for you all. Ravyn, I apologize that my brothers are not introducing themselves." She gave them each a piercing glare along with their food. "You know Kaelem, sitting across from you. He's a year older than me, and the one sitting to your left is the next oldest, Raimond. Next to Kaelem is Nash. These two at the head and foot of the table are the oldest, Hagan and Haldar. Of course, you can see they're twins."

My eyes went wide with shock. "Twins?" My head pivoted back and forth between the two identical brothers. I hadn't noticed at all. The brothers all shared such similar features that I'd completely overlooked it.

Laelynn furrowed her eyebrows in confusion. "Yes, of course. Have you never seen twins before?"

"Only once," I murmured, ducking my head and trying not to stare. Camellia and I were not identical like Haldar and Hagan so it was startling to see two faces that looked exactly the same.

Laelynn sat down next to me at the table with her plate of food. The brothers were busy eating but I knew they were still actively listening. "Well, they must not be that common where you come from."

I narrowed my eyes slightly. Laelynn had an innocent enough expression on her face, but she was digging for information. I could feel the question in the tone of her voice.

"And?" I challenged.

Everyone paused and eyed both of us.

"Laelynn, stop probing." It was Kaelem who'd chided her.

He studied me again with those penetrating eyes and I felt exposed in the worst way. It was as if he'd said exactly what I'd been thinking. Glaring at him, I mentally put up walls inside of my head to block him from reading my thoughts ... if that's what he was doing. I didn't want him knowing my secrets if he had the ability to read minds.

When the corners of his mouth turned up in a hint of a smile, I nearly gasped.

"You're one to talk, nosey," Laelynn muttered to her brother. I didn't miss the smirk they shared.

Everyone went back to their food. I took a deep breath and tried to relax. Laelynn was only being polite and I was being paranoid.

"*I'm* a twin, actually," I said finally, attempting to be polite in return.

"Oh?" Laelynn said lightly, trying not to seem pushy.

"I had a sister. We were the only set of twins in our clan."

This time the brother sitting next to me, Raimond, spoke up. "You *had* a sister?"

I nodded and lowered my eyes. "She's probably still alive. I haven't seen her in eight years." Why was I telling them this?

Ravyn, stop talking! I thought, mentally scolding myself again.

Laelynn gaped at me. "How ...? I mean -"

Kaelem rescued her from her stuttering. "Lae wants to know why you're wandering the Valley alone and not with your family."

When I glanced back at Kaelem, his expression was not as severe as before. In fact, he looked eager to hear the tale.

"It's not a story I like sharing," I replied, attempting to shut down the conversation again.

Nash, the brother next to Kaelem, leaned forward. "Were you banished from your clan?"

I heaved a deep sigh and muttered, "Something like that."

"Nash, she said she didn't want to talk about it," Kaelem repeated.

The remainder of the meal was more of the same. Laelynn pestered me with questions and I gave them vague answers or dodged the questions altogether. It was obvious I was frustrating her. She still wanted me to join them, but I couldn't stay here this close to the compound. In order to protect them, and myself, I had to leave as soon as possible. They couldn't know my secrets. It would be dangerous for all of us. General Wolfe would send his soldiers to punish them if he knew I'd been here.

After dinner, Nash was in charge of keeping an eye on me. Better him than Kaelem, who gave me a troubled glance before he filed out the door with the others. When Laelynn stepped out of the room in an effort to clean up, she left me alone with a brooding Nash.

The uncomfortable silence was too much. I spotted another door off the main living area and asked Nash, "Does that lead to a balcony?" I thought I'd seen one from the ground. It would be the perfect place to get away from everyone and relieve my tension.

"It does," he replied.

I rose to my feet and gestured to the exit. "Do you mind? I'd like to get some air."

"Stay by the window where I can see you," he said, warning me with his eyes that he would still be watching.

Stepping out onto the balcony, I gripped the wooden rails, closed my eyes, and breathed in the crisp, evening air. It was just what I needed to clear my head. The sun's final rays of the day were still peeking through the trees. The mixture of warmth and the cool breeze felt wonderful on my face.

As I basked in the remaining glow of the autumn sun, a knot formed in my belly. The feeling that someone was watching overwhelmed me. It was probably one of Laelynn's snoopy brothers, making sure I wasn't slaughtering the village, but when I opened my eyes and looked over the railing, it was not one of the brothers at all.

Her brothers were strong, but not like this man, the one staring up at me. This warrior's posture was arrogant. He knew without a doubt that he was a magnificent fighter. Those sharp eyes didn't miss a thing, even in the dark of the evening. For a moment, I was worried he might be one of General Wolfe's soldiers, but he still had a light in his gaze that the soldiers did not have anymore. His height was impressive, much taller than any of the soldiers. Despite the fact that he wasn't as broad-shouldered and hulking as Two, he still looked like a powerful force. His dark sleeveless shirt and pants were well-suited for blending in to the forest and there were daggers strapped to his thighs.

What held my attention most were the scars that ran down the side of his face. Permanent marks of valor, probably from a battle won against a Night Howler or a Saber. He wore them well, and they only enhanced his handsome warrior's form.

The evening light failed to reveal more of his details, but I couldn't stop staring at him. Maybe it was only my silly imagination, but I felt drawn to this stranger. It was something I had never felt with Kieron. Kieron and I had been childhood friends growing up in the compound. We'd grown to care for each other over time. This was different. A compulsion inside me begged to go and speak with him, but I couldn't seem to break eye contact long enough to move.

"Ravyn!" Laelynn exclaimed. "There you are!"

I looked over my shoulder to find Laelynn joining me on the balcony. There was a sense of relief in her voice, as if she'd expected me to be gone. I probably should have attempted an escape. Her exuberance was starting to wear on me, or maybe my irritation was due to her interruption of the intensity of the moment.

When I glanced down again, the man had disappeared. Disappointment filled me. I felt as if I'd just lost something important, and I didn't know why.

"What are you doing out here?" Laelynn sidled up next to me and gave me a wide smile.

"Just getting some air," I replied. "It's nice out here. And no offense meant, but your brothers all seem to think that I'm going to massacre everyone."

"They don't think that."

"Then why haven't my weapons been returned?"

"They don't trust as easily as I do. But you saved my life today. All they saw was you beating up some men twice your size." She dropped her voice to a whisper and added, "And you *did* kill one of them."

I couldn't feel bad about what I'd done. If I hadn't killed him, the Valley surely would have. I had only spared some other innocent from his thieving and whatever else he'd planned for Laelynn.

Instead of making excuses, I simply said, "I can't stay here for long. Will I be able to get my things when I leave in the morning?"

She smiled again, but I could see the disappointment in her eyes.

Why do you want me here? What do you want from me?

"I'll make sure that you do," she assured me. "I meant what I said earlier. We could use another fighter like you for our village. My brothers would come around, especially Kaelem. I think he likes you."

I snorted. "I think you may be imagining things. And … I'm very thankful for your offer, but it's better for everyone if I go."

"Alright then, but just know that you will be welcomed back. I think we'd be good friends, Ravyn."

"Maybe," I mumbled, giving her a half-hearted smile.

Laelynn thinks *I* would be a good friend? Except for Kieron, I'd had no companions at the compound. But that was before everything had changed – before *he* had changed. There had been no camaraderie or loyalty within our group. We were just a bunch of kids pretending to be adults, learning how to fight and shoot guns. The memories of the General's training made me shudder.

Friendship demanded a certain amount of trust between two people. That was too risky for me. Maybe she *could* be my friend, with time. I could get over the constant cheerfulness, but it would mean living here for a while. Staying here in Linwood could be fatal for them.

I could never stay in one spot so long, I thought. *The General would find me and punish them.*

Laelynn grinned again, oblivious to the horrifying thoughts running through my head.

If I were a good friend, I'd leave and get as far away from them as I could. That was the only way to make sure they'd be safe from General Wolfe and his soldiers.

"Well, let's go get some tea and call it a night, huh?" she said.

I nodded in agreement. "Sure."

8
Thorne

I rose early as I always did, at least three hours before sunrise. This time was usually spent drinking coffee or going for a long run, but my coffee was getting cold and I still couldn't shake the memory of her.

Ravyn was her name. It was pure luck that I had even found out that piece of information. That brown-haired female had interrupted … whatever that was last night.

Ravyn's hair was the darkest I had ever seen, hanging in soft waves down her back. She was tall and strong, like Tallon, and nearly as young. When the sun had lit up her every feature to me, I was struck by how flawless she was. There was not a scratch or bruise on her face or hands, which I found odd for someone who had been roughing it in the Valley. Then, as if she had known I was there, she opened her eyes and found me standing out in the open like an idiot. No alarm was raised. In fact, she'd barely moved. Her gaze never wavered and she didn't even flinch at my unsightly scars, which I typically tried to hide.

I had never given this much thought to any female before. Gunter was going to give me serious grief when he found out. It *had* to be a passing thing. Just yesterday, I was adamant that I did not want or need a female companion, but I could not get Ravyn's image out of my mind.

The other thought that nagged me was the conversation I had overheard. Were those two brothers talking about Ravyn? She didn't seem very welcome in their village. They guarded her every second. What was I missing? I stared into the flames, searching for answers that I knew would not come.

After about ten more minutes of debating against myself, I decided to return to the village and find some answers. Dumping the cold coffee in the dirt and leaving the cup by the campfire, I marched over to Gunter's tent. He would need to take charge of the hunt at sunrise.

Crouching down, I peeked inside his tent. "Gunter." My voice did not wake him so I reached for his shoulder and gave it a gentle shake. He muttered something indecipherable, but still did not wake so I tried again, saying his name a little louder. "Gunter, wake up."

He groaned and squinted up at me in confusion. "Did I oversleep?"

"No. I'm going back to the village I told you about last night."

"Do you need me to come with you?" Gunter started to rise up out of his blankets.

I shook my head. "Lead the hunt at sunrise. Make sure to leave someone at the camp."

"What time should I expect you back before I send out a search party?"

I scoffed at the insult but didn't take the bait. Something in my gut was telling me not to waste any more time. "Midday."

"It's that girl, isn't it? That's why you're going back."

"Humph."

Gunter grinned mischievously. "It is. You don't have to admit it, but I could hear it in your voice when you spoke of her last night. You're interested in her." Gunter chuckled a little. "So, is Max right? Is she a demon?"

"Don't be ridiculous," I said, rolling my eyes.

"Listen, just be careful. You don't know anything about her."

"We never know anything about any of our captives from the Valley," I pointed out.

"You're going to take her captive then?"

"It's possible."

"I don't believe you. You're a terrible liar." He lightly punched my shoulder and then said, "Still, be careful."

I nodded and left the campsite immediately. If I hurried, I could be there just before dawn.

9
Ravyn

I had woken up to total darkness, barely able to see my hand in front of my face. The trees hid whatever light the moon was giving off out here in the Valley. Panic was choking me.

It had only been a week since I'd run away from Terran and, honestly, I couldn't believe I'd survived this long. The food that I'd packed for the trip was almost gone. At sunrise, I had to hunt for more.

But first, I had to live through the night.

While living in Terran, I had heard stories about the Sabers and Howlers and their affinity for human flesh, but I never believed them. What would the Terran people know about it, having never been outside the electric fence around the city? I had figured they were just stories to keep the kids away from the fence. My second night in the Valley I was proved wrong. I spent the night up in a tree, but still the Yellow-Eyed Sabers had come calling. They circled my tree all night. I didn't get a wink of sleep for worrying that I might fall off the branch and into their waiting jaws. Their eyes watched me hungrily, saliva dripping from their dagger-like fangs.

Tonight, I wasn't as lucky. I'd found a tiny hollow carved out of a tree. The opening was just wide enough for me to slide inside. I'd covered the mouth of the little cave with a large stone and covered my body with dirt and leaves, trying to disguise my scent. The boulder didn't shield the opening completely, but I was hoping it was good enough to keep out the Sabers. They'd been stalking me every night since they'd found me.

The sound of a branch snapping had jarred me awake. Quivering in fear, I covered my mouth with my hand to muffle the sound of my whimpering. They had found me. Nothing would save me this time. That boulder wouldn't hold back those hungry beasts.

They paced just outside. I wasn't sure how many there were, but I was sure it was more than one. They hunted in packs, though one would have been enough.

I closed my eyes and prayed ... for a miracle ... for anything. I didn't want to die.

Opening my eyes again, I tried to peak around the stone and, there at the entrance, staring at me, were bright, hungry, yellow eyes.

I didn't scream or cry, but my heart plummeted in my chest, knowing that I wouldn't survive this. I shook uncontrollably as the beast dug at the ground around the stone, trying to get to me. He growled, anxious to have me within his grasp.

In just a little while, I wouldn't exist anymore. So much for being brave and independent. So much for freedom. I was trapped and alone. There was nothing and no one to save me from this.

BANG!

***

Gasping as I woke, I sat up so quickly that I almost bumped heads with someone.

"Ravyn?" Laelynn whispered urgently, revealing her identity.

Feeling disoriented, I scanned the room. I recalled that I was in Linwood, staying the night with Laelynn and her brothers. They'd allowed me a pallet on the floor of the main living area, close to the stove so I would stay warm. I was grateful to them for it, especially since the nights were getting colder with the winter months drawing near.

The room was dark. No light was peeking through the windows yet.

"What time is it? Did I wake you up?" I asked quietly, trying to shake my nightmare and the sound of the rifle firing. The dreams always felt so real. It was possible I'd called out in my sleep. My stomach clenched at the thought. Crying out in the middle of my nightmares when I slept out in the forest could lead the soldiers right to me.

Laelynn knelt beside me on the floor and placed my rucksack beside me. Surprised, but also relieved, I rifled through the bag. I felt for my two trusty daggers and the pistol I'd carried since I'd been running from the General. Everything was still there, including all the spare magazines and some food Laelynn must have added.

"Ravyn," she whispered. She put her hand on my shoulder and squeezed. "You need to go. Quickly. They're coming."

My heart clenched tight in my chest and my tattoo began to tingle again as I heard the sound of gunshots in the distance. It wasn't just the crack of the rifle in my dream that had woken me. The village was under attack.

10

Thorne

The sky was just beginning to lighten when I found the village again. A thick fog had settled between the trees, a common occurrence in the damp forest. The shadows of the early morning and the fog kept me well-concealed as I continued my approach. I wasn't sure what I would find this morning or why I felt such urgency to get there, so I moved cautiously.

Just on the outskirts of the community I heard the unmistakable sound of rifles firing through the trees. The shots came from the far side of the village and they seemed to be getting louder – drawing closer. People in the village were shouting and scrambling to pull up the ladders. There were some women and children who cried in fear at the coming danger, but the village had been designed for this very reason. It kept its people hidden away in the safety of the tree tops.

I found cover under some brush that grew at the base of one of the smaller trees and surveyed the area for enemies. Movement out of the corner of my eye caught my attention. Someone was shimmying down the side of one of the huge sequoias not twenty feet from me. It was an act of sheer madness. There were no branches to grab hold of so close to the ground. This person must be hanging on to the bark and moss by their fingernails. When the climber edged down a bit more, my stomach dropped as I glimpsed that long, black hair again. It was Ravyn. The woman had a death wish.

My first instinct was to help her, but the instant I moved, I was fired upon. I ducked and rolled toward the next tree as bullets whizzed by, shattering the trunks of the sequoias around me and spraying wood fragments everywhere.

Having heard the shots rip through the trees around her, Ravyn must have panicked and lost her grip. When I saw her fingers slip from their hold, time seemed to slow down. I watched in horror as she plummeted to the ground. It was at least a fifteen-foot drop, but she did not utter a sound as she hit the dirt; no scream of pain or crying as I had expected. She was on her feet almost immediately and leaning against the tree without any sign of an injury.

Feeling some relief, I released the breath I had been holding. We were not out of danger yet, though. I peeked over my shoulder through the brush to see three men headed straight for us. In a matter of minutes, they would march directly between the trees that hid me and Ravyn. All three appeared to be strong fighters by the looks of them. They wore uniforms with caps that matched and carried rifles similar to ones we sometimes used in Peton. The largest of the three seemed to be the most worrisome. He was built much like Pierce, except this man's skin was dark like a storm cloud.

We would have little protection against bullets if these men were decent shooters. I signaled to Ravyn but she was rummaging through her bag, of all things. I noticed then that she was pulling out weapons of her own. She swiftly tucked a dagger into each of her boots, then pulled out a pistol and checked the magazine. Slipping the gun into her belt, she slung her bag over her shoulders in preparation for either an attack or retreat. Even in such a dire situation, I could not help but admire how swiftly she prepared her weapons. She handled them with ease, a skill many of Peton's youngest Warriors were still learning.

Turning to peer around the tree, Ravyn finally made eye contact with me. There was a spark of recognition in her eyes and relief on her face.

My hand signals to her were quick and to the point. I gestured over my shoulder in the direction of the shooters, and then held up three fingers. Nodding in understanding, Ravyn began her own motions. After a few jabs of her finger I frowned. Was she actually telling me to make a run for it? That was an absurd plan. There was no way she would be able to make it on her own; not with those three men closing in.

They had to be getting close. Their footsteps were noisy, stepping on leaves and branches, not caring if we could hear them or not. Because they were armed, they thought they had the upper hand. They were in for a surprise.

Ravyn drew her pistol again, and then it dawned on me what her plan might be. That foolish woman was going to make herself a target to draw those men away from me. So much for being chivalrous. She was going to sacrifice herself.

I was not going to let that happen. I tried to get her attention again, but her forehead rested on the barrel of her pistol, focusing on the task ahead. Then, almost quicker than I could blink, she wheeled around to take position between the trees, firing three shots in succession at the men coming up behind me. She turned on her heel and raced away into the forest. They fired at her repeatedly through the sequoias, but she veered too quickly between the trees for them to get a clear shot. Her agility was remarkable.

When she was finally out of range, the shooting stopped, but the men were yelling at each other.

One of the shooters uttered a foul curse and said, "She took out Eight. Almost between the eyes!"

My jaw nearly dropped in astonishment. Gunter was right. Ravyn was a mystery, but what I was learning intrigued me more and more.

I held my position behind the tree and listened for signs of movement.

"Come on, leave him! We can't let her get away," the other shouted in a deeper voice. They ran through the brush, following

Ravyn's trail, the dark one leading the way. My dagger was out of its sheath in an instant. When they ran by I gripped the blade gently, as I had done a thousand times before, and sent it hurtling toward the man that lagged behind. His body jerked as the knife pierced him in the spine and his rifle slipped from his grasp. He was dead before he hit the ground.

Ducking down into the thick ferns again, I waited to see what the dark fighter would do. He turned to study his companion for a moment. Snatching up the fallen rifle, he dismissed the man as if he meant nothing and continued on after Ravyn.

Cautiously, I stepped out from under the brush that had been concealing my presence. No shots were fired. There must have been only the three shooters raiding the village. If there were any others, they had followed Ravyn, just as she had intended.

I prowled over to the fallen man. Crouching down beside him, I yanked the dagger from his body and wiped the blade on the man's uniform to remove most of the blood.

I frowned and stared off into the forest. Should I follow her? It was not about taking a new captive this time. If it were my sister, Tallon, or any other Warrior, I would never leave them out here alone. Those shooters had been targeting her specifically. I wanted to find out why.

The fog was thicker than ever. I could no longer see the dark fighter through the trees, but his trail was easy to track. Moving slower now, I listened for snapping branches and footsteps: anything that signaled an enemy might be near. I inwardly cursed this foolhardy impulse, but I could not bring myself to leave Ravyn alone with this villain.

The silence of the forest was ominous. I felt presences all around but I could not see them through the murky fog. Adrenaline rushed through my body and my grip on my blade tightened in anticipation. Just as I was beginning to think I had lost them, the barrel of a gun was jammed into my back.

11
Ravyn

I lost the soldiers in the heavy fog. There were three of them, just as the blonde warrior had indicated, and I was certain that Two was among them. I had seen his dark, menacing form for a split second when I had fired off the three rounds. It was a shame he wasn't the one I killed, but that had been a lucky shot anyway.

Sitting here on the ground, covered in the thick, green undergrowth, I continued to think about the warrior. It was completely crazy to be so relieved to see him and know that he was somewhere out here with me. I probably shouldn't have left him back there, but there was no way of knowing if he would be a help or a hindrance to me.

Okay, that wasn't entirely fair. I'd never seen him fight, but he didn't know these soldiers like I did. He didn't know what they could do, and he definitely didn't know what *I* could do.

"Well, well, well…what do we have here?"

My body froze over. The voice I could hear belonged to Twelve and, for a second, I thought she had found me. She was one of the few women that General Wolfe had recruited into his program. She wasn't a great fighter in hand-to-hand, but she was sneaky and very light of foot which is why I hadn't heard her coming. She wouldn't be stupid enough to stand around and chit-chat with me. She'd be dead before she said anything else.

"Hey, I got someone!" she shouted to another soldier. I prayed it wasn't Two.

My stomach churned as I realized who she might have found. I was hoping to escape without delivering any more death today, but I was starting to believe that the only way to be free of the soldiers was to kill them all. That way, they wouldn't be able to hurt me or anyone I cared about.

My throat went dry when I realized what I'd just considered. Did I care about that blonde warrior?

I cared that he lived. That was all.

Oh, stop it, you big liar, I thought. It was more than that. There was something about him. I couldn't explain it, but I cared very much that he lived.

I prowled beneath the undergrowth in search of Twelve and her mocking voice. She couldn't be more than twenty feet away. When I reached the scene, the warrior was there as I feared he would be. Twelve was behind him holding a pistol to his back, and a bald soldier – I couldn't remember his number – was standing in front of him. The bald soldier's rifle was lowered, arrogantly thinking that they had complete control of the situation. That mistake was going to be their downfall.

This was why the warrior was a hindrance to me. I didn't know what he was thinking, what he would do, or if he even had a plan at all. There was no way to know for sure if he would react quickly enough if I attacked.

I should have just jumped out from the bushes and taken care of those two soldiers myself. It would have been easy. Realizing how foolish that plan was, I disregarded it. There was no possible way to kill them both without using my pistol. Even if I decided to use it, the warrior might shift the wrong way and get shot by mistake.

Biting my lip, I held my position and waited for an opportunity.

"Where is she?"

The sound of Twelve's lifeless voice was irritating. The words would have come across better with some sarcasm, but the soldiers couldn't speak with emotion anymore. All of the General's soldiers sounded this way now.

"Who?" the blonde warrior replied.

The bald soldier responded. "Don't play dumb with us, we saw you follow her in this direction. Where is she hiding?"

"What is she to you?"

Keep them chatting, warrior, I thought, preparing to attack.

"She is General Wolfe's …"

“Shut up!” Twelve ordered the bald soldier before he gave too much away.

I needed to make a move soon. They wouldn’t stand around and chat for much longer, and I knew they wouldn’t leave the warrior alive. I clutched both my dagger and my pistol. The pistol was risky. The noise would most certainly attract Two and any other soldiers this way.

“I am going to give you till the count of three to tell me what I want to know, then I’m going to pull this trigger,” said Twelve.

I hoped the warrior was ready.

“One.”

Clutching my dagger, I took aim.

“Two.”

The warrior moved so swiftly to attack, I barely saw him turn.

His timing was perfect.

I sprung out of the bushes and sent my dagger hurtling toward the bald soldier. He crumpled to the ground with my blade buried in the side of his skull just as the warrior knocked the pistol from Twelve’s hands.

The warrior shoved Twelve back a few feet, then spun to confront the bald soldier. His brows furrowed with confusion when he spotted him on the ground.

“I’ve got this under control,” I assured him.

He gave me a quick nod and turned back to continue the fight with Twelve.

It should have been easy for the warrior to make the kill, but instead he let her attack. Twelve advanced again and again and he easily blocked her punches and kicks, but never finished the fight. I didn't understand his hesitancy.

What is his game? I wondered.

The warrior used his feet to knock her legs out from under her and she rolled away from him. Getting back to her feet, Twelve reached for the knife hidden inside her boot. Sighing over this turn of events, I raised my pistol and fired one shot to her chest. She dropped to the ground.

The warrior turned to me and I was met with ice-blue eyes. He was just as tall as I thought he would be; well over six feet. His white-blonde hair was cropped short and slightly curly. The next thing I noticed were the tattoos. A matching set of thorny vines curled around his muscled arms, starting from somewhere beneath his sleeveless shirt, then winding around his biceps and forearms, all the way down to his wrists. Glancing back up at his striking face, his expression had turned as chilly as the color of his eyes.

I raised an eyebrow at him. "Don't look so annoyed."

"I had it under control."

"You were being too defensive …"

The muscle in his jaw ticked. "By choice. I wasn't trying to kill her."

"She didn't deserve your mercy … even if she *is* a woman."

Turning my back on him, I ignored whatever protest he had and returned to crouch down beside the bald soldier I'd killed. I didn't recognize him so I carefully rotated his head to see the tattoo I knew would be permanently etched on the back of his neck. The markings were on every soldier, including me. Same letters; different numbers. His said 'TS39'.

I felt bile rise up in the back of my throat. General Wolfe had managed to create over forty of them.

"What does that mean? TS39?" The warrior was hovering over my shoulder. He smelled like rain with a hint of something else I couldn't place.

"Nothing."

The soldier called TS39 was bleeding out from his temple. I wouldn't need to worry about him, so I left him lying in the dirt. The female soldier, Twelve, I couldn't be sure about. I stepped over to her body and knelt down to inspect her wound. The shot had been to the chest. She seemed dead. Just to be certain I ran my dagger across her throat to slice her carotid, the largest blood vein in the body. She'd bleed out in seconds.

I had to be sure.

After cleaning my blade on her clothes, I tucked it back into my boot and slid my pistol into my belt again. I searched both bodies quickly for anything of value. There were a couple of nice daggers, a few more magazines that I could use, and some food. I stuffed it all in the rucksack that was still slung over my shoulder. When I looked back at the warrior, he had already armed himself with the pistol that belonged to Twelve and a rifle was slung over his shoulder. He looked even more impressive with all that fire-power.

"Here." I tossed him a spare magazine which he snatched out of the air easily. "We should leave. I'm sure there are more soldiers nearby. The shot I fired will lead them here."

"One soldier for certain," he agreed. "Big man. Dark skin."

"Dark skin?" I scanned the area nervously. The sun had finally risen, its rays shining through the trees. The morning fog had lifted as well, but the shadows of the sequoias continued to make the forest seem ominous. I looked at the warrior again. "You're sure?"

When he nodded, I cursed under my breath and started jogging away from the two soldiers I'd killed. If the warrior was smart he would follow me.

The ferns were thick around the sequoias and difficult to maneuver through. The branches slapped my arms and legs as I ran. Large roots jutted out from the base of each sequoia and there was no shortage of branches and logs to avoid as I fled. I had no clear destination in mind so I simply ran east, moving closer to the coast.

"Why did you do that?" the warrior asked, keeping pace with me easily.

"Do what?"

"Cut that female's throat?"

"Seemed like a good idea. Those soldiers can never be too dead to suit me."

He frowned and his brows pinched together. "Dead is dead."

I laughed hollowly, and then mumbled, “Sure.”

He was still jogging beside me, which made me a little uncomfortable. His stride was smooth and effortless. He hadn’t even broken a sweat earlier in the skirmish with the soldiers.

Why was he still following me?

I put that question out of my mind. Two was the bigger concern. He might still be tracking me, but without his back-up, he may have returned to General Wolfe again. If that was the case, I almost felt sorry for him. Returning to the General empty handed was dangerous.

After about a mile, I slowed to a walk, but kept my pace quick. Sweat dripped down the sides of my face and down my back. Veering through the sequoias was beginning to aggravate me. There was no definite trail through the trees and their trunks were so wide, it forced me to meander around them instead of simply walking in a straight line.

“So, who are you?” I asked him. “You were not from that village?”

“No, I did not live there. I’m from Peton. A Warrior.”

Slapping another branch away from my face, I stepped out of the undergrowth and turned around to face him. The warrior wasn’t prepared for it and nearly barreled into me. He took a step back and put his hands on his hips.

“I’ve heard of that clan,” I said as I glanced around the area for signs of any soldiers. We were sheltered within a circle of four giant sequoias. Their trunks were at least twenty feet across. I glared back up at the warrior again and muttered, "Now it all makes sense."

While I wasn't looking he had shifted his body so he was only partially facing me. He peered out of the corner of his eye so only the unmarked side of his face was visible to me.

"What makes sense?" he asked.

"You're a slaver."

The warrior snorted at my accusation, but I wasn't letting him off the hook.

"That's why you didn't kill Twelve," I said, frowning with disgust. "You wanted to take her as a slave." I held up a hand to stop him from interrupting. "Were you going to take some of those villagers as slaves? Is that why you were there?"

I crossed my arms over my chest and waited for his excuses.

"First of all, we do not deal in slavery. Second of all, no, I was *not* going to take the villagers as captives. They belong to a clan. My people only take the exiled or deserters that have no place." He folded his arms, mimicking me. "And what do you mean 'twelve?' What's with all the numbers?"

I pinched my lips together, turned away, and started hiking through the thick undergrowth of the forest again. Why couldn't I have kept my stupid mouth shut?

The warrior stayed right on my heels, continuing to hound me. "Answer the question, Ravyn."

I wheeled around to face him. Once again, he stumbled to a halt and angled his face away.

"How do you know my name?" I asked, narrowing my eyes at him.

"Your friend spoke it when you were standing on the balcony." The warrior waved his hand in dismissal, as if that weren't important. "Now tell me."

With a reluctant sigh, I answered, "That was her name. It's what she was called."

He scoffed. "A number? That's ridiculous."

"I agree. And what do you mean, 'all the numbers?' What other numbers did you hear?"

"Just after you fled into the woods, I heard one of them say 'she took out Eight.' They call each other by numbers?"

I grudgingly nodded.

The warrior held my gaze for a moment. His expression had thawed, the anger gone. Now he seemed to be studying me. "You shot him almost between the eyes," he muttered.

I shrugged and ducked my head. What I had done wasn't something to be admired. "Sometimes I get lucky." My head snapped up again. "What happened to the other two? You said that the dark one was still out there, but what about the third one? Did you kill him?"

The warrior lifted his chin arrogantly. "Yes."

"How did you kill him?"

"What does it matter?" Irritation laced his voice.

"Just tell me!" I demanded.

"My dagger severed his spine at the neck," he explained. "Now, it is time for you to answer some questions. How did you know this Twelve person and those other numbers? Who are they?"

I started hiking again, weaving between the trees and high-stepping through the brush. This line of questioning was dangerous, regardless of how I'd felt earlier about rescuing him.

"Do not walk away and pretend you know nothing." He kept up with me easily with his longer stride. "You didn't recognize the man, but you *did* know the woman."

I rolled my eyes and admitted, "Fine, I knew her."

"Yet you killed her?"

"She was not a friend," I explained. "They were sent to find me and take me prisoner."

His brows pinched together and his mouth turned down in a worried frown. "Prisoner?"

"Yes," I said sharply.

The warrior ran his fingers through his tousled curls. "What of the man?"

"Like you said, I didn't know him." Once again, I started walking east.

"You're not answering my questions." The warrior gently grasped my arm, breaking my stride, and turned me around to face him. "Be truthful, Ravyn."

I liked the way my name sounded when he said it. His deep voice demanded honesty. Though his face was partially turned from me again, his eyes bored into mine, urging me to tell him what was on my heart … but I couldn't. Could I?

"It's not fair that you know my name and I don't know yours," I said a little breathlessly. His hand was hot against my arm and it made me feel warm all over. I could feel heat rush to my cheeks.

"My name is Thorne."

He let go of my arm but didn't step out of my personal space. I got the feeling that this man was accustomed to getting his way.

Glancing around me, I searched for signs of danger; mainly Two. I didn't feel any tingling in my tattoo, but I wasn't going to depend solely on that passing twinge. Thankfully, the thick fog had lifted. It would be more difficult for someone to surprise us.

"Come on, let's keep walking." We began hiking again, this time side by side. "Those two back there and the others near the village … yes, I know most of them. They're soldiers."

"For this General Wolfe?"

I bit my lip to keep from cursing. Thorne was digging for information again. It wasn't safe.

Thorne heaved a sigh of frustration. "Why can't you answer me? These are simple questions."

"Because it's none of your concern. That's why."

When he didn't respond, I glanced at him to see his reaction. He wasn't paying attention to me at all. He looked like he was trying to sort out a complicated puzzle.

A few minutes later, he gave me a calculating stare. "So you were their prisoner before?"

Through gritted teeth, I confessed, "No, I was one of them. Alright?" I couldn't stand him thinking I was some victim – someone who was weak. Most of all, I didn't want him thinking he'd be able to take me captive.

"Humph," he retorted. "You don't seem very soldierly to me. Not like them. They seemed … off, somehow."

"Like they were sleepwalking? Just going through the motions?"

Thorne nodded. "They had no emotion in their voices at all. You're not that way."

"No," I whispered, stopping in my tracks and staring off into the trees, remembering. "Those soldiers are broken."

"He couldn't break you."

Unable to look at him, I shook my head. I was afraid there would be pity in his eyes. "He did his best."

When I started moving again, so did Thorne. "So, this General Wolfe is in charge of these soldiers. Who is he?"

An evil, evil man, I thought to myself. "I don't know much about him, honestly. He's not exactly the friendly sort, so I didn't get to know him."

He looked at me thoughtfully. "It sounds like he didn't want you to leave."

I laughed dryly. "No, he didn't, but I won't go back. I'll die first."

We entered the clearing where I'd first met Laelynn, Thorne just a step behind me. I didn't know why I'd come back this way.

My feet must have unconsciously brought me here, where yesterday's adventure had first begun. My eyes automatically searched for the man I'd killed, but I was completely unprepared for what I saw. I gasped loudly, covering my mouth with my hands. The man I'd killed had been picked clean to the bone during the night by the beasts of the Valley. Closing my eyes against the gruesome sight, I spun and barreled straight into Thorne's body. His arms caught me and encircled me protectively. His earthy scent was so comforting, I never wanted him to let go.

"Night Howlers, most likely," he murmured into my ear as I continued to hide my face in his chest.

"*I* did this," I breathed sadly, keeping my eyes pinched tightly.

"You killed him?"

Feeling ashamed of my weakness, I slowly backed out of his arms to meet his eyes. "I had to. Those two men were attacking Laelynn – the woman I was with on the balcony," I explained. "That's how I met her and why I was in the village."

"You brought them *both* down? By yourself?"

I clenched my jaw. "Just because I'm female, doesn't mean I can't kill. You saw that for yourself."

Thorne said nothing, but I could see him trying to fit all the pieces together as he studied me. His body was angled away from me again, so I couldn't admire him fully. I thought the claw marks from whatever beast had so foolishly attacked him were … not 'beautiful' – that was the wrong word – but they were certainly not ugly, and they didn't make him unsightly in the least.

Being in this clearing, knowing what was lying on the ground right behind me, made me cringe inside. I sincerely hoped that Laelynn was safe and that this death that I'd dealt out was not in vain. Hopefully the soldiers had abandoned the village now that I was no longer there. There was no way to return now. I would only put them in danger again. It was best to just move on alone. As much as it pained me, I knew the same was true for Thorne. I must walk away and never see him again, for his own good.

"I cannot stay any longer. If you were planning to take me as your slave, you can think again."

"I told you, it's not slavery. We rescue exiles who want a better life than what can be offered in the Valley – running from Sabers or slowly starving to death. The Valley is a dangerous place. In Peton, we feed them. We give them jobs, clothing, and shelter. They earn their keep. We call them captives for no other reason than we have always called them such. Everyone in Peton works to earn their keep."

"And what if they don't want to go with you?" I challenged.

He narrowed his eyes at me, understanding exactly what I was asking. "You do not want a life out here."

"You don't know what I want."

We both attempted to stare the other down, but I had a feeling we'd both still be standing there in the morning if I didn't give in.

After shrugging my shoulders at him, I crouched down to reload my pistol. "I'll warn you now. Those soldiers would not be good captives." I kept talking while I worked. "They are machines.

They've all been brainwashed and won't take orders from anyone but General Wolfe. If they were in their right minds, they would have given up on me two weeks ago. They'll keep hunting me just because he says so."

Straightening up, I looped my bag over my shoulder and shoved my pistol back into my belt. My eyes wandered down to the intricate patterns etched on his arms. "I get it now; the thorns." I gestured to his tattoos. "You're a leader, aren't you?"

"Commander," he simply said.

When I smiled at him, his eyes flicked down to my mouth. I had to stifle the urge to lick my lips. Only Kieron had ever wanted to kiss me before, but we were younger then; kids, really. Soldiers at the compound had attempted to corner me, but their intentions were less than honorable. I had quickly put a stop to it. My experience with males was limited, but I knew why my mouth was suddenly a point of interest.

"You know, the last man to try and kiss me ended up with a bloody nose."

He gave me a cocky grin. "Is that so?"

I narrowed my eyes. "Don't even think about it."

His expression sobered. "Where will you go, Ravyn?"

"I don't know," I admitted. "I was heading east, to the coast. Whatever I do, I can't stay here."

"Peton is near the coast. You would be wise to join us."

I shook my head. "I don't think so."

"Why not?"

“It would be dangerous for you. The soldiers will be gunning for me again soon.” I looked him dead in the eye so he understood how serious I was. “They’ll *always* be gunning for me.”

12
Thorne

As we parted ways, I mulled over our strange encounter. To say that Ravyn was interesting would be an understatement. She was both beautiful and fierce. I could just drown in those liquid, blue-green eyes. It was the same extraordinary color of the Fairuza Sea; the waters that backed up to Mount Asa and my cabin on the far outer edges of Peton. Her hair was even lovelier up close. She did not tie it back or braid it as many of my female Warriors did. Only the front half was tied back, while the rest fell over her shoulders and down her back. 'Stunning' was the only word that came to mind when I thought of her.

And absolutely maddening! I truly believed she was talking me in circles on purpose. Was answering a simple question so difficult, or was she deliberately being obtuse? Whatever her secrets were, I was determined to uncover them. *If* I ever saw her again.

I struggled during our conversation, wondering if I should take her as a captive, but I rebelled inwardly at the idea. With her stubborn nature, she would have fought me every step of the way. Making her one of our captives just would not do.

It was only mid-morning when I returned to camp. The other Warriors had not returned from the hunt yet, so I washed up and found some food and drink. Archer was busy tinkering with the weapons in the cart. The man we took captive the night before was sitting up in his cage glaring at me in contempt.

"Why do you look so angry? We have not harmed you."

"I want to know when I'm going to get out of here," he snarled. "I haven't done anything wrong."

I stepped closer to the cage. "Where are you from?"

The man merely glared at me.

"How long have you been exiled?" I asked, crossing my arms over my chest.

The muscle in his jaw clenched. For some reason, he was refusing to answer.

"Well, we are taking you to Peton. You will have a home there, a job, new clothes, and food to eat. What does your life out here offer that is better than this?"

He glared at me in return. "I just want my freedom."

"And you will have it. After you have completed your service and have become a proper citizen." I moved even closer to him and leaned against the cart. "All freedom comes at a price."

The exile huffed and kicked out at the cage, shaking the bars.

I shrugged my shoulders and walked away to await the other Warriors.

***

I awoke to the sound of the men coming in from the forest. Gunter greeted me while the rest moved to the supply wagon to find food for their midday meal.

"Well?" I asked him.

Gunter shrugged. "Nothing happened. It would have been more interesting if you were there to keep me company. Pierce had a bug in his britches ... probably over you running off and not coming on the hunt. There were no exiles to be found to the north, though we didn't travel more than three or four miles."

I nodded. "We'll hunt northwest tomorrow. Get some rest this afternoon."

"I'll get some rest after you tell me what happened this morning." Gunter grinned and crossed his arms over his chest. "Did you find her?"

"Get something to eat, and then I will tell you."

We sat down by the remains of the morning's campfire and I recounted my adventure. Gunter was rendered speechless, which was an astonishing feat.

"All that happened this morning? In what, just an hour or so?"

"I didn't keep track of the time. I promise to do so next time."

Gunter rolled his eyes.

"At first, I thought there might be an opportunity for a few captives at the village, but I was amazed that they were forming a new clan of their own. They've built all their homes and shops in the trees. It was exceptionally done. I wonder how they keep the Night Howlers away," I murmured, thinking out loud.

"I think you wanted to see that Ravyn again."

The sarcastic retorts hanging on the tip of my tongue were only lies I wanted desperately to believe. Gunter was right. Part of me *had* wanted to see Ravyn again.

"She intrigues me," I finally admitted to him after weighing my words.

"So, you talked to her, then?"

"Yes, in between the running and the fighting, we had a nice chat about the weather."

He ignored my barb again. "Why not take her captive? Then you could bring her home."

"I thought about it, but I do not want that; not with her."

"So, you *do* like her." Gunter smiled widely. "It sounds like destiny was with us on this hunt. Just yesterday you were against taking a life-mate, and now you are shirking your hunting duties to search for one. She must be a fine woman to warrant so much attention. What is she like?"

"She is …" I stared into the fire pit. "She is a warrior and beautiful, but … stubborn as a thick-headed mule! Obstinate, arrogant, and too clever for her own good!"

Gunter choked on his drink when I started railing about Ravyn and then roared with laughter. "She's the female version of you! Sounds like just the thing you need."

After glaring at his annoyingly cheerful remark, I reluctantly nodded.

“Then claim her, Thorne,” Gunter declared, slapping me on the shoulder.

I shook my head. “That is an old tradition …”

“But it is still a Peton law. If you claim her, the clan would accept her under your authority. You are the commander. Your position demands their respect. They would not question you.”

“My father would have plenty of questions.”

Gunter said nothing about the discord between me and my father and gave me time to think on his words. It had been a long time since anyone had claimed someone from outside of Peton, but I was familiar with the custom and rules. While the captives were guarded and governed by any number of Warriors, a claimed person would only be under the authority of the Warrior who claimed her. No formal words were required, unlike the Binding Words that were said to join two people as life-mates. Claiming was merely a mutual understanding between two individuals and usually led to a serious courtship.

Ravyn was no ordinary exile. From what I gathered, she needed a place to escape to, but had been forced to stay on the run from the General those soldiers had mentioned.

“I will think on the matter. Even if I see her again, she might not consider it.”

"You never know, and don't look so downtrodden." Gunter studied me carefully, then asked, "How did she react to your scars?"

I clenched my jaw at his question.

"Don't get a bug in your britches, too!" He held up his hands in surrender. "I'm only asking because I know how sensitive you are about them."

Lightly touching the marks on my face, I thought back to the short time I had been with Ravyn.

"She didn't even flinch, did she? I can see it in your eyes." Gunter grinned. "I like her already. Look, she won't reject you. At least …" he hesitated, finding the right words, "she won't reject *you.*"

"That makes no sense."

Gunter wiped a frustrated hand down his face. "What I mean is, she may have her reasons to reject the offer, but it wouldn't be because of you. From what you've told me, she was trying to protect you from those soldiers. She didn't *have to* save you."

"She did not save me," I huffed.

Gunter snorted at my attempt to argue. "She could have just left you to die out there. Perhaps she *does* care about you. If she does say no at first, it's only because she's being stubborn. But you are the most stubborn person I know, so you will simply have to convince her."

"Humph." Gunter was beginning to irritate me with his logical arguments.

"And just for the record, I would have been extremely annoyed if you had died."

My lips twitched in amusement. This was why Gunter was my best friend. He was brutally honest, even if it was infuriating at times. I pounded him on the shoulder and retreated to my tent to find some solitude and to ponder what was to be done about the stubborn, spirited woman.

13
Ravyn

I didn't actually believe that Thorne was going to let me walk away, what with all his talk of captives. I figured he'd try to lure me into his camp and have his Warrior buddies throw me in a cage. I guess I was wrong about him. Not that I liked him *at all*. He was pushy and overprotective.

You are such a liar!

So I liked him a little, but that didn't mean the other stuff wasn't true. Besides, I barely knew him. I'd known Kieron for six years, had trusted him like no other, and he betrayed me to General Wolfe. It was ludicrous to trust or have feelings at all about a person after only knowing them for twenty-four hours.

He probably thought I was a crazy person, cutting people's throats after they were undeniably dead and charging into the fray without a thought for myself. Maybe that was why he'd let me go. He didn't want a captive who was completely mad.

Maybe I *was* crazy. I was sitting high up in a tree, spying on the man. There was no way to hear what was being said, so I just observed. There were six tents in various places in the clearing. Through the branches of the trees, I spotted two wagons at one edge of the clearing. One of them held the exile I had knocked unconscious two days ago.

Thorne seemed to be alone, except for his captive. Couldn't say I was sad about the exile being locked up. He deserved it. I still didn't agree with Thorne and his clan's custom of taking captives, but from what little I'd learned from the General, the tradition went back generations. If what Thorne had told me was true, then they were actually rescuing people. That didn't seem so bad.

Thorne approached the captive in the wagon several times, bringing him food and water and sometimes speaking with him. He was never abusive or disrespectful. The Warrior disappeared into his tent for a while, most likely to go to sleep. I spent that time eating some food that Laelynn had packed for me. She'd stuffed blackberries in my bag along with some walnuts and a couple of fruits that looked like small apples. Some of the leftover potatoes and rabbit she had roasted last night had been thrown in my bag as well. I ate about half and saved the rest for later.

Just before midday, four men, who must have been Warriors, entered the camp. Their size was fairly equal to Thorne's and it made me wonder if every man in Peton was built like a fighter. Were the women just as fierce? I was tall for a female, but still thin. Perhaps that was why Thorne had trouble believing that I had taken down those exiles?

Thorne emerged from his tent and immediately approached one of the men, most likely his second in command. The other three marched straight to one of the wagons and began preparing a meal. Thorne and his Warrior friend talked for a good half hour. I wondered what they were saying or if Thorne mentioned me at all. I mentally scolded myself for that silly thought.

There were times during the conversation that Thorne seemed flustered or embarrassed by the way he turned red around the ears. His friend laughed frequently, which irritated me. Thorne wasn't a comedian so the man must be laughing *at* him. I scowled and wondered if he'd laugh after I broke his jaw.

Later in the day the Warriors sparred together. It was no wonder he was their commander. He moved with a lethal grace and swiftness that could not be matched, and his strength was truly remarkable. I felt foolish for thinking that I needed to protect him. How ridiculous I must have seemed to him.

The rest of the day was uninteresting and I knew I should get moving, but the sun was already beginning to set. Resigning myself to another sleep sitting up, I settled in to the branch and lashed myself to it, praying that the night was dreamless.

***

"You are Test Subject 1."

I looked up at General Wolfe through my blood-soaked hair. I didn't know if there was anywhere on my face that wasn't bleeding. He'd been beating me for a while. I couldn't even remember how long it had been.

"Say your new name," he said menacingly. I didn't reply.

He backhanded me across the cheek again. My head snapped back and, for a second, I saw stars. I slowly returned my head to its original position and stared back at General Wolfe. His own knuckles were bleeding from striking me so many times.

I hadn't been outside this isolation chamber in days. Smoke had filled the room this morning to put me to sleep. When I'd woken up, I was tied down to a silver metal armchair. The walls were bright white and the fluorescent lights buzzed above me. One of General Wolfe's scientists cowered in the corner by a long surgical table. I had been strapped down to that thing too many times to count.

"You are Test Subject 1. Say. Your. New. Name," the General growled. I still didn't reply.

Using his fist this time, he punched me across my other cheek. Blood filled my mouth. He'd been starving me for days now. The scientist observing in the corner of the room looked green with horror. I could see the pain in his face. He felt sorry for me. He felt the guilt every time the General punched, cut, or stabbed me.

I'd still rather be me than him. If he failed, the General would kill him.

"Who are you? SAY IT!"

He'd gotten so angry that saliva spewed from his lips when he spoke. He'd gotten out of control again. The scientist would have to stop him soon. They couldn't afford to let me die.

"WHO ARE YOU?!"

"Ra-vyn ..." My words slurred because my mouth was swollen. I was pretty sure my jaw was broken too, but my hatred for this man drove me to continue fighting.

"I ... am Ravyn. Never ... be your ... slave. You ... never be ... master."

His face turned purple with rage. It had been weeks since he'd been trying to break me. He'd been attempting to change me into one of his soldiers; one of his mind-slaves. I wouldn't do it. He'd taken everything from me. He couldn't have my name, too.

"My ... name ... Ravyn. Not ... test subject!"

General Wolfe raised his fist, ready to punch me again. The scientist approached the General to stop him but was slammed against the wall. The General had definitely gone over the edge this time. That was never good. The General stormed over to a table that was lined with his tools of torture to grab a large blade.

This was it. He was finally going to do it. Surprisingly, I felt a wave of relief that the time had come. I sat up as straight as I could in my chair to meet my death with dignity. The General swung the knife down and ...

***

I grabbed for my heart and gasped loudly as I awoke from my latest nightmare.

Resting my head in my hands I wondered, *When are these horrible dreams going to leave me?*

The tears I had woken up to kept dripping down my face, even as I wiped them with my sleeve. They were not just nightmares. I had actually lived through each one, and re-lived them over and over in my sleep. At least I'd slept the entire night this time. The sun's first rays were peeking through the trees.

I wondered how Thorne would react if I *did* confide in him about my past; if I trusted him with my secrets. It made me feel sick to my stomach imagining being so vulnerable with him. Even so, he didn't seem to be the sort to look on me with pity or judgement. He hadn't reacted that way when he learned I'd been a soldier once. The only emotion I could detect in his eyes had been concern for me. Maybe he only looked that way because he saw me as a potential captive.

I looked down into the Warriors' camp. Perhaps it wasn't such a bright idea to remain so close to them, but it made me feel like I wasn't so alone in the Valley.

General Wolfe had isolated me from everyone and had tried to break me too many times to count. My face and body didn't hold any scars, but I worried that my mind and heart always would. I wondered again about the scars upon Thorne's face. Did bearing the scars minimize the memories of the pain somehow? His scars were not from torture, but from battle. I didn't think I'd mind having some scars from a great battle. But lasting marks from torture – they would be a constant reminder for me and anyone else who saw them.

Then it suddenly hit me: Thorne was hiding his scars from me.

He had purposefully angled his body when we spoke yesterday in order to hide his scars from my sight. Was he afraid that I would shrink away or pity him? The thought that anyone would respond to him in that way infuriated me. There was no other reason why he should be ashamed of them, unless there were citizens in Peton that made him feel weak because of them. I wouldn't know for certain why he was hiding his scars unless I confronted him about them.

I scoffed at that plan. Thorne didn't want me to *see* his scars. Asking him about them would probably not go well.

The camp below was quiet. I hadn't seen a soul wandering around since I'd woken up this morning. Thorne seemed like the kind of man who would be out of bed well before dawn to get to work; training, taking captives, and doing whatever else they did out here. If they were gone, possibly to find more captives, then it was time for me to go. I'd stayed too long anyway. I was putting them in jeopardy simply by being here. Two had been given plenty of time to pick up my trail and follow me here.

I leaned my head back against the sequoia and let out a deep sigh.

You're procrastinating now, I thought. *You have a plan. It's time to get out of here and follow through with it.*

Thorne had mentioned that Peton was on the coast. I glanced down at the camp again.

Don't even think it.

I shook my head over my own foolish thoughts and climbed down from the tree. I was packing up my rope and checking my weapons to continue my journey to the coast when I heard a strange sound in the camp. It sounded like an animal; one I'd never heard before. There hadn't been many kinds of animals in Terran: small goats, chickens, and a few pigs. There were none at all at the compound, so I was interested to see what sort of animals the Warriors of Peton valued.

I surveyed the camp carefully for any sign of the Warriors. It was hard to believe that Thorne had left his camp completely unattended, but that was convenient for me. There was no one in sight at the moment. I was going to take a quick peek to satisfy my curiosity and then leave for good.

The Warriors' camp was fairly small and surrounded by thick undergrowth that grew rampantly beneath the canopy of sequoias. There would be plenty of places to hide as I approached the clearing.

I circled the camp until I saw them. Just on the edge of the clearing, there were six beasts that I'd never seen before; not in real life anyway. They were horses. I stared at them in wonder. There had been pictures of them in the Terran history book and I remembered seeing them as a child, but our teachers had told us these animals had gone extinct. I should have known better. What did the Terran people know of anything outside their electric fences? The pictures did not do justice to these proud animals. They were magnificent creatures.

Cautiously, I drew near the largest of them; black with white legs and a smooth white stripe down the length of its head to its nose. Its black mane and tail flowed long and silky, making me want to run my fingers through it. His onyx eyes watched me as I slowly crept toward him. When he suddenly snorted and bobbed his head up and down, I paused and looked around carefully. It would be just my luck to have an animal give away my position to an enemy. I had no clue if this behavior was friendly or not, but I was too curious to care, so I continued slowly edging forward.

I thought, maybe I could tempt him with something to eat? But what did I know of animals and the things they ate? I couldn't remember what the book in Terran had said, so I took out one of the small apples from the bottom of my bag. I held it out to him, hoping he wouldn't take off my fingers. I chewed on my lower lip and squeaked fearfully when he snorted again. He leaned forward to sniff the contents in my hand. After what seemed like forever, the horse pressed his wet snout into my palm and snatched up the fruit with his teeth and lips. As soon as he withdrew, I jerked my hand back and held it close to my chest. I laughed breathily in relief that I still had all my fingers. The gorgeous creature seemed to be enjoying his treat.

Before I could stop myself, I extended my hand again, moving even slower so I wouldn't startle him. My fingers grazed the tip of his nose. When he didn't move or react, I smiled widely and continued to stroke the animal's long snout.

"You are amazing," I whispered to him. I giggled again when he snorted and nudged me with his nose, looking for more treats. Still grinning, I backed away, having lingered long enough.

When I reached the outer edge of the Warriors' camp, I suddenly felt strong arms wrap around me, pinning my arms to my sides.

"Thorne, let me go!" I shouted, believing it was the Warrior sneaking up behind me. I didn't struggle against him. My first instinct was to break his hold, but I knew he'd never hurt me.

He didn't let go. In fact, his grip on me only tightened. Then he started dragging me backward, into the woods.

"You sure did make this easy for me," he mumbled into my ear.

My heart dropped to my belly. It was definitely not Thorne.

14

Thorne

I woke up well before dawn again. Sitting by the small fire, I sipped my coffee and listened to the sounds of the birds and insects making their sweet music as the sun rose. It was quieter here than in Peton. It was even quieter than my home up in the hills away from the village. From my mountain retreat, I could hear the sounds of the waterfall that flowed down the hillside behind my cabin. There were mornings I would hike out to the very edge of the mountain that overlooked the Fairuza Sea, listening to the sounds of the waves crashing against the shore. I would watch the water turn incredible shades of orange, yellow, and red as the sun came up in the east. After a few hours, the water transformed into the vivid blue-green that I loved so much.

All I could see now were the blue-green of her eyes.

Was it only two mornings ago that I had considered this time alone before sunrise a gift? I could not sit here any longer with nothing else to keep my mind occupied except a black-haired female.

Dumping my unfinished coffee in the dirt, I roused the men.

"Thorne, what has come over you?" Gunter grumbled. "It's not even dawn yet."

"Let's get on with it. If we leave now, we could catch a few sleeping and be back before lunch again."

"If you say so." Gunter sighed but got himself ready anyway. "I think you're just bored. I'm telling you, a life-mate would relieve you of this need to work so hard."

I scoffed. "Work must go on regardless."

"You know, Thorne, I look forward to the day that you eat your words."

***

"We hit the jackpot, men!" Brock announced excitedly after we had stumbled upon four exiles this morning. "Day three! Archer won his wager."

"Quiet," I hissed. The soldiers that had been tracking Ravyn could be anywhere and I did not want to bring them here by mistake. I gave Gunter a knowing look and he nodded back.

"Right, let's keep it quiet on the trip back. No need to attract unwanted attention," Gunter ordered.

Brock and Max merely shrugged. Archer was nonplussed over the command, but Pierce glowered at me before returning to help the exiles. I shook my head and ignored him.

"Are we going to keep all four, Commander?" Brock asked more quietly. "We already have the one back at camp."

"We never leave one behind alone. There is always room for one more."

We had chanced upon some sleepers, just as I had been hoping. There were four of them living together just southwest of our camp. They had taken shelter within a cave-like crevice in the trunk of one of the sequoia trees. Pierce was the one who had located them. It was a lucky coincidence because I never would have spotted them in their hiding place.

These exiles would do well in Peton. They would have been dead in a week as starved as they looked, or the Sabers would have found them. At first they had resisted, but the offer of food and shelter silenced any arguments about coming with us.

This was why we came on the hunt three times a year. Not only did we add numbers to our workforce in Peton, but we were also saving people who would die without help.

As we travelled back through the thick forest, I stumbled upon a new trail; one that did not belong to us. I beckoned Gunter over.

"What have you found?" he asked.

"Take a look here." I pointed to the trail.

"Looks like a man's footprints. Large boots, I'd say," Gunter speculated. "The man is probably a good six feet tall. Why? You want to track this one too?"

I started getting a bad feeling as I crouched down to get a better look. The footprints were heading in the direction of our camp and my gut was telling me that they belonged to one of the soldiers. Even if it was not a soldier, it could have been a thief after our horses or supplies.

"I'm going to run on ahead and check it out," I told the Warriors. "I will see you back at camp."

The trail was easy to follow. Too easy. Whoever had left these tracks did not care if anyone followed him. This either meant that he was arrogant, ignorant, or extremely dangerous. I was hoping for the first two options.

Fifty feet away, the trail turned and headed away from the camp, which confused me even more. It was possible that some barbarian had been wandering around in this area. That would explain the tracks left behind for anyone to spot.

I still felt uneasy. Ravyn had warned me that the soldiers would follow her; that they would keep coming for her no matter the cost. If this was a soldier …

But she told me she was leaving this area. She had mentioned heading east to the coast. Ravyn should not be anywhere near here.

Maybe I was being paranoid, but my mind would not let it go. I was consumed with images of Ravyn being hurt or captured and, for once, I was torn in my sense of duty. Following the trail would be a simple way to lay my misgivings to rest.

I ran my hand over my messy curls. The commander in me knew that I should go directly back to camp. The Warriors should come first. Making certain our supplies and horses were secured took precedence over everything else. Even Ravyn.

She was a well-trained warrior, like me. Ravyn had proved that she was capable of taking care of herself in a fight, especially with only one opponent. I should not be worrying or having any sort of feelings for this woman. It was absurd that I had even thought about claiming her and bringing her back to Peton. I did not need a life-mate.

Finally, I made up my mind. Returning to camp was the responsible thing to do.

When I reached the edge of the clearing, I saw movement out of the corner of my eye. Anticipating an attack, I hid quickly behind a tree until I caught a glimpse of the flowing black hair that had been haunting me.

Ravyn was standing on the other side of the clearing amongst our horses and petting my own beast; the most temperamental of the bunch. He hardly ever took to strangers so easily. Her mouth moved, soothing him. I nearly shouted a warning when she reached up and stroked his head, but my stallion stood perfectly still. When she laughed, it was a pure delight to hear. I frowned when I realized that I wished it were me. I craved her touch and her laughter.

Gunter was right. I wanted her and I couldn't ignore it anymore, but I would not be able to force her to come with me to Peton. I must earn her trust.

My heart pounding inside my chest, I stepped into the clearing. This was an entirely new sensation. Was I … nervous? I had never felt nervous in my life, not even when I challenged for the right to be Peton's commander. I swallowed back my anxiety and kept going.

Suddenly Ravyn stiffened. I thought she might have detected me drawing close, but then I heard her shout, "Let me go, Thorne!" That's when I noticed the man behind her. He had wrapped his arms around her middle, holding her prisoner and she believed it was me.

Ravyn's face went white when he whispered something inaudible in her ear. When he began dragging her backward into the dark of the sequoias my gut twisted up in knots.

Quickly drawing my dagger, I was after them at once. It was not the darker soldier that Ravyn feared, but I was certain it was one of them and was eager to bring him down.

The man struggled to keep hold of Ravyn's thrashing limbs as he dragged her through the brush and between the sequoias. She stomped down on the instep of his foot and elbowed him repeatedly in the ribs. He cursed loudly at the pain she dealt, but still he didn't loosen his grasp. A white hot fury surged through me when he twisted Ravyn's arm up behind her back in an attempt to restrain her.

I charged through the brush just along the opposite edge of the clearing. The man froze in alarm when he spotted me sprinting toward them. He had made it only a short distance because of the fight Ravyn was giving him. In sheer desperation, he rearranged his grip on her and drew the crossbow that had been hidden behind his back. I recognized him at once and ached to throw my dagger straight into his heart, but I couldn't do so without hurting Ravyn. She slammed his arm down with her elbow before he could shoot and, with a simple twist of her hands, she had him disarmed.

I was nearly upon them and preparing to attack when I heard Ravyn cry out in pain. She screamed a second time when the man yanked his blade out of her side. My bellow of rage echoed through the trees as I watched her body crumple to the ground at the man's feet. After giving her a look that could only be described as repentant, the man fled into the woods with his bloody knife and crossbow.

My footsteps faltered momentarily at his sudden retreat. I didn't understand it. I continued to gape at him until he disappeared into the dark forest. Every instinct in me screamed to chase him down and tear him limb from limb, but that would only leave Ravyn injured and alone, so I let him go.

Why would he flee rather than fight? And why try to drag her away alive if he only meant to kill her? If he had truly wanted her dead, he had missed his opportunity when she was distracted by the horses. He could have stabbed her right then and saved himself a fight.

Dismissing my concerns for now, I turned my attention to Ravyn. Her hand pressed down on her side where the wound was bleeding heavily. Her lungs drew short, painful breaths and her eyes were full of unshed tears. When I knelt down at her side, she sweetly reached for me with her free hand. I clasped it tenderly and held it to my chest.

"Thorne," she whispered, "you're here."

My voice was gruff with pent up anger. "I'm sorry I wasn't here sooner. You're badly injured."

I was not the skilled healer like my sister, Kemena, but I had seen enough injuries to know that Ravyn's could be life-threatening if it was not treated.

"I'll be alright." She smiled weakly.

The tears began to trickle out of the corners of her eyes. I used my thumb to wipe them away and smoothed her hair back from her beautiful face. If she died, I would hunt this man down to the ends of the earth.

"You've lost too much blood. I must take you back to camp."

"No!" Ravyn shook her stubborn head at me. "Leave me."

I ignored her ridiculous argument. "You will come with me. I won't let you die."

She needed stitches. Even that much was obvious, and I knew Gunter always brought his needle and thread for emergencies like this. Reluctantly, I released her hand so that I could tend to her wound. I slipped off my shirt in order to bind it with the material.

"That's nice," she said dreamily.

If she had not been in such a dire situation, and I had not been so furious, I would have laughed. Her gaze lingered on the tattoos that covered my chest and shoulders as I worked to wrap the cloth around her body. When her eyes met mine again, her cheeks flushed.

"Sorry," she choked out. "I think the blood-loss has made me light-headed. I wouldn't normally say that."

I grinned. "If you do not die, you can look at me all you want."

She smiled and blushed again. "I promise I won't die." Her eyes shut for a second as if she had passed out and then opened wide with rekindled fear. "Leave me here, Thorne. I want you to be safe. Please, go!"

"You're a stubborn little warrior, but I am more so. You *will* come back to camp with me. No more arguments."

Careful not to disturb the wound, I lifted Ravyn from the ground and cradled her in my arms. There was no struggle from her. She wrapped her arms around my neck and tucked her head under my chin as I made the trek back to my tent. As much as I wanted to enjoy the feeling of her body pressing into mine, I knew her lack of physical protest was not a good sign.

"I'm going to pass out," she murmured against my skin.

"I'll take care of you," I assured her.

"That man; he wasn't a soldier."

My jaw clenched, still angry over his attack. "He was one of those brothers from the village."

"Why would he do that?" she asked, her voice raspy and weak.

"We'll discuss it later, when you are healed."

"Thorne?"

"What is it, little warrior?"

She whispered so quietly I could barely hear her. "Please don't be afraid of me."

My brow furrowed at the curious remark. Why would I be afraid of her?

"Don't …" She took a deep breath and exhaled. "Don't let the General …"

"No one will harm you," I promised her. "I give you my word."

When I felt her body relax in my arms, I knew she had finally passed out.

When I reached the camp again, Gunter and the other Warriors were back with the four captives. I barely gave the captives a second thought since I was more concerned for Ravyn.

"Gunter!" I shouted urgently. "Bring your needle and thread, quickly."

When he saw me carrying Ravyn, he reacted immediately. I took her to my own personal tent. Moving carefully through the tent flaps, I set her down on the fur blankets inside, making her as comfortable as possible. Stitching a wound was painful, even when asleep.

I removed my makeshift bandage and lifted her shirt to reveal the wound, but careful to keep her body decently covered. She would not thank me for exposing her to anyone, myself included. Gunter stepped inside with a lamp, prepared with his needle, thread, some water, and bandages.

"I take it this is your Ravyn. What happened?"

While cleaning away the blood, I rehashed the events leading up to the incident. The retelling was not any easier than watching it happen. I was furious all over again. Gunter took it all in stride of course, asking for details along the way.

"How deep would you say it is?"

Pinching my eyes closed and clenching my jaw, I visualized how the man's knife had slid out of Ravyn's side, covered in blood. "Maybe four to five inches."

"From the angle of it, he could have hit any of her major organs. I can stitch her up, but we'll have to wait to know for sure."

I felt the blood drain from my face. Even Kemena, with all her skill, would not be able to save her if that were true.

"I'm sorry, my friend." He rested his hand on my shoulder. Then he added, "Also, I wanted you to be aware … the captive that we found yesterday is gone."

My brows pinched together in confusion. "Gone?"

"Escaped. The cage was empty when we arrived back at camp."

I frowned at the news and glanced down at Ravyn.

When Gunter saw my puzzled stare, he asked, "Do you think she did it?"

"I would like to think she did not interfere with our doings, but she was strongly opposed to our tradition."

When I was nearly finished cleansing her skin, I noticed the bleeding had slowed significantly. I paused and, sure enough, the gash was smaller than I remembered.

"I'm ready." Gunter leaned in with the needle pinched between his fingers.

"Wait," I said abruptly, stopping him before he pricked her skin. "Something is wrong."

Gunter moved the lamp closer and inspected the tear in the skin. "I'm not sure what you mean. She definitely needs stitches from the looks of this, but … that's odd. Are you sure about the depth of the knife? This doesn't seem to be fatal. Perhaps all that blood was just bluster."

I shook my head, gently touching the pink skin. "The wound was wider."

"You might have been mistaken in what you saw, Thorne," he said. "You looked livid when you came back into camp. Sometimes in our anger we see things as larger than what they truly are. That happens all the time."

I checked Ravyn's pulse at her neck. "Feel her pulse, Gunter. It should not be that strong after losing so much blood. Kemena tells me often that a heartbeat will become weaker because there is less blood to push through the body."

Gunter took a peek at the gash again. Some of the redness had disappeared entirely.

"You know, Thorne, I don't think you're seeing things after all." He gaped at her torso. "The wound is closing up on its own much quicker than is natural. How is that possible?"

"I don't know."

"Look at it there." Gunter pointed to the edges of the gash, his mouth gaping. "Her skin is closing up. It's very slow, but you can see it happening." He shook his head and rubbed his chin thoughtfully. "It's … miraculous."

Gunter's face held the same look of disbelief and shock that was undoubtedly on my own. Who was this woman who could heal so quickly? I did not believe in magic or witches, but there were many people who did. It could be dangerous for Ravyn.

"Please don't be afraid of me," she had said.

This was what she had meant by that puzzling request. Unfortunately, I would have to wait until she woke to get answers to all my questions.

Gunter began packing up the supplies, leaving the water and some of the bandages. "I don't believe she will need my services, not that they match your sister's." He grinned at me. "Wouldn't life be much easier if we could all heal like this?"

My stomach roiled at his flippant comment. This was the reason she was on the run. I felt it deep in my bones.

"Say nothing to the Warriors of this," I said. "This stays between us."

"You know, she might be the reason for all those stories."

I narrowed my eyes. "Stories?"

“Max’s tale? The black hair; the way she doesn’t die. Could she be the demon?”

15
Ravyn

When I opened my heavy-lidded eyes, I had no idea where I was. The room was dark, but not pitch-black. It was difficult to see if it was day or night, so there was no way to know how long I'd been unconscious. I remembered struggling with someone. The man had been strong, never buckling under my assault on him. I hadn't tried to kill him since he only seemed bent on taking me captive, but I was regretting it now. My scalp ached where the man had yanked on my hair and my side was throbbing … he'd stabbed me! And Thorne …

I was suddenly very alert, but I continued to lie motionless. My tattoo was silent on my skin. Thorne had never felt dangerous to me, but he'd surely seen my secret. He had seen me heal at a supernatural rate, something I had been hiding since I was a young girl in Terran. Even my family had never witnessed it. Well, there was no going back now. I was still alive, which meant that maybe … just maybe … he wasn't afraid of me.

I touched my side gently to make sure that the Warrior hadn't stitched my skin back together. Stitches would be useless to my body. The skin was probably near to closing over by the time he got me back to camp anyway. I really hated lying around, but it was better for the healing process and much less painful. Eating would help, but I couldn't do that while lying flat on my back. It was best to just wait.

The next thing I noticed were the soft, thick furs covering the ground beneath me. They felt wonderful. I dug my fingers into the silky tendrils and, like a kitten, I nestled my cheek into the comforting blanket.

"Are you purring?"

Pain surged down my side when the unexpected sound of Thorne's voice made me gasp and tense up. He chuckled from somewhere close by in the darkness.

"I didn't realize I was," I admitted.

The rustling of fur and clothing could only mean one thing. He was moving closer. Another soft gasp escaped me and I flinched when I felt the warmth from his body on my shoulder. Having Thorne so close, and unable to see anything but a shadow of him, unnerved me.

"You look worried," he said.

"I tend to be cautious around people who know my secret."

“I have had some time to get over the shock,” he muttered. “Do you want to sit up or will you continue to lie there as I question you?”

“I need to stay still for a while longer.”

“Your wound has been closed for a while now.”

“You’re only seeing the outside,” I explained. “The skin usually closes over even before the rest begins to mend, but there’s still pain on the inside. That means I’m still healing.”

He startled me by brushing his fingers across my bare flesh. Goosebumps flashed across my skin in response.

“You are as skittish as my stallion.”

“Well, I can’t really see you,” I pointed out.

“Did General Wolfe make you this way?”

“No.” My voice quivered from his touch. “I’ve been able to heal like this for as long as I can remember.”

Thorne pulled his hand away. “Am I hurting you?”

“No,” I answered quickly, silently cursing my silly behavior.

“Then why does your voice tremble?”

I giggled awkwardly. “It’s nothing. It’s not because of pain.” There was no way I was revealing why his touch made me so anxious. After all, I was nearly seventeen; old enough to know what typically occurred between men and women. It had been different with Kieron; not quite so sudden. Still, Thorne wasn’t the first male I’d admired.

“I *will* have some answers from you now.”

I smirked at Thorne. “Well, aren’t you a bossy-pants.”

"You talked me in circles yesterday and did not answer me directly. Today, I will be direct, and I would like the same in return."

I supposed I shouldn't be so shocked by his demanding tone. He was commander of a great many people in Peton and he had bossed me around in the same way yesterday, after the clash with the soldiers. He'd been brought up to speak so.

"Ask away," I said, conceding just this once.

"Explain how you healed so quickly."

I shook my head. "I honestly don't know."

"Are you a witch? Or some sort of demon?"

A short bark of laughter escaped my lips. "A demon? Are you serious?"

"Answer the question."

"I said I don't know," I snapped. "I've been this way since I was a child."

"I needed to ask," he said, oblivious to my anger at his ridiculous question. "Some traders from another clan brought stories to Peton not too long ago about something new roaming the Valley. Something that was even deadlier than a Night Howler. It kills easily and doesn't die, and then leaves behind long strands of pitch-black hair."

"Oh dear," I croaked. "That does sound like me, doesn't it?"

"It does." Thorne chortled at my answer. "That is what people are calling you. The traders said that when you looked at them, they believed you would suck out their souls."

"Do you believe that?" I swallowed nervously. These rumors about me were even worse than the reality.

"I do not have a superstitious nature."

"I think I remember those men," I muttered, thinking back. "It was, maybe, ten days ago. The soldiers got me good that time … before I killed them. The traders caught me piling up the bodies to burn. When they saw me, I'm sure I looked like death warmed over. My clothes were torn up from the bullets I had taken and I was covered in blood."

"You *were* shot? I assumed that was an exaggeration."

I couldn't see his expression, but if I gauged his voice accurately, I was certain he was gaping at me in shock. I didn't blame him. How could anyone believe such a tale?

"How did you -?" he started to ask.

"- Survive? I have to take the bullets out before I can heal properly. I heal faster when I'm well fed, and it also depends on the severity of the wound. How long did I sleep?"

"About two hours."

I considered the information for a moment. "Usually being stabbed only takes about an hour's time to heal, but I haven't eaten since last night. That might be why it's taking so long this time."

His body tensed beside me. "Usually? How many times have you been stabbed, woman? And shot?"

I was torn between laughing at his outrage and shouting at him for calling me 'woman'. I settled for glaring in his general direction.

"You can't change what's already been done, *warrior*. Besides, it could have been a lot worse. Most of them are terrible shooters."

For a full minute there was nothing but silence. I could almost hear the wheels turning inside his mind.

"Is this why General Wolfe hunts you?"

I pinched my lips together and nodded.

"What does he want with you?"

The genuine concern in Thorne's voice gave me butterflies and muddled my thinking, but I had to keep it together. There was no good reason for him to know everything.

"It's not safe for you to know my secrets, Thorne."

"So you will not tell me." The bitterness in his tone made me wince, as if I'd injured him somehow.

I bit my lip and stared into the dark. Confessing everything to Thorne would be so easy. I wanted to. As a compromise, I decided to only to give him part of what I knew.

"He wanted to use me as a weapon, more or less. He wanted me to be like the other soldiers; brainwashed like a mindless machine. Without my free will I could be used to kill on command."

"And being able to heal unnaturally fast makes you a valuable asset," he reasoned.

I nodded. "His mistake was assuming that I would bend to his will like the others."

"What was he planning?" His demanding tone made me bristle up like an angry Saber, but I supposed his concern was valid. His clan, and perhaps his family, needed to be protected.

"There's no telling what goes on in the General's evil mind," I said vaguely. "He didn't entrust his secrets to me. The other soldiers are expendable. They're just bodies that do his dirty work for him. But whatever purpose he's creating them for, it's not good. Destroying them will destroy his plans."

"The captive that we had caged … did you free him?" Thorne's voice had gone chilly.

"What?" The sudden change in topic caught me off guard and so did his accusation. "He's not there?"

"No and, since you were in our camp while my Warriors and I were not present, you would have had the opportunity to set him free."

"He was there the last time I looked. It might have been yesterday evening when I saw you speaking with him. I didn't think to look this morning."

"You did not care for our taking of captives," Thorne said doubtfully.

"I swear to you, I didn't let him go. I may not agree with it, but I would never interfere with your clan's business."

"What were you doing in the camp, if not to free him?"

Staring up into the dark, I heaved a sigh of frustration. "I wanted to see the horses. I had never seen one in person. I wanted a closer look, that's all."

"So you've been close to the camp since we parted?"

"Yes. I'll admit that much," I confessed. "I was hiding up in a tree nearby."

"What were you doing?"

"Just watching," I said, shrugging.

"Spying?"

Annoyed with his skepticism, I rolled my eyes and huffed. "No, of course not. I wasn't close enough to hear anything that was said. I was only curious." It would have been more difficult to explain that just being near normal people made me feel a little less lonely for a change. "It's my turn to ask questions. Why did you help me, Thorne? What do you want with me?"

There was suspicion in my voice at that last question, but I had to know. Did he still harbor the idea of taking me captive? I would not become a victim because of my blood again. All I wanted was to get to the coast and live in peace.

"I helped you because I wanted to."

I narrowed my eyes at him. "And you have no ulterior motive?"

He chuckled. "We have already met our quota of captives for this year. *You* would not make a good captive."

"That sounded like an insult."

That deep, throaty laugh escaped Thorne again. "Only if you take it that way, little warrior."

Butterflies fluttered through my stomach again at his pet name for me. This was not a good sign. The overbearing brute seemed to enjoy quarrelling with me, and I needed him to keep his distance. Having friends had consequences, just like with Laelynn and her brothers. One of them had just tried to kill me. It seemed no one could be completely trusted.

"I think I'm done now," I said, hoping to gain some physical distance from him. I raised myself up to my elbows. Thorne grasped my hand in an attempt to help me, but I shook him off. I was fumbling around in the dark trying to find a comfortable place to sit when Thorne grabbed hold of me again.

"Just let me help, woman," he huffed, clutching my waist and pulling me down beside him. "Is that more comfortable?"

"No, it isn't! I'm nearly in your lap." I tried to escape his grasp and inch away.

"You are not in my lap. But that can be arranged."

"No!" I protested, even as he sniggered in amusement. "It's not funny!"

"The look on your face is quite entertaining."

I went still in his arms. "How can you see my facial expressions in the dark? I can't see you at all."

"I don't know," he said thoughtfully. "But I can see you clearly. I suppose I've never had trouble with my vision at night. And now you are frowning for no reason."

"There *is* reason," I argued. "You are touching me."

"You had no trouble holding my hand earlier."

I felt my cheeks redden at the reminder. "I was delirious. Now that I'm not bleeding to death, it's unnecessary. Your touch makes me uneasy."

"You do not like me touching you?" he said, even as he tucked stray hairs behind my ear.

"I'm not accustomed to it," I whispered, shivering at his touch again.

Showing him that weakness was a new experience for me, but it was true. I hadn't been touched in kindness in a long time. Mother tried to be affectionate, but Father always admonished her for it. He hadn't wanted her to become attached to me because he knew that I would be gone one day. Then there was Kieron …

"I think I should probably go. Me being here … the soldiers …"

"I think you are about to insult me and my Warriors," he interrupted, his breath warm in my ear.

When I turned to face him, we were inches apart. His eyes were dark and his face was nothing but a shadow. I could barely make out his scars in the dark, and I had the sudden urge to run my fingers over them. Only his obvious attempts to hide them earlier stopped me from doing so.

"You don't know who you're dealing with. My problems with the soldiers aren't going away. They won't stop hunting me."

He merely shrugged. "It doesn't matter. We'll handle whatever comes."

"Have you always been so arrogant?"

"Confident," he corrected me. "It is only arrogance when you lack the skill to back up your words. Has running away always been your answer?"

"I've had no other choice. I've been alone for a long time."

"You are not alone now," he said gently, squeezing my shoulder. The gesture was an unspoken offer of protection. "You have a different choice you can make. And, regardless, you will not be going anywhere for a few days. The other Warriors do not know of your gift. If we are to keep them unaware, then you must pretend that you are still injured. You'll stay here for now."

I ground my teeth together at his command.

"Why do you now look ready to throttle me?" he asked.

When I growled, he merely chuckled. It made me clench my jaw even more. "I'm annoyed."

"Why?"

He seemed genuinely at a loss for why I was so irritated. I rolled my eyes and said, "Because you're probably right about me staying here."

"And that made you angry?"

"You're bossy, too," I mumbled. "What do you propose I do in this tent for so many days?"

Thorne shrugged his shoulders. "Whatever we want."

His tone did not suggest anything inappropriate, but I still voiced my concerns. "You're not thinking that we're going to -" I waved my finger back and forth between us to signify what I meant. It was a good thing it was so dark because my face was surely turning ten shades of red.

Thorne bellowed with laughter. "That is not what I meant, woman. I meant sleep, eat, or talk."

"Talk?" I said skeptically.

"Yes, little warrior. Are you now uncomfortable with talking?"

I should not be so trusting of Thorne but, for some strange reason, I felt an instant rush of relief. He was still an overbearing brute, but at least he was treating me with respect.

"Talking is fine," I said finally. "You said I could trust you?"

"You are about to insult me again," he said gruffly. "I gave you my word that no harm would come to you while you are under my protection and the protection of my Warriors."

My throat thickened with emotion and I felt my eyes pooling up. No one had ever offered to protect me before, nor had I ever felt in need of protection. Kieron was the only boy I'd ever been close to and the General took him from me. It suddenly terrified me that the same could happen to Thorne. I could not ask for his help or depend on him to hide me. This was not his fight.

"You will stop battling with this for now, Ravyn. You will remain in this tent for three days and then you can decide. Now, stay here while I get us something to eat."

16
Thorne

The other Warriors were settled around the fire pit, talking and eating, as I left my tent. The fire was small, only burning to heat the stew Max had thrown together in a pot. Pierce murmured quietly with Archer on one side while Gunter, Max, and Brock chortled over some secret joke.

Their conversations abruptly ceased as I strode over to join them. Standing rigidly, I suddenly felt as if I were on trial.

"What?" I demanded.

Of course, Gunter could be counted on to speak up first. "You seem like you're in good humor, that's all."

Brock and Max nodded in agreement. Curling my fingers into fists, I felt the overwhelming urge to pound the smirks off their faces.

"Humph." I plopped down beside Max and leaned my elbows on my knees.

"You were laughing, Commander," said Brock, peering around Max, still grinning like an idiot. "I don't think I've ever heard you laugh." The other men mumbled their agreement.

My jaw clenched at their scrutiny. I had always taken my job as commander seriously. There was no time for foolishness. Warriors had a job to do and I did mine well. I did not earn my place by laughing and joking about with the men. Showing any weakness might lead to a challenge for my position.

The only sound for several minutes was the scraping of spoons inside bowls. The silence was uncomfortable, and I knew they were waiting for me to tell them something. Anything.

"Is the woman alright, Commander?" Brock finally inquired, showing genuine concern.

"Ravyn will be fine," I assured him.

Chewing his food at the same time, Gunter added, "She didn't even need stitches."

"When you brought her into camp, you acted like she was going to die in your arms."

I glanced over at Pierce, who had spoken. His blue eyes, just a shade darker than my own, were full of cool hatred. He had challenged me for the position of commander after Hawke stepped down a little over a year ago, but I had defeated him. The bitterness he had always shown made me think he had not accepted his rank beneath me. Elevating Gunter to second-in-command above him did nothing to win him over either. Hawke *had* raised Pierce as his own son since he was a young boy. Perhaps Pierce assumed he'd be the next commander, or at least the second-in-command.

In response to Pierce, I merely shrugged my shoulders. "Her wound was not as bad as I had initially thought. Just a lot of bleeding. Kemena sees this all the time." I sent Gunter a knowing look to keep him from mentioning anything further.

"You two talked quite a bit," Pierce said, almost as an accusation. "If she is well enough, we ought to send her away or take her captive. We do not need trouble."

"She is not well enough to be sent away yet. She will not be one of our captives, either."

Pierce was not convinced. "I was just wondering what our purpose for staying was since we have the captives we need."

I rubbed the two-day-old scruff on my chin. "I have questions about this village where I met the woman. It is an established clan."

Gunter remarked, "I'm surprised we didn't run into it on the last hunt."

"Perhaps it hadn't been built yet," Archer pointed out. "Three months is plenty of time to construct primitive shelters if they worked all day, every day."

Max shrugged and added, "Or maybe we just missed it."

It surprised me that Max had even spoken. As one of the youngest in our group, he typically kept his mouth shut, deferring to the others' wisdom. But his logic was sound.

"This is true," I agreed with them both. "It could be a coincidence. Their location is well-hidden and primitive, as Archer suggested. I would not have found it by chance."

"Does the woman belong to them?" Archer asked.

I shook my head. "Ravyn ran into them by chance as well. She was the one who brought down those two exiles."

"You're serious?" Brock's brown eyes widened. "That's impressive."

"She was rescuing a woman; a member of the village. Ravyn made friends with her and her brothers, though it was one of those brothers that injured her."

Archer raised his eyebrows. "That's a strange way to repay her."

"And what of the exile?" asked Pierce. "Did she free him?"

"No." But I had a strange sense of satisfaction knowing that Ravyn had stayed close by.

"He's smiling again," Gunter murmured to Brock with a grin on his cocky face.

I cleared my throat and glowered at them. "There are also soldiers stalking her. I fought a few of them at the village. They take orders from a man she calls General Wolfe."

"What does she say about him?" asked Gunter.

"He was responsible for her training and is desperate to have her back."

"It is unreasonable for them to waste resources to take back one woman, no matter how good a fighter she is," argued Pierce.

"Unless she uncovered something important," Archer deduced. "He wants her silenced."

Archer's reasoning was on target, as always. I had a terrible feeling that her healing gift, something that this General coveted, was at the center of it all.

"And you are willing to protect her?" Pierce asked resentfully. "Even if it means putting us in danger?"

I snorted. "Is anyone here afraid of a fight?"

Brock laughed and clapped his hands eagerly. "I was hoping for some excitement on this hunt!"

"Let's not be careless," I said quickly, holding up my hands. "We will stay three days; enough time to allow her to heal and decide her next move. In the meantime, Archer, set more traps around the camp."

"You got it," he said with an excited grin on his face.

"Gunter, you and Max divvy out the heavier weapons," I ordered. "I want everyone prepared."

Archer nodded to Max. "Come find me when you're done. I'll teach you my latest tricks."

Young Max lit up at the opportunity. I was glad to see Archer passing on his wisdom to others.

I fixed a stare at Pierce. "I want you and Brock to go back to the village and spy on those brothers. Go back to that clearing. You will be able to track them from there. The five men you will watch all carry crossbows. Be back before sunset."

"Let's get moving!" Gunter ordered.

Brock hopped up immediately, excited for his mission. The rest of the Warriors followed suit. All except for Gunter. He drew closer to me so no one could overhear our conversation.

"I hope you know what you're doing," he whispered.

"Would you have us leave, knowing there are threats in the forest?"

"There are always threats in the Valley. We have no fight with these soldiers and, I hate to agree with him, but Pierce is right. What if she leads them here?"

"Then we will do what needs to be done," I said firmly. "I will not leave her to that fate."

"She should be perfectly fine by now at the rate she was healing."

I shook my head. "It is for appearances only, to give us a chance to sort out these new obstacles."

"You didn't tell the other Warriors about how fast she heals. Do you not trust them?"

"I trust them."

"Even Pierce?" Gunter raised an eyebrow at me.

"Whatever Pierce has against me, it's personal. He would never let another Warrior die because of that." I waved my hand, dismissing the subject. "Ravyn is very private about her gift. That is why I said nothing. She feels frightened of people knowing, and for good reason. From the information she shared, it seems that the General has a certain affinity for causing pain. These soldiers are brainwashed and broken. Tortured."

“You believe he did the same with her?”

“All the signs tell me that he did,” I confirmed. “Ravyn is not broken as those soldiers are, but she flinches at my touch. There is fear in her eyes when the General is mentioned, and I doubt this woman is afraid of much in this world. Can you imagine what it must have been like to be hurt over and over, only to heal and go through it all again?”

Gunter muttered a curse. “This General sounds like a Saber that needs to be put down.”

I knelt down to ladle stew into two bowls, thinking that Gunter would get to work overseeing the distribution of our firearms, but I could feel him hovering over me.

“Go ahead and spit it out,” I said, without even looking at him.

“Will you claim her then, knowing all this?”

I shook my head. “I don’t know.”

“I know you have feelings for her, whether you’ll admit to them or not.”

“She will only be here three days.”

“That’s three days to get to know her, court her, and get her agreement.”

Gunter stalked away to distribute the weapons before I could make another argument. He made it sound so simple. But I might just drive her away in three days.

17
Ravyn

"You are quite the piglet," Thorne said, chuckling.

He watched me out of the corner of his eye as I finished up my third helping of stew. I could see him clearly now since he'd brought a lamp inside the tent. Unfortunately, he was a master at keeping his scars hidden. I didn't know why it bothered me. I supposed it was only fair since all my scars were hidden from sight as well.

Pushing the thought aside, I gave him a sly grin and licked my fingers unashamedly. "I'd say I was sorry, but I'm not. I have to eat a lot, and often, to keep up with the healing. It saps my energy."

"I am glad you are not picky."

Thorne moved my empty plate toward the tent-flap and then stretched out on his side, his elbow supporting him. The tent was just long enough to accommodate his impressive height.

"Why? What did I just eat?" I asked curiously. "It was delicious."

"The meat was mutton. We raise Mountain Prongs for their meat and milk. They do well in our mountains," he explained.

"Mountain Prongs?" I asked curiously.

"They are very gentle animals. The males grow to half the size of a horse. The females a bit smaller. They have shaggy brown coats that we sheer to make clothing. They're named for their long, straight horns."

These animals sounded like large goats. There had been a herd of goats in Terran, at least while I'd lived there.

"And the vegetables?"

"The green, slimy leaves were sea-kale and some type of seaweed I do not know the name of."

My jaw dropped in astonishment. "Sea-kale? Seaweed?"

Thorne grinned at my bewildered expression. "I understand. There are times I have to choke down the seaweed."

"No, that's not it." Leaning toward him, I asked, "You can really eat those things from the sea?"

"Well, the sea-kale only grows *near* the sea, not in it. The seaweed -" he scrunched up his face in disgust. "Most of us hate it, but my sister, Kemena, says it is good for us. She packs many of our food supplies for these hunts."

"You have a sister?" My smile widened at the thought.

"I have three sisters."

I raised my eyebrows and my jaw dropped. "Three? So your people are allowed to have large families then?"

With a puzzled expression on his face, Thorne said, "Large families are common."

"They're common?" I whispered in awe. His clan probably had plenty of room to grow in population. "Will you tell me about them? Your sisters, I mean?"

He swung around into a cross-legged position before answering. "Kemena is the oldest sibling. She is a healer, and so is her husband, Aaron. Tallon is fifteen, just four years younger than me."

"Is she also a healer?"

Thorne roared with laughter.

My mouth dropped open again. "What did I say? What's so funny?"

"If you knew Tallon, you would know." Thorne scratched his scruffy chin. "Kemena is strong-willed, but she's gentle. Tallon decided to become a Warrior, if that answers your question."

"Women are allowed to be Warriors too?" I choked. Peton was vastly different from Terran.

"There are not many, but if they so desire and train properly, then we do not deny anyone."

"So Tallon is more like you then?" I smirked at him.

Ignoring my taunt, he said, "Then there is Lenna. She is nearing ten. She is training to be a healer under Kemena."

For a long minute I sat in silence, wondering what it might have been like for me if I'd been born and raised in Peton. Of course, I didn't take my healing ability into account. As far as I knew, no one from Terran knew about it. I wondered, based on Thorne's reaction to me, whether people from Peton would be more accepting of my gift.

"Your parents must be very proud," I said, smiling at him.

A shadow passed over Thorne's face, but it was gone just seconds after.

"It is my turn again, little warrior. Where is *your* family? Do they know what has become of you?"

I lowered my eyes, for Thorne would surely spot the pain that still lingered there. "I *had* a family. I'm sure they're still there, in Terran."

Thorne raised his eyebrows. "Ah, the isolated ones. Did they banish you?"

"Yes and no. I ran away before they had a chance."

I proceeded to explain the laws governing the clan, how I'd been a twin to Camellia, and the plan to take me away the evening before our ninth birthday. By the time I finished my tale, Thorne was frowning fiercely.

"It should not be this way with families."

"I wasn't meant to stay there anyway, Thorne." I shrugged away his anger. "Mother really did try to accept me, but Father clearly favored my sister. The healing ability didn't help, either.

They never said anything about it, so I don't think they knew. If they had known I might have been banished even sooner."

"What about your sister?"

My stomach clenched at the memory of my twin. "I think Camellia didn't know what to make of me. I was always breaking rules, sometimes on purpose. We fought a lot over my rebellious nature. She wasn't mean to me, but Father liked for her to keep her distance from me."

"It hardly seems possible that your parents could keep the two of you separated all the time."

"It was," I agreed. "We were forced to share a bedroom because our home was so small. We talked some when father wasn't around. Mostly about school." In that moment I missed my sister. I missed the scent of flowers throughout the house. I sighed and shook my head. "She was the complete opposite of me, that's for sure; everything that the Terran people appreciated in a girl. Meek, submissive, ordinary."

"Ordinary is boring," said Thorne. "So she did nothing to defend you?"

"We were just girls. What could she have done, or said, to the Elders or my Father to stop them?" I shrugged my shoulders. "It wasn't her fault. Everything is as it should be now. She's safe with her family and probably married by now."

"So young?"

"We are nearly seventeen. Sixteen is a marriageable age there."

“And you were only nine years when you left Terran? I am surprised you survived in the Valley alone.”

“I almost didn’t.” I shivered at the memory. “Soon after I left, the Sabers picked up my scent.” I heard Thorne mutter a foul curse under his breath. “There’s a den not far from General Wolfe’s compound. They stalked me for days until I was rescued by the General’s soldiers. I was lucky, though.”

“Explain,” he demanded in that bossy tone again.

“If they had decided to take me away when I was younger, or I’d waited and hadn’t packed supplies, I would have died. The Elders take the infants into the forest to die. I saw the truth for myself the night that I ran away.”

Thorne’s blue eyes froze over and his hands curled into fists in his lap. “You saw one of your Elders do this?”

His voice was fairly terrifying. I’d hate to ever end up on the wrong side of his temper.

“The night I ran, I followed one of them to the fence. That was actually how I managed to escape. He was carrying a newborn child in his arms and left him out on a stone, like a sacrifice.”

Thorne wiped his hand down his face. “I cannot believe any person, any clan, would stoop to such things.” He cast his eyes in my direction, forgetting even to hide his marred face from me. “If he had not been there, how would you have managed to get through the fence?”

“Well … the wires of the fence ran horizontally. There was about a foot of space between each wire. So,” I drawled. “I was going to get a running start and dive through the wires. I've never been electrocuted before, but I was hoping that I would heal like I had always done."

He spat out a curse and ran his fingers through his hair. "You could have been killed!"

"I was nine," I said with shrug. "It was my only plan and a chance I was willing to take."

Thorne shook his head in contempt. "If we had known in Peton, we would have taken all those children," he murmured regretfully. "There are many families that cannot have children. They would have gladly adopted them. Those Elders ..."

I held up a hand to ward off the dispute I knew was coming. "I understand. I do. It never sat well with me what the Elders did, but the people felt they had no choice. The law was the law. They were not fighters and no one wanted to be exiled for defying the law. Those people wouldn't have survived one day in the Valley. Giving away a baby was easier than forfeiting a safe and comfortable life in the clan. Most people only had one child, just to be safe."

"Still, it is unforgivable," he said gruffly. There was anger in his eyes, but also pity.

"Don't look at me that way!" I hissed. "Do not feel sorry for me. I've come to terms with what's been done and I wouldn't go back even if I wanted to."

"I don't pity you." He took a moment to choose his words carefully. "The life that you have lived has made you who you are.

This I respect and admire. I just …" his jaw clenched with barely concealed fury, "... just thinking about someone trying to take one of my sisters away … I would kill the one who tried."

As he continued to ponder my story, I let my eyes linger over his form. The thorny tattoos gleamed in the light on his lean arms. His white-blonde hair curled wildly on his head and I had the feeling he liked it that way. When I glanced up, he had hidden his scars from me again.

"Don't do that." The words fell out of my mouth before I could catch them and his eyes hardened immediately. "I'm sorry, but you – you don't need to hide them."

The muscles in his jaw ticked again, and I felt guilt over my remarks. I hadn't intended to make him uncomfortable or angry.

"You should lie down and rest," he muttered, ignoring my comments and the awkwardness between us.

"Aren't you worried about the soldiers?"

"I have ordered the others to take shifts for the next twelve hours. I will take a shift closer to morning."

Dismissing me completely, Thorne stretched out on his back and closed his eyes. Leaving some space between us, I curled up on my side, facing him. He was between me and the tent flaps, another act of protectiveness. I had called him overprotective two days before, what felt like a lifetime ago, but I knew it had been instilled in him due to his sisters. He had been their guardian.

My thoughts were still in a whir about accepting his protection tonight and the next three days. It was not like me to play the woman-in-distress. Of course, every time we had stumbled upon each other, I *was* in distress. The first time we had met I was chased by three or four heavily armed soldiers, and then yesterday, I was stabbed and left for dead. Just a normal day for me.

I couldn't help but think of what he'd told me. *You have a different choice you can make.* It was impossible to deny that I was intrigued by the freedoms I could have in a place like Peton. I could be a Warrior, like Thorne; like his sister, Tallon. It was the goal of my journey to live by the ocean, and they had that in Peton.

However, there was no way to know if they would be so accepting of my healing as Thorne was, but I wouldn't find out unless I made the decision to go.

18
Thorne

It did not take long for Ravyn to drop off to sleep. I continued to lay motionless on my back, just listening to her breathe and pondering all she had said. The story of her past was unbelievable and appalling. My blood was still boiling over her tale of all the infants left out in the Valley to die. Could that really be true? I ran a frustrated hand through my hair and down my face, imagining that happening to any of my sisters …

I sat upright and swallowed back the bile that threatened to rise up from my belly, then turned to gaze at Ravyn. She was curled up on her side, arms tucked to her chest. Even as she slept she was protecting herself. Her hair was spread around her in disarray, leaving her perfect face completely exposed. There was not a blemish on her, thanks to her gift, and despite all the horrible things she had told me, her spirit remained unbroken.

Her ability to heal left me feeling rattled. I still could not quite believe what I had seen with my own eyes and wondered how on earth I could take her back to Peton. Everything in me knew that what her body could do was an extraordinary gift, but not many would see it that way. As a Warrior, having the ability to heal quickly was an advantage. I imagined others growing envious of her gift and wanting to exploit it, as the General had done. Some would see only the demon that the rumors told of. The thought of Ravyn being banished again or executed made my stomach turn. I did not want that done to her.

There had to be a way to hide it from the clan, especially the Elders. My own father was likely to detest her simply for being an outsider. He was only interested in his political standing within Peton and would squash anything that came between him and his aspirations. That included his expectations of me.

Despite all the problems, it felt right having Ravyn near. At first it was only curiosity. I thought my interest would diminish after meeting her, but she continued to intrigue me. She had an instinct for survival but contradicted it by risking herself to shield everyone around her.

I was still at a loss over her reaction to hiding my ravaged face. It was a habit I had developed to keep people from insolently staring at the marks, but she had berated me for doing so. I did not know whether to shout at her or kiss her for calling me out.

Heaving a sigh, I knew deep down what I should do. It was my duty to protect her, just as I would the exiles we brought home.

Ravyn needed a safe place, and what better place than behind our strong walls? The General would need to have a long reach to track her and capture her there. My mountain cabin was isolated enough to keep her healing a secret and close enough to the sea to entice her to stay.

Beyond that, though, Gunter was right. I wanted to claim her as my own, to keep her safe with me. I felt a tightening in my chest when I thought of her walking away from me.

I rolled my eyes and clenched my jaw. Gunter never had this problem. He always had the females of Peton sighing and tripping over him with his looks and his charming words. My words alone would never help me win Ravyn over. During our conversation, I had bumbled around and made her angry at every turn.

Unable to sleep just yet, I left Ravyn to rest and went to find Gunter for an update. He was sitting alone by the fire, sharpening his blade.

"All is quiet," Gunter said, never looking up or breaking the rhythm of scraping his blade over the stone. "Pierce and Brock are still gone, but they still have a couple of hours yet till sunset. Archer is somewhere on the perimeter, setting up traps with Max. Everyone is armed."

"Good," I replied, joining him by the fire.

"I've been thinking about that captive that escaped."

"And?"

Gunter finally peered up at me out of the corner of his eye. "He had to have help getting out. I inspected the cage. The lock was cut with a tool."

"Ravyn does not have anything like that in her bag," I assured him.

"Someone else must have come to his aid, then." He continued his scraping. "One of those crossbow-brothers, or a soldier perhaps. Another exile wouldn't have a tool like that, either. It doesn't add up."

"There is definitely something strange going on. I intend to find out before we go back, Gunter."

Gunter glanced up at me out of the corner of his eye. "Did you claim her yet?"

My eyebrows shot up. "Are you crazy?"

He shrugged. "I'm just going to keep asking until you do. What are you afraid of?"

I gritted my teeth together and stared into the open flame.

"Are you still worried about your scars?" Gunter said angrily. "I'm going to beat you to a pulp, and I'm sure the other Warriors would help me." He gripped my shoulder. "Stop worrying so much, Thorne. You are a good man. Any woman would be lucky to have you as their protector."

"Ravyn is just as skilled as many of our Warriors in Peton. She does not need a protector."

Gunter pondered for a moment. “Maybe ‘protector’ is too strong a word. You told me you didn’t want someone who nagged and worried all the time. You need a partner.”

I was stunned by his observation, and I found myself nodding in agreement. Now I just had to find a way to convince Ravyn.

19
Ravyn

My body was aching from standing so stiffly. But that was what I had to do to make them think that I was a soldier. I stood like a statue and stared straight ahead. If I even blinked too many times he would notice. He noticed everything.

We were all lined up today for a final test in one of the many training rooms. This one was not very large. It had just enough room for about fifteen of us to be lined up from end to end. There were bright fluorescent lights overhead and the walls had been painted bright white. The only piece of furniture in the room was a table at the other end of the line of soldiers, opposite me. From the corner of my eye, I saw a wide selection of guns and knives. General Wolfe had warned us that this day would come. The day we would finally become 'active-duty' soldiers, ready for combat.

I was filled with dread when I saw the General strolling past the line of soldiers toward the table, inspecting us all as he went. I could not falter. I was so close to gaining my freedom.

"Today is the day, soldiers," he said with a vicious sneer. He enjoyed watching us suffer. "This is the final part of your training. After this, there is no going back. DO YOU UNDERSTAND, SOLDIERS?"

"YES, GENERAL!" we all shouted together in unison.

He was just as deadly as a Saber, and resembled one too. He stood at five feet, nine inches ... just an inch taller than me. His hair was a mix of black, silver, and gray, giving him the coloring of the Sabers I'd seen in the Valley when I was just a child. His cruel, gray eyes saw our weaknesses and took joy in exploiting them.

In the line of soldiers, I was first. I was TS1. That was my rightful place, according to General Wolfe. Two stood beside me to my right, enjoying every moment of this. The General stood at the far end of the line by the last soldier in this recruiting class.

All of them had been turned. They had all been broken by the General's methods. But his mental attacks and constant beatings had not had the same effect on me. I survived, and I was still in control of my own mind. I could never let him know.

The door to the room burst open and several older soldiers marched inside. They were escorting what looked like prisoners. Each of the prisoners had black covers over their faces, hiding their identities from us. They placed one of those prisoners in front of each of us.

And then I knew.

The General's footsteps marched closer. He was coming for me. He was always coming for me. Fear flooded my heart because I knew what he was going to order me to do, and I would not do it.

"TS1," he barked at me. "Take this weapon and kill." He held out a knife with a deadly serrated edge, expecting me to set the example for the others.

My body had become so tense I thought my spine would snap. My heart pounded in my chest. My deception was finally at an end. I had done a lot of things that I wasn't proud of, but I would not do this.

The General leaned in until he was barely an inch from my face. "TS1, did you not hear me? Take this weapon and kill that man."

When my eyes turned to his, he flinched in surprise.

"No."

***

With a frightened gasp, I sat up instantly upon waking, much like I always did. The darkness was thick, like solid black walls closing in on me. My heart pounded inside my chest and my hands shook.

Where was I? Why was it so dark?

"It's not real," I whispered, trying to take deep breaths. "Not anymore. It was just a dream."

I crossed my arms and hugged my middle, making myself smaller to get away from the overwhelming darkness around me. Breathing deeply was not helping. My chest tightened up even more and my panting quickly turned to sobbing. Like a jittery bird, I swiveled my head back and forth, straining my eyes to find anything that was familiar.

"Ravyn?"

I gasped again and recoiled at the sound of Thorne's voice before I remembered that I was inside his tent. Relief flooded my mind. I wasn't at the compound. I was safe.

"Where are you?" I whispered between my sobs. I reached my hand out into the inky blackness, searching, trusting that he would find me. Without a word, he grasped my hand and drew me into his lap, wrapping me up in his arms. I hid my face in the crook of his shoulder, but I knew he'd noticed the tears that were streaming down my cheeks. There was no hiding my trembling body either.

"Tell me what's wrong," he murmured into my hair as he stroked my back.

My breathing was out of control and the tears wouldn't stop flowing. Regardless, I had no idea what to say to him. The memory of that day sickened me beyond words.

"Can we get out of here? Please? I can't breathe."

Thorne was quick to comply. He cradled me in his arms easily and carried me out into the night air. Normally this would annoy me, but with the way I shook, I wouldn't have made it two steps.

Relaxing against him was impossible. We'd only gone about twenty feet from the camp when I felt my stomach churn and Thorne's stride was only making it worse.

"Put me down," I said, pushing myself out of his arms. "I'm going to be sick."

When my feet hit the ground, I stumbled to the nearest tree, pulled back my hair, and emptied my belly onto the ground. Once I was done retching, Thorne took hold of me again and led me away. I didn't care much where we went. There was no strength left in me to resist.

The sound of rushing water perked me up just when I thought my legs were going to buckle. Then I saw it. Light glinted off the choppy surface of the stream. I dropped to my knees at the edge and rinsed the disgusting taste from my mouth. The water was freezing, like newly melted snow. Slowly swallowing, I let the cool liquid linger on my tongue and lips and then splashed my face to clear away the remaining tears and sweat. My breathing finally calmed as I stared at the water bubbling by.

"Feeling better?" Thorne asked, breaking into my thoughts.

Sitting back on my heels, I peered at him out of the corner of my eye where he lounged against the base of a tree just a few feet from me. His body was totally relaxed with his arms folded and his feet crossed at the ankle. The light from the moon shone brightly through the foliage, splashing slivers of light on his face; his entirely unhidden face.

My response should've been something like "I'm fine" or "it must have been the meat," but seeing his wonderfully imperfect face staring back at me gave me courage to speak the truth.

"No," I murmured. "I don't feel better."

"Is it an infection in your wound?"

Thorne's eyes were filled with a tenderness I recognized. It was one that beckoned me to confide in him. I used to see the same expression on Kieron's face.

But trusting in Kieron had been a mistake.

Facing the stream again, I pinched my lips together, feeling a lie form on the tip of my tongue. I could do it easily. I could tell him anything and he would never know the truth, but I did not want to lie to him.

Thorne was not Kieron. Thorne didn't belong to the compound.

"It's not an infection," I admitted finally. I wasn't brave enough to look him in the eye when I confessed, so I stared at the stream instead. "It was a dream. A horrible nightmare. I have them almost every night, but this one -" I choked on my words.

"What kind of bad dream makes a person sick?"

"The things I dream about are things that once happened to me." I glanced over to measure Thorne's reaction, but he sat perfectly still, waiting for me continue. "They were real."

"Tell me," he said gently.

"The morning we met, do you remember how I told you that I used to be a soldier?"

Thorne nodded.

I looked away into the trees again and began my horrifying tale. "When the General brainwashes the soldiers, his technique is brilliant. Cruel, but brilliant. He spends weeks tearing down a person's mind until they no longer know who they are. Then he creates for them a new identity. Most of them break easily."

"He tried to do this to you?"

I nodded. "I didn't understand at first, what he was trying to do. The others began to act differently. I felt … violated … for an hour or two. Up here." I tapped my forehead. "But then I would heal again and everything was back to normal."

"Your mind healed what the General tried to destroy?" Thorne inquired curiously, barely keeping his anger in check.

"It's the only explanation I could come up with," I said. "My mind is part of my body. What he did to them; none of it ever worked on me."

A muscle in his jaw ticked again, a sure sign of his growing fury. "That was when he started hurting you."

My voice quaked at the recollection. "He thought that a more brutal approach was what I needed. After a while, I decided to act as if he had finally won, so he wouldn't hurt me anymore. I made it till the end of his training, but the final test – that was what I dreamed about tonight. He ordered each of us to kill someone."

"I have seen you kill before, ruthlessly, and without hesitation."

"Those were soldiers," I pointed out. "They are not innocent, not anymore. And they were after me. I'm not seeking them out for revenge. The men they brought to us had hoods over their faces; tied up so they couldn't fight back. They were merely tools for the General's purpose." I sent Thorne a piercing stare. "I have *never* killed anyone in cold-blood. Not like that."

Bringing my knees up to my chest, I rested my head on them and closed my eyes, though it did nothing to ward off the painful memory. Then, without any warning at all, I felt Thorne sitting down behind me. He grabbed hold of me before I could bolt, and put my back against his chest.

"You move like a ghost," I whispered, tensing up at the feeling of his body pressed against mine.

"As a well-trained Warrior should."

His powerful fingers gripped my shoulders and kneaded them in slow circles. Soon enough I was relaxing against him. I liked feeling him so close to me, and hated that I needed his warmth so badly.

"You're always touching me," I pointed out, peering over my shoulder at him.

"You'll get used to it."

"Oh, I will?" I said testily.

"We will discuss that topic later. For now, tell me what happened next in this nightmare. Are you afraid to tell me, little warrior?"

"Of course not."

He stilled his hands and leaned in closer, breathing into my ear, "Then trust me."

After taking a deep breath to ready myself, I finished my story. "It wasn't the actual dream that sickened me, it was what happened after. I woke up before I had to relive that part."

Thorne kept contact with me the entire time. He rubbed my knotted shoulders for a while and then switched to combing his fingers through my tangled mess of hair as he listened.

"I *didn't* kill that man, whoever he was," I pointed out. "But in refusing to do it, I revealed to the General that I'd only been pretending. For months, I'd fooled him. Do you know what my punishment was?" His hands stilled at my question. "I thought he'd just let a couple of the soldiers beat up on me for a day or two. *That* would have been more merciful than what he did. He had me -"

I took a deep breath and blew it out slowly, fighting the tears that pricked my eyes again. Thorne stopped stroking my hair and settled his hands on mine instead. Heat rushed to my cheeks when I realized my own hands had been gripping his thighs while I'd been talking. When he laced his fingers through mine, I had to bite my lip to keep from resisting. Holding his hand felt nice.

"Tell me," he murmured.

I swallowed the lump that was hung in my throat. "He had me strapped down to a chair and forced me to watch as each soldier took turns torturing and killing those men. He had them do it one at a time to extend the suffering, both for them and for me. He warned me that for every time I closed my eyes, he would inflict even more pain on them."

After several minutes of simply breathing in the cool night air, Thorne finally broke the silence.

"Why was that so difficult to tell me?" he asked, his lips grazing my neck.

It wasn't the intimacy or the question that had me bolting out of his arms and out of reach. He'd been so close to uncovering the place where my tattoo was etched into my skin, and I wasn't ready to show him.

Thorne stood up as well, looking perplexed and almost hurt. "Did I anger you?"

"No, I just -" I started, uncertain how to continue. "It's not easy to talk about my pain. I have to relive the very worst moments of my life night after night. I can't get away from it."

"I'll help you," said Thorne confidently.

"You don't know what you're saying. The things I've been through, they're burdens that *no one* should have to carry."

"And if I want to help you carry them?" He took a step toward me.

Shaking my head, I took a step back to counter his approach. "You don't want that," I said, my voice thick with grief. "I should leave."

"So you will run again."

"People that get too close to me always get hurt," I warned him.

"I can take care of myself." He closed the distance between us and cupped my face with his hands before I could backpedal away. "Let me decide what I am willing to risk."

This wasn't supposed to happen. I didn't want to be drawn to Thorne any more than I already was. The General destroyed Kieron and it nearly broke me. I could not let that happen to this man.

"Don't do this," I whispered.

"It's too late, little warrior." He was but a whisper away. "It was too late the moment I first laid eyes on you."

I closed my eyes at Thorne's words. A lone tear finally escaped, spilling down my cheek and over his thumb. He rested his forehead on mine. My senses were filled with the comforting, earthy scent of him. I knew then that I would do anything to save him.

Even if it meant leaving him.

20
Thorne

The piercing cries of Night Howlers in the distance brought us both out of our silent reverie. Though they were not close by any means, it was foolish to be standing out here in the dark with hardly any weapons. Anything or anyone could be stalking us. We were so distracted by each other, neither of us would notice until the enemy was upon us.

"We ought to be getting back to camp, little warrior," I murmured. "Are you tired?"

"I couldn't sleep now."

I felt her shiver.

"We'll just talk, then." I grasped her hand once more and began leading her back to the tent. "I have more questions."

Having Ravyn at my side, her hand in mine, felt natural. I knew that I had just missed a perfect opportunity to reveal my intentions, but she had been backpedaling so much I did not want to frighten her away. I still had time.

The stories of Ravyn's past continued to get worse and worse, and I had the feeling that this horrifying memory was not the only one she was holding onto. My stomach was still in knots over the brutality she had experienced on that final testing day. Ravyn had suffered more than I had first imagined. It was no wonder she had gotten sick in the bushes earlier. My body was trembling with rage simply from listening to her tale. Moving to sit with her, stroking her hair, had been an attempt to calm myself. I was aching to kill Wolfe and any other soldiers who hunted her, but running off recklessly into the Valley would accomplish nothing.

It was clear the General needed to be dealt with. Would my clan support such a decision? With winter coming in a month or so, an attack on him would need to wait until springtime.

As we closed in on the camp, I stopped to scan the area. Archer and Max did an excellent job setting up the perimeter around camp. We did not often need to use explosives but, when we did, I could always count on them to have some extra surprises up their sleeves.

"What is it, Thorne? Do you hear something?" Ravyn looked around us, warily.

"I'm looking for the tripwire. Archer and Max laid down traps around the camp. Trust me; we will not enjoy what happens to us if we touch it."

"What will happen?"

I chuckled and squeezed her hand in reassurance. "Who knows what those two cook up as traps these days, but they are extremely effective. I have seen them set up crossbows that shoot when the wire is triggered. They have even concocted tripwires that cause landmines to explode, spraying shrapnel in every direction."

"Why didn't you warn me about it on the way out of camp?" she huffed.

"I was carrying you. There was no need to tell you."

I moved forward carefully, keeping Ravyn behind me to keep her from setting off the traps unintentionally. Finally, I saw the almost invisible wire. It was barely a foot off the ground stretching in both directions, making a wide loop around the camp. Only someone who knew it was there would be able to find it, especially with so little moonlight coming through the trees here to reflect off it.

"There." I pointed so Ravyn could see for herself. "Come. I will carry you from here."

"I can walk just fine, thanks," Ravyn snapped. "I know I was a blubbering mess back there, but I'm not as weak as you think."

My lips twitched when I faced her, trying to suppress a grin at her irritated expression. "I do not think you are weak, little warrior. I am carrying you because the other Warriors are still under the impression that you are wounded."

"Oh, sorry," she said regretfully.

I reached for her with my free hand and grazed my fingers down the side of her face. Remarkably, she did not flinch away from me this time.

"I would not want to be with anyone who was weak."

I scooped her up into my arms before she could make any other protests. She did not understand yet, but I was not letting her go without a fight. We would argue over it later.

Stepping carefully over the tripwire, I marched straight into the clearing. Brock sat at his post by the fire, which meant I was next on watch till dawn.

"Everything alright, Commander?" he inquired, nodding his head at me in acknowledgment.

"Nothing to worry about, Brock," I assured him. "Signal me when it's time for me to relieve you."

Inside my tent, I set Ravyn down on her feet. She settled down on the layers of furs as far from me as possible. The tent was small and uncluttered. There was only enough room for two people to sleep side by side, so Ravyn's efforts to remain distant from me were amusing.

I scanned the inside of my tent to be sure everything was as it should be. A few extra blankets were piled in the back corner. Ravyn's rucksack and the lamp had been placed near the tent's opening. I looked over at Ravyn. She was dragging her fingers through her hair, attempting to untangle the knots. Her cheeks were bright red again. The mischievous side of me wanted to sit right beside her to watch her squirm. Instead, I took a seat near the tent's opening across from her, my legs crossed at the ankle.

"Are you cold?" I asked her. I thought I had seen her shiver, though it could have been from fear and not the chill in the air. "There's a blanket in the corner behind you if you are."

I raised my eyebrows and fought back a grin when Ravyn reached for it and wrapped herself up. I figured she would stubbornly refuse my offer. The fact that she didn't made my heart beat faster. Maybe I was making progress with her after all.

"I'd like to speak in more detail about that village in the trees," I said while lighting the small lamp. This time I did nothing to hide my face. "What do you know about it?"

Ravyn sat with one leg folded beneath her and one knee pulled to her chest. She watched me intently.

"Not much. I was only in Linwood for one day."

"Tell me what you *do* know. Gunter and I have been trying to make sense of all that has happened today with the man that stabbed you and the exile that escaped."

"You believe there's a connection?" Ravyn frowned with concern. I could see her mind working through the puzzle.

"It's only a theory. Start when you first met the brothers."

Ravyn recounted how she had rescued Laelynn and the brothers had taken her as a temporary prisoner. Most of what she recalled about the village I had seen for myself: the buildings in the trees, the water-wheel the brothers had built, and the pulley system they had crafted.

"What about the two exiles you knocked down? Did either of them speak to you?" Exiles and deserters spoke differently from barbarians that had never seen the inside of a clan.

"No, I didn't give them a chance." Ravyn shifted so both her knees were pulled up to her chest.

"Is there anything else you remember that might have been out of place, in Linwood or in the clearing with the exiles? Anything at all?"

Ravyn pondered the question while idly running her fingers through her hair. "The two exiles reminded me of soldiers. I can't put my finger on it … they didn't wear the uniforms … but their haircuts and their boots were very similar."

I leaned back on one hand and scratched my scruffy chin with the other. "That is something to consider," I muttered. "Anything else?"

"I do recall thinking how odd it was that they'd formed their own new clan from nothing. I've never heard of that happening before."

"The Warriors all agreed they could have built it within the last three months. We didn't see it last hunt, though … we weren't looking for it."

"It must be new because it's not on any of General Wolfe's maps. He has every clan marked on his maps."

Leaning forward and narrowing my eyes, I asked, "All of them?"

Ravyn nodded. "He's meticulous about it."

I was uneasy about General Wolfe having every clan on his maps but I didn't know why. How would he know their exact locations and why? And how did Ravyn know that he was so detailed with them? She had told me the first day we met she didn't know much about him. I suppose that fabrication could be excused since she hadn't trusted me then.

Unaware of my thoughts, Ravyn continued. "I assumed they'd been banished from their clans or had run away, like I'd run away from Terran, but Laelynn said they're all from different clans. She and her five brothers collect strays, so I imagine they do what you and your Warriors do," she suggested.

Thorne shrugged. "We won't know the answer until we are able to question them."

Ravyn nodded. "Laelynn and her brothers puzzled me some, I'll admit. Laelynn accepted me easily in that short time, but the brothers never did fully trust me. Kaelem was the only one that seemed to relax around me, other than Laelynn. She said that he *liked* me," she added, rolling her eyes.

"I am not sure you should believe that, though." I could not help the bitterness that crept into my voice.

Ravyn snorted. "Why not? Don't tell me you're jealous."

"It has nothing to do with jealousy," I argued, bristling at her accusation and the idea that someone else might pursue her. "That night I saw you on their balcony, I overheard him and his brother, Hagan, talking. Kaelem mentioned that he had something he must do, that he had no choice. His words were, 'it's the best thing for the village.' Hagan disagreed, but didn't try to stop him."

"And you think that it was about me?" Ravyn asked, raising her eyebrows skeptically. "That could have been about anything! Did he even mention my name?"

My shoulders slumped. "No, but what if he was the one who sent word to those soldiers? Don't you find it strange that soldiers suddenly happened upon the village firing their weapons?"

Ravyn gulped, her mouth turned down in a frown. She rubbed the back of her neck and murmured, "Laelynn knew they were coming for me. She awakened me to give me a chance to run."

"Kaelem said he had no choice. The General could be forcing them to comply," I pointed out to her. Then cocking my head to the side, I inquired, "Does Wolfe have the means to destroy a village of that size?"

"Easily," Ravyn whispered.

She was looking at me, but her eyes were unfocused, as if she were imagining the carnage the soldiers would leave behind if they had wanted to destroy every citizen of Linwood.

"Kaelem may have turned you in to save his family if he knew the General was looking for you."

Ravyn's brows pinched together in disappointment. "I hope that's not true."

"Maybe they left Laelynn in the dark about their intentions until she saw with her own eyes what they had done," I told her, trying to give her something – anything – positive to hold on to.

"Even I do not share things with my sisters when it is for their own safety or if it will hurt them."

Ravyn's eyes were filled with sadness. I wanted to take back my words, but Ravyn was too intelligent not to see the truth in my theory.

"I'll accept that it's one of the possibilities." She raised her eyebrows and held up a finger. "But I still have faith that Laelynn would have never knowingly betrayed me."

I nodded. "Fair enough."

I did not want to destroy what little faith she had in others and especially in me. I was grateful that she had trusted me at all with the torture she had gone through.

Ravyn shook her head in disbelief. "I would have put my money on one of the twins, either Hagan or Haldar, turning me in to the General – not Kaelem. But you're right. I don't know them well. It could be that the General has them in his pocket, but I don't see how."

I rubbed my chin, thinking it through. "You said you didn't know much about the General. Is he wealthy?"

"I'm not sure, but I would assume so," Ravyn considered. "He and his scientists were always working on new technology, new weapons, and such. That has to come from somewhere."

"Do you think he may be trading with other clans?" I asked, sitting up straighter. I felt as if we were about to stumble upon something important.

"Perhaps. Do your Warriors train with more than just daggers? Do you use rifles?"

"Of course."

Ravyn leaned forward, her blue-green eyes ablaze with curiosity. "Where do they come from? Do you have a factory that makes your weapons and ammo?"

"No, we do not." I stopped to think about all I knew of Peton and its workings. "My Father is an Elder of Peton, and he has never made mention of any such factory. He does talk a lot about our trade routes with other clans."

"Tell me about them."

"I know well of the trade that we have with the clans Murray and Ahern. They are the two clans located closest to us. We trade with Ahern for our horses."

"What do they get from you?" she inquired.

"Medicines; gold, mostly. The mountains are filled with gold throughout, but it is a soft metal. We do not use it for armor or weapons so it is of little use to us. We trade it to Murray as well. They use it for decoration and for currency within the clan."

"And what do you get from Murray that you don't already have access to?"

"The people of Peton are not fisherman," I told her. "We do not have boats or docks. The people of Murray have large, strong ships they take out to sea for weeks at a time to catch all kinds of sea creatures for a source of food. They are delicacies in my city and another source of meat for our bellies."

“So no ammunition or weapons, then?” Ravyn shrugged out of the blanket that had been wrapped around her shoulders. “Where is *my* satchel? *My* weapons?”

When I retrieved her rucksack, she pulled out her gun and placed them in front of me. “You are familiar with this?”

“Every Warrior in Peton has a pistol like yours. We don’t normally carry them on the hunt with us because we don’t want any accidents.” Exiles, for the most part, were not difficult to subdue or convince to join us. There had been some who had become savage in their attempts to get away and made a grab for our weapons. We always brought rifles and pistols in the wagon in the event we ran into a rogue Saber or Howler, but none of us had ever needed anything more deadly than a dagger in many years.

Ravyn narrowed her eyes. “These are made by General Wolfe, in his compound. I’ve seen the assembly line myself.”

I scoffed. “That does not mean …” My words trailed off when I saw Ravyn’s skeptical expression.

“You accused me of being close-minded about Laelynn and her brothers, yet now you want to argue? If Kaelem and his brothers are spies for the General, isn’t there a remote possibility that your clan is trading something to the General for weapons?”

“It’s just not possible,” I muttered to myself. “I would know about it if we were.”

“What if they left you out of the loop?” Ravyn asked, turning my own argument against me. “This had to have started long before you became commander. You're young. How long have you held the position?"

"Just a year."

"How long have you been familiar with these types of weapons?"

I stared at Ravyn in disbelief. Her speculations were like a punch in the gut. Was it possible that the Elders didn't trust me with this information? Was this why Commander Hawke had stepped down so suddenly? Did our Elders know what kind of man they were doing business with?

"I'm sorry," she said regretfully, keeping her eyes locked on mine. "I understand what it is to feel betrayed."

Running my fingers through my hair in frustration, I said, "I do not know for certain, but -"

"I know," she agreed without needing to hear the rest. "Thorne, the General is a greedy swine. He loves power and control. I don't understand why he would willingly give another clan weapons that could be used against him unless there was a reason."

My gut was telling me that Ravyn was right. I just did not want to believe that my own clan could have strings attached to this madman.

Ravyn unexpectedly reached out and rested her hand on my knee to comfort me. It was a small show of affection, but a step forward for her. I ought to be reveling in it, but was completely unwound by what she had revealed to me.

"You must consider that there could be someone communicating with the General. It may even be an Elder. I hope it's not true."

Before I could argue against it, I heard the flap to my tent flutter behind me.

"Commander?" It was Brock, letting me know that it was my shift for the watch.

"Thank you, Brock," I answered him. "Get some rest."

"Yes, sir," he said, and then quietly retreated.

Ravyn's hand still rested on my knee and I could see how saddened she was by all that we had discovered.

"I must take my shift," I muttered, still in a state of shock.

"One more thing," she insisted, squeezing my knee to halt me. "Did anyone compete with you for your position?"

"Why do you ask?"

"If your clan is in communication with the General, and they did, in fact, keep this information from you, perhaps the Elders, or whoever is keeping secrets, were hoping for someone else to fill the position. Someone they could control."

The image of a bitter and angry Pierce filled my mind immediately. I stood abruptly, anxious to get away from Ravyn's probing questions.

"Thorne, I'm sorry …"

"I will see you at first light."

Without looking back at her, I stepped out of the tent, into the night.

***

Sitting at the edge of the fire pit, I stared into the yellow and orange flames as dawn approached. For three hours, I had been on watch. Only the shrieks of the Night Howlers could be heard from far off.

Pierce and Brock had returned from a successful journey to the village. No sign of trouble, but they did not have much to report. There was no sign of the soldiers, and the villagers seemed to be going about their business in the usual way. They both confirmed that the crossbow-brothers were nowhere to be found, either.

Nothing was adding up the way I thought it would. There were more questions than answers. Did father know about the trade with the General? Did Commander Hawke? Surely, he would have been privy to this kind of information. Who could I trust to ask? If there were spies inside Peton, it would be dangerous to start poking around. The General could have turned anyone, even one of my Warriors. Pierce, I could believe. He had never been a friend. Could Ravyn be right? Could the Elders have been hoping for Pierce to fill the role of commander instead of me?

I had to tread carefully with this information. Only Ravyn and I knew, and that was how it must stay until I had a chance to speak with Hawke. I trusted him more than my own father.

The sun's rays were peeking through the sequoias now, and I could hear the other Warriors stirring in their tents, preparing for the day. I dumped out my coffee onto the grass since it had gone cold. That was three mornings in a row I could not enjoy its flavor.

Hoping Ravyn would be awake, I strode back to my tent. She would help me find the truth. She had a strong sense of justice and loyalty to the people she cared about. If there was one person I could trust now, it was her.

Anxious to see her, I ducked inside. I expected to find my little warrior cleaning and oiling her weapons out of sheer boredom, or even sleeping, as there was nothing else to do inside my tent. Pretending to be wounded was going to be tough on her spirited nature.

What I found instead was an empty tent. Ravyn was not there, and her weapons and satchel were missing.

She had left me.

21
Ravyn

After sneaking out of Thorne's camp, I traveled roughly five or six miles until I reached a beautiful part of the Valley. There were no massive sequoias here. These trees were friendly and almost playful, as if they were made for a child to climb upon. Their leaves had changed from green to a fiery red during the autumn months. Multiple sprays of sunlight passed through the branches to the forest floor, lighting up the rose bushes and other flowering shrubs scattered across the ground.

This must be Crabapple Grove. I'd seen it a few times on the General's maps but hadn't given it much thought since I'd never believed I'd make it this far.

Just ahead, Blackrock River cut a path through the trees, winding its way east to the sea. However, this part of the river was a short segment of rapids. Swimming in these waters would be dangerous. Jagged stones lurked just beneath the flow. Downriver, a stone's throw away, the rapids ended and the water fell into a deep, slow-moving pool of water.

Taking a seat on the river's edge, I ate quickly, hoping it would sustain me for another few hours. I'd have to hunt again, and I was unfamiliar with the game in this area. I was further east now than I had ever been before. My only hope was that I had left the Saber dens back in the heart of the Valley.

As I watched the water flick off the boulders and onto my boots, I thought about Thorne. He had to know that I was gone by now. Would he be angry? Relieved? I didn't know, and I shouldn't care, but guilt crushed me for some reason.

Staying with him would have been risky. He was beginning to dig too deep into my secrets. They could get him killed, or worse, captured and tortured by the General's soldiers. Wolfe would think nothing of using the innocent in order to get to me. It was the right thing to do, leaving like I did. A clean break was best.

Then why was I trying so hard to convince myself?

If there was one thing I'd learned with the General it was that anything I held close could be taken from me in an instant. I had held Kieron too close and now he was gone. Even my freedom was a fragile thing.

Then why did you risk your life for Laelynn? For Thorne? I asked myself.

That was simple. I hated seeing people suffer, especially because of me. It was a weakness that the General had used against me time and time again.

I shook my head, trying to clear the errant thoughts away, especially of Thorne. The Warriors from Peton were better off without me. I needed to focus on where I was headed next. Perhaps continuing east, further away from the compound, I could find an isolated place to live next to the sea. I could stay hidden, never to be seen or heard from again. The rumors of a mysterious demon would finally die, and I could live out the rest of my days.

Deep inside, the thought of never seeing Thorne again had my heart aching with loss and loneliness, much as it had those first few weeks without Kieron.

After finishing off the last of my food, I moved downstream where the water was calm and lazy. I knelt down and scooped water to my mouth with my hand, always alert to my surroundings. The birds and rodents of the forest were rustling around in the trees and bushes. The cicadas' songs were trilling all around me. The music of the forest was sweet in my ears; a clear signal that no threat was near.

Bathing helped to clear my head and wash away my guilt. I could imagine Thorne giving me that mocking little grin, reminding me that I was running away again. It was not really him that I was running from though.

Liar.

His strength and fighting spirit drew me in, and his silver-blue eyes melted me at every glance. I had ached to run my hands through his blonde curls and trace his scars with my fingers. All at once, I was miserable that I hadn't kissed him even once.

I dunked my head under the chilly water in an effort to scrub Thorne from my thoughts along with the dirt from my hair and body. Afterward, I donned my second set of clothes and braided my hair. It had been a long time since I'd pulled my hair back completely. The tattoo had always bothered me, so I had left my thick hair loose to cover it, but I knew it was time to let that shame go. It was because of Thorne that I felt this way. My tattoo wasn't a disgrace and neither were his scars. I vowed to never deliberately hide my tattoo again, just as I'd challenged him not to hide his face.

While packing up my dirty clothing, I suddenly stilled. Everything had gone eerily silent. The birds and bugs had hushed their singing. I cursed myself for being so distracted by Thorne, snatched up my belongings, and scurried away to hide. My neck finally began to tingle. I hoped that it had warned me in time.

Since the brush was useless to hide in, I moved further downstream. The banks of Blackrock River had cut deep through the earth creating shallow caves along the edges. That was my best chance. I slid down the embankment, careful not to tumble into the water. There on the narrow ledge, I stepped carefully until I found a niche under the ridge above. It was just large enough for me to curl up in. With any luck my trail wasn't obvious. I muttered another quiet curse at my carelessness.

A few minutes later, I heard their boots stomping heavily on the forest floor. Holding my breath, I knew that at any moment they could be cornering me here on this tiny ledge. I wiped my sweaty hands on my pants and then drew my pistol. After all this time, I should not be so fearful of these soldiers. They had proven again and again to be slow, even thoughtless at times, making it easy for me to escape without much effort. Two was the only one I wanted to avoid at all costs.

The footsteps grew louder, but they stayed on the grassy ledge above me. It sounded like only one or two soldiers, and probably males with their heavy boots. Regardless, it made my chances of escape a little better.

Gravel and dirt rained down in front of me, splashing on the embankment and into the river. They'd halted almost right above me.

"I thought you said you had her."

I covered my mouth with my hand as my heart sank. Of course it was Two, the one I'd been trying desperately to avoid.

"The river is too overpowering," said the other. "There's too much water in the air here."

There was something odd about this man's voice, or rather, something that wasn't odd. He was not a soldier like the rest. His voice was not lifeless, nor did he sound like an uneducated barbarian.

"I did not save your worthless hide from those savages just to watch you botch this hunt," said Two, his voice menacing like the rest of him.

"Don't blame this on me. It's not my fault that she escaped," the man foolishly argued.

"General Wolfe gave you one job to do. You are to use that talent of yours to scent out the girl. He wants her back."

Scent me out? A heightened sense of smell? Perhaps I was not an anomaly after all. There could be others that had special gifts and talents. My mind shifted to Kaelem and the way he'd seemed to read my thoughts. Then there was Thorne with his ability to see things clearly in the dark. Could there be many out there who possessed unique abilities?

"Like I said, if she's anywhere around this river, I'm not going to be able to pinpoint her location because of the moisture in the air. It covers up her scent. So I suggest you find her a different way."

Two grunted and then there was only silence. He must be struggling to think. The soldiers didn't do that very well for themselves anymore. They only took orders.

"We will go back then," Two decided.

"Back where?" the tracker whined. "I'm tired of trudging through the mud, especially with you."

"Back to the camp of those savages. According to the General's informant, she was welcomed into the leader's tent. We will gather more soldiers and question them."

"I am going back to the compound," the other man huffed. "You and the other mules can hunt her on your own."

"No, you are coming with me," Two snarled. "I promised not to let the savages hurt the General's pet. Now come on!"

After they'd departed, my heart was still pounding in my chest and my legs shook from crouching down for so long. The savages Two spoke of could only mean the Warriors.

"Thorne," I whispered.

His name alone was enough to get me moving. I knew this was my chance to be rid of the soldiers for good, but Two had snatched the chance from me. I had to warn Thorne.

Clutching my bag and tucking my pistol back into my belt, I climbed out of the shallow ravine and raced west again, back toward the Warrior's camp that I'd left just hours ago. My heart ached when I thought of what the soldiers might do. Thorne and his Warriors would be completely unprepared. I could never leave them to that fate.

As I ran, a vision of Thorne and his commanding presence filled my mind. There wasn't much of a choice for me to begin with, I supposed. Perhaps I was destined to meet him. The General always bragged to his soldiers, and to me, that our lives had a greater destiny and that fate had brought us together. His idea seemed crazy, especially after the torture he'd put me through, but now I thought I understood what he was trying to say. I was meant to find Laelynn and her village, because it had led me straight to Thorne.

This was going to be a hard run back to the camp if I was going to make it there before the soldiers, but I had to try. I gritted my teeth and willed my legs to move faster. I wouldn't fail him.

Even if he turned me away later for leaving him, I would not let anything happen to my Warrior.

22
Thorne

With arms folded across my chest, I stared into the trees. Morning had come and gone. The scant rays of light shining through the foliage had finally burned away the morning fog.

"Thorne," Gunter called out behind me. "We're ready to move out."

I peered over my shoulder. The wagons were packed up and the horses were saddled. The four captives sat calmly in the cart, anxious to leave the Valley behind. The clearing was now just another patch of soil, indistinguishable from the rest of the forest. It made me feel hollow inside. For the first time since I had been coming on the hunt, I was not ready to return to Peton.

Had it only been four days? It seemed like weeks ago that I was standing beneath that balcony, seeing Ravyn's face for the first time. My shoulders hunched and my jaw clenched at the recollection. I turned to stare into the trees again and scowled.

Pierce could be counted on to chide me about it.

"She's not worth it," he'd said. "There are other women in Peton that you can trust."

The triumph on his face was irksome, as if he had hoped that this would happen. The others had been more understanding and subdued in response to my brooding, especially Gunter. Having encouraged me at every turn, he kept his distance, probably because he was feeling partially responsible.

A hand clamped down on my shoulder. "You cannot do this to yourself," Gunter murmured.

I could not decide whether I wanted to punch someone or go after Ravyn just to shake some sense into her. Last night I was so sure ...

"I know what's going through your thick head," Gunter scolded. "Don't even think about it."

I ducked my head and sighed. He knew me all too well. The only part of me I had much confidence in was my fighting skills.

"Did she tell you that she wanted to come back to Peton? Did she give you any indication of her acceptance?"

I frowned as I thought back on the night before.

"I do not believe it was you she was rejecting, no matter what you're telling yourself," he said more gently. "You would both be miserable if you forced her to do something she didn't want to do."

I lifted my chin and threw back my shoulders. "I do not need a life-mate."

Gunter gaped at me. "Saints above! Are you back to that? That's not what I -"

"Enough." Waving away his retort, I turned on my heel with renewed determination and marched to my stallion. There was no sense in speaking of it anymore. If the woman was going to run every time I tried to get close, I did not want any part of it. It was time to go back to Peton; back to what was familiar. The strange things happening here in the Valley would hopefully right themselves before spring. If the General planned to mount an attack on Peton, the Warriors would defend the city and keep its people safe. That was what we were born to do. That alone was my soul purpose in this world. Not chasing after some female.

My stallion nickered and nipped at me as I checked his bridle and girth. I glared at him. "I will not be lectured by you, either." The beast took pleasure in snorting and then side-stepped, knocking me off balance.

"Commander?"

The hesitant voice of Brock kept me from retaliating against the stubborn animal. Out of respect, I stopped to listen, but I could not face him.

"Are you going to leave her out there? Do you think she will survive out there on her own?"

I pressed my lips together and clenched my hands into fists again. Ravyn had made her choice. It was not my problem if she did not survive.

Without bothering to answer, I returned to checking my saddle bags to make sure they were secure. Brock shifted his weight nervously from foot to foot, but he did not retreat and leave me to my bad humor.

"I know that I'm in no position to give anyone advice about females." He laughed timidly. "But my father once told me the story of when he courted my mother. She kept turning him down, again and again. Of course, my father, stubborn man that he is, wouldn't take no for an answer."

I stopped working and listened to his story. Brock had never mentioned his family's history before.

"He found out later that my grandfather was a drunk and had been beating my Gran. Fortunately, my grandfather died of whiskey consumption. But my father was finally able to understand her hesitancy." Brock took a step closer to me and said quietly, "Maybe you don't know all the facts. We agreed yesterday that she must know dangerous secrets about this General. And Archer is right. He will silence her eventually to keep anyone else from finding out. You'll never know if you return to Peton without her." Brock paused for a moment and then finally added, "You seemed different when she was in the camp. Happier … for what it's worth, Commander." Brock nodded and strode away.

A groan of frustration rumbled through my chest. In order to find the answers, I had to find her. Did she even want to be found?

Brock was right about one thing. She did have information that was dangerous.

The part of me that was still angry at Ravyn wanted to pummel Brock into the ground. Only Gunter had ever spoken so freely with me, but I could not shake the truth of his words. Ravyn had made it perfectly clear that the soldiers would never stop chasing her. Maybe that was her fear. By tracking her, the trail would lead them straight to me and my Warriors and Peton. Was she trying to protect herself, or us? Perhaps it was a bit of both.

I swore under my breath. My stallion turned to stare at me and nickered his agreement.

I sought out Gunter by the cart of captives and gave him my decision. “Fine. I am going after her.”

Gunter’s eyes lit up immediately. When he saw my furious expression, he quickly cleared his throat and put a frown back on his face.

“I’m glad you have come to your senses,” he said, pretending to be serious.

Rolling my eyes at him, I began arming myself with lightweight weapons. I could feel the stares of the other Warriors, especially the suspicious eyes of Pierce. I did not owe them an explanation.

I carried five daggers and two pistols on my body. I thought about adding a rifle but it would do me no good at short range. I was prepared for anything, whether it was beasts, barbarians, soldiers, or even an enraged Ravyn.

My lips twitched when I thought of the look on her face when I caught up to her. I had been tracking since I was a boy. There was not much in the world that could hide from me if I put my mind to it.

Gunter handed me a small pack full of food and water and then I turned and faced the other Warriors. Gunter was still struggling to suppress his grin over my decision. Brock was not smiling, but he looked satisfied. Archer and Max did not seem to have an opinion about it. Pierce's rigid stance and stone-cold glare made his feelings obvious.

Dismissing his contempt for now, I announced, "Start back toward Peton. Set up camp just before sundown. I will join you before dawn."

Pierce's lip curled in disdain at the order. I expected a challenge for my position here and now, but Gunter came to the rescue by backing me up. "Alright, you heard the commander. Let's move out!"

When the Warriors hastened to obey, Gunter turned back with a troubled look.

"I will give you until dawn, and then Brock and I …"

"Do not worry about me, Gunter," I interrupted. "Just keep the Warriors headed in the right direction. I'll catch up soon and I won't be alone."

"You're certain of that?" he grinned.

I snorted. "Even if I must carry her over my shoulder."

Gunter rolled his eyes this time. "An excellent start to the union."

Chuckling over the image, we pounded each other on the shoulder in farewell. Then I turned back to the dark forest. Ravyn had a few hours head start so I would have to move quickly.

Whether she wanted to be found or not, a new hunt was on.

***

Following Ravyn was not as easy as I had planned. Hardly any of my Warriors could move this stealthily through a wooded area, but my well-trained eyes could still see traces of her path. The corner of a boot here. The bend of a blade of grass there. She stepped so lightly that her tread was easy to overlook.

If it were me, I would be heading toward the next good water source. Hawke had brought me out for a trek through the Valley before I had taken my place as commander, and I recalled the river that meandered through this area. Hawke warned me that it was not a good place to camp for the hunt because the Sabers and Howlers tended to stick close to larger bodies of water. Between the rapids and the beasts, I typically stayed away from it, but there were some deeper waters that would be good for bathing. I would bet anything that Ravyn was there, possibly following it to the ocean.

I had been tracking her for a little over an hour when I began to hear something tearing through the forest in my direction. The snapping of branches and rustling of the shrubs was loud. It could be a barbarian or exile. They were notoriously stupid and noisy. The approach did not sound like an animal. Even a Saber would move stealthily as it stalked its prey.

There was no time for a battle. Every time I paused, I wasted precious time and energy in my search for Ravyn. I sunk into the shadows of the tree trunk beside me and waited. The footsteps grew louder, moving quickly through the undergrowth of the forest. The person ran as if they were being chased by the devil himself.

As he moved closer, I readied my dagger. Bringing down one lone person was easily done. If it was a soldier, it would better the odds for Ravyn. If it was a barbarian, then the loss would not be great. My blade would end things quietly.

Just as he ran by, I pounced. Everything was a blur. I heard a muffled grunt as the person hit the ground beneath me and my momentum sent me crashing down on top of him.

The person beneath me coughed and struggled to take in air, having had the wind knocked out of him, but he did not fight back. With my knife still in hand, I rose to my feet, and I found myself staring down into livid, turquoise eyes.

23
Ravyn

"What are you doing, Thorne?" I shouted, a sharp pain surging through my torso.

"Me?" he bellowed right back. "I should be asking you the same question, woman! I could have killed you! Do you have a death wish or do you secretly enjoy getting injured?"

I'd recognized him as soon as he had popped out from behind the tree. His white-blonde hair was so unique and it stood out brightly in the shadows of the Valley. Overwhelming joy had exploded in my chest at seeing him. Of course, I was not expecting him to slam into me so hard. My body felt bruised all over, like I'd hurled myself into a stone wall. I made no effort to move. I breathed as deeply as I could, but my chest was too tender to do much more than inhale in short, painful gasps.

"I think you might've done *less* damage if you'd just shot me," I grumbled.

Thorne raised an eyebrow at my overly dramatic remark. I fought the urge to laugh because it would've been too painful.

"Are you alright?"

"No, I am not alright!" I croaked. "I was just flattened by a giant, stubborn, brute of a man!"

"I would never have thought it was you making so much noise. I thought you had better skills than this, especially when you snuck away so silently in the night."

I winced at his sarcastic retort, and then muttered, "Oh, shut up. I think my ribs are cracked."

Thorne knelt down beside me. My gaze traveled over his face, wondering how on earth he could be here. I never thought he'd lower his towering pride and come looking for me. The thought had me feeling fluttery all over.

After I was certain my body had healed, I held out my hand and let Thorne assist me to rise. His touch was gentle, despite the tightness of his eyes. Once I was on my feet, Thorne kept me snug against his chest, his hands gripping my shoulders possessively.

"I agree it was careless, but I was in a hurry."

His voice was gruff with emotion. "How do you expect to stay alive out here making such a racket? The soldiers …"

I reached up and cupped his scarred cheek with my hand, effectively halting his rant. "The soldiers aren't after me right now. They are after you and your men, which is why I wasn't taking care." Thorne's eyes darkened into dangerous storm clouds. "Two almost found me by the river. He had another man with him, one who is gifted like me. He was using my scent to hunt for me. Luckily, they didn't find me, but I overheard Two saying he was going to gather more soldiers and go after you."

"You're certain?"

"Yes," I said regretfully. "He also mentioned that there was an informant among you."

"An informant?" He ran his fingers through his unruly curls. "Then I must go …"

Before he could say another word, I swiftly pressed my mouth to his. It was absolutely the wrong time and place for it. Kieron would have laughed at my impulsivity but then would also agree that the timing suited me: right in the middle of a crisis. But I wanted to kiss him right then, just one time. I wanted to taste his lips before something happened to one of us and it was too late.

When I broke away, I covered my tingling lips with my fingers. Thorne gaped at me, stunned speechless by my impulsive act.

"Well … sorry," I stuttered.

He widened his eyes and gave me a lopsided grin. "You're sorry?"

"Yes. *No*! The soldiers. We should go." I ducked my head to hide my heated face and started running again before he could say anything more.

***

I allowed Thorne to lead the way back toward the camp. As we ran, I couldn't help but admire his form. He had trained his body, not just for strength, but for speed and endurance as well. It took him little effort to leap over fallen limbs and veer through the shrubs that blocked our path.

He peered over his shoulder several times to make sure he hadn't lost me, but I was with him step-for-step. I had trained my body well, too.

Thorne's pace finally slowed and then halted. I recognized our surroundings. The tripwire used to stretch through the trees here. Stepping up beside him, I grazed my shoulder against his without flinching.

"Do you see anything?" I whispered.

He shook his head. "The men have already begun the journey back. They will be on the road now."

"Are they prepared for an ambush?"

"They were trained by the best," he said, grinning with that familiar arrogance. "They are prepared for anything."

I snorted at his boast, but I knew I wouldn't have him any other way.

"I'll take your lead on this one," I told him in a hushed voice. "You know this area better than I do."

"We will circle around and meet them ahead on the road. If there is an ambush waiting, we will be there to stop them."

We ran slower than before, still hoping to catch up while moving silently. With any luck, we could deplete the General's numbers enough that he would be forced to give up his pursuit of me. Then I'd be free to go to anywhere. I could even go to Peton.

Suddenly, I felt it. The tattoo on my neck came alive with that predictable tingling sensation, warning me of danger.

And then I heard it. The familiar booming of rifles reverberating through the trees.

When I picked up my pace, so did Thorne. There was no need to move quietly any longer. Pure instinct kicked in. I sensed Thorne running at my side and shouting something, but I didn't hear his words of caution. All I felt in that moment was adrenaline and the desire to fight and win.

I knew what I must do. The soldiers' orders had always been to bring me back alive, so they would hesitate to fire their weapons at me. That gave me a distinct advantage.

When we finally saw the Warriors ahead, we both stopped in our tracks. They'd taken cover behind the trees. Two horses lay dead on the road, and the captive's cart had been driven off the path into the trees to protect them from the crossfire. I grabbed a couple of spare magazines from my satchel, slid them into my pockets, and hid my bag in the brush at my feet. I'd have to come back for it later.

Sweat was trickling down my face and back. Thorne was behind me, perspiration glistening on his forehead, but he didn't seem out of breath at all from our sprint back to find his Warriors. I didn't bother asking if he was ready. He was a Warrior. The man would probably give me that cocky smirk and tell me that he was *always* ready. The thought made me grin.

I was about to rush into the foray when I felt Thorne's hand grip my upper arm.

"What are you planning, woman? Just going to run in recklessly, guns blazing?" He asked angrily.

I mentally kicked myself for my blunder. "I'll go in first and draw them off. Once they see me, they'll lose interest in your Warriors."

Thorne clutched both of my shoulders in a painful grip and glowered down at me. "So you *are* planning to sacrifice yourself … *again*. Just like you did at the village."

I was puzzled by Thorne's expression. There was panic in his eyes. Fear.

"I don't need your protection. It seems reckless to you, but I'll be alright," I reassured him, placing a hand on his heart. "Their orders have never been to kill me. Once they see me, they'll be so distracted chasing me down that it'll be easy for you and your Warriors to take care of the rest of them. Trust me."

Thorne grazed his fingertips lightly over my hand and reluctantly nodded. "I will rally my Warriors and follow behind. Do not be careless."

I quickly nodded my promise and then raced into the trees. There was a moment I worried that Thorne might try to follow me, but I couldn't look back. I had to trust him to follow through, just as I'd told him to trust me.

I saw a few of the other Warriors out of the corner of my eye. At least fifteen soldiers were across the path, slightly uphill from where the Warriors were hunkered down. The Warriors were overwhelmingly outnumbered. I ignored the Warriors' wide eyes as I ran across the path toward the line of soldiers on the hill. They would surely believe I was the demon I'd been rumored to be after this.

As I broke through the trees on the opposite side, a soldier locked eyes on me and began shouting orders to the others.

A near-hysterical giggle burst from my lips. My plan had worked perfectly. The shooting stopped so suddenly I felt like I'd gone deaf. The soldiers were now fixated on me, just as I'd anticipated.

I fired off a few rounds in their general direction. One might've been a hit, but it didn't matter. The game was on, leading them through the trees like a cat playing with a mouse. They might think I'm the prey, but I had no intention of being caught.

At least six soldiers were following me. Their shots hit the trunks of the sequoias around me, but I was weaving through the forest so swiftly it was a waste of bullets. After a quarter of a mile, I hid and prepared to go on the offensive.

My heart raced with excitement. I gripped my pistol tightly as I waited, tucked away behind a tree. The soldiers made no effort to be stealthy. Six against one should be easy but these soldiers did not think or strategize well on their feet.

The first one found me before he realized I was there. I kicked his rifle out of his clumsy hands and put two bullets into his chest before he could blink. I used his slumped body like a shield as I fired my pistol at the remaining soldiers. Three more went down before I ran out of bullets.

The last two soldiers were closing in. It was too late to reload so I dropped both the dead body and my pistol. The first soldier swung his rifle at me like a club, but I ducked swiftly. While crouching down, I drew the dagger from my boot and shoved it deep into his gut.

In my peripheral vision I saw the other soldier lift his rifle. I dropped to the ground just as the shot was fired, but not before I felt the flesh tear across my shoulder. Ignoring the sting, I jumped to my feet and fled, leaving my blade behind. The soldier continued to fire off shots as I ran for a place to hide. I thought I might get lucky but just before I escaped behind another tree, a bullet ripped through my thigh. I cried out as excruciating pain surged down my leg. Doubling over, I gritted my teeth and clutched the bleeding wound. It was a through and through, but my body would weaken substantially before it healed.

With sheer determination, I drew my last dagger and grasped the cool steel of the blade. There was just the one soldier. I had to be fast and accurate. Carefully, I inched around the thick sequoia. Like a deadly sniper, he was peering through his scope, waiting for me. I jerked my head back just as a shot rang out. Wood fragments exploded around me. When I took another glimpse, he was still ready. This time, the familiar click of an empty cartridge was all I heard. It was over for him. Without hesitation or remorse, I stepped out and threw my dagger. The rifle slid out of the soldier's hands as he stared down at the blade piercing his chest. A few seconds later, he crumpled to the ground.

I hobbled over to the man's prone form and tore a strip of his shirt away for a makeshift bandage. While I dressed the wound in my thigh, I listened carefully to the forest around me for incoming threats. I worried for Thorne, even though I knew he was capable of handling himself. Still, I wanted to be sure. As quickly and silently as possible, I retrieved my weapons, reloaded my pistol, and started making my way back to the road.

It was slow going. My leg throbbed as I staggered through the shrubs. The sky darkened with a coming storm, making the forest look even more sinister than before. I stayed vigilant, expecting soldiers to pop out of the shadows at any time. Two was still out there, stalking me. There was going to be a day when he finally challenged me but I didn't want it to be today. Not while I was wounded and weak.

The forest was too silent. The branches seemed to bear down on me, making me feel claustrophobic. Something wasn't right. Someone was watching me.

Then I felt it again: that familiar tingle.

I turned in slow circles, checking the trees around me for any sign of movement. My mouth went dry at the thought of meeting Two like this. I gripped my pistol and dagger a bit tighter, one in each hand.

A clash of thunder shook the forest and, at that precise moment, I was slammed into from behind. The force of the soldier's body sent me sprawling to the ground, knocking the pistol from my hand. I managed to hang on to my dagger, but it did me no good since I was face down with the man's weight on my back. When I felt his hot breath on my neck, I reached back and jabbed my fingers into his eyes. He howled in pain, giving me the chance I needed to wriggle out from under him.

"Six," I muttered, preparing to battle him despite my damaged leg. "I wasn't expecting you."

If Two was the best tracker and fighter of the remaining soldiers, then Six was second-best. The other soldiers between Two and Six had either been executed by the General or killed by me during the last four weeks. They had always been my fiercest opponents back at the compound. The General had forced us to fight each other one-on-one in order to rank us. For Two and Six, it had been a competition to see who could beat up on me the most in that challenge ring.

Six rose quickly, infuriated by my cheap shot to the eyes. I had never considered Six as much of a threat as Two. He was not as bulky and certainly not as tall, but his mind was just as twisted. Sneering at me cruelly, he tapped his serrated knife against his thigh, taunting me.

"Looking good, One," he said contemptuously. "Long time, no see."

Listening to his lifeless voice was sickening. Six had joined up around the time I had. I could remember him before he was corrupted into a monster.

"General Wolfe misses you. So does your precious Two," he sneered. "Come back with me now or I'll be forced to hurt you."

I didn't bother to respond to his remarks. Two did not remember me from before and neither did Six, not really. The General had probably ordered him to say it. Cruelty was a specialty of his.

Six charged me like a bull. Shifting my weight off my injured leg, I sidestepped him and skimmed my dagger across his ribs. It wasn't enough to slow him down. He roared in outrage and retaliated by backhanding me across the face with his fist. The warm, coppery taste of blood filled my mouth and my weak leg buckled beneath me. Before I could get to my feet, Six grabbed me up by the back of my shirt and smashed me into the nearest sequoia. The earth seemed to spin end over end as I dropped to the dirt. My head throbbed and my vision blurred from the impact. The blade I'd been carrying was gone; lost somewhere in the undergrowth of the forest during the scuffle.

Six's mocking laugh filled my ears. Though the forest was whirling from my knock on the head, I knew he was hovering over me. When he dug his fingers into my wounded thigh, I screamed in agony.

"Why is the General so fascinated by you?" he asked with obvious derision.

I cried out again and attempted to kick him away when he gripped my leg again, but I was too weak to fight him. My body wasn't healing quickly enough.

Six leaned over me, his face spinning in circles. I used whatever was left of my strength to punch him, but he easily clutched both of my wrists in one hand and held me down. The familiar ring of steel being drawn from its sheath made my heart race and my mouth go dry.

"Perhaps I'll just carve you up into pieces before I deliver you to him."

"Please, Adron!" I pleaded with the boy I once knew. "Don't do this! I know you are in there!"

His laughter mocked me. I struggled against him, but his weight was immovable. As he rested his cold blade on my cheek, I pinched my eyes shut and prepared for the pain to come. I would not give him the satisfaction of seeing me cry.

24
Thorne

After watching Ravyn tear across the road like a wildcat, it took me a full minute to pull myself together.

I don't need your protection.

Her words kept echoing in my mind. She may not need protection, but it did not change the fact that I wanted to protect her. Her thinking was completely backward. It should be *my* job to draw the soldiers away; to keep her safe from them, but she continued to put herself in danger.

The stroke of her hand across my cheek and her spontaneous kiss was what kept my hope alive. The tightness in her eyes had softened. She did not flinch at my every touch. I would have to wait until this battle was over before we could speak of it again.

Ravyn was right about the soldiers. Once she had made her presence known, all common sense left them. The other Warriors left their cover to follow after the retreating soldiers. I joined them in the fight, quickly killing two of them. We took care of the rest just as swiftly. A total of ten minutes had passed since Ravyn had left my side.

"Good to see you alive, Thorne," Gunter said, joining me.

Pierce and Max followed suit, but there was no sign of Archer or Brock.

"Brock caught the first bullet from the ambush," Gunter explained, reading the fear in my expression. "I had Archer stay behind to make sure he didn't bleed out before we could get him some help."

"How many soldiers did we bring down?" I asked them.

"I counted fourteen soldiers," Pierce surprised me by speaking up. "But there had to be more than twenty of them when they first started shooting at us. There was too much confusion to know for sure."

That meant there were at least six following Ravyn. She was a good fighter, but against six soldiers? Alone? I reloaded my pistols with full magazines.

"Whatever you're planning, I'm coming along," said Gunter, checking the rounds in his own pistol.

"Not this time. If I know Ravyn, she will have done away with most or all of them by now. I will go alone." I gave both Gunter and Pierce a pointed stare to keep them from arguing. "Go back and tend to the wagons and Brock. I will be back shortly and together we will discuss our next move."

I started following Ravyn's trail through the undergrowth and sequoias, away from the road. Thunder rumbled loudly overhead and the forest was growing darker with every minute as the storm drew closer. Her tracks were easy to follow despite the shadows. It was only seconds later that I saw them.

Ravyn and a male soldier were both scrambling to their feet to face each other within a circle of sequoias. She gripped her dagger tightly in her hand. I couldn't see her pistol. It had either been knocked from her hand in the fray or she had ditched it after she emptied the magazine.

My first instinct was to rush into the clearing to help her, but I hung back. Ravyn would not thank me for rescuing her when she believed she could handle things. Crouching down, I crept through the ferns to get a better look and assess the situation. Stopping about thirty feet away, I peered around the trunk of a tree to watch. The man she faced was not the dark one that she seemed to fear most and, from what I remembered, he was not as large either. It should be no problem for her.

The soldier muttered something to her with a disdainful grin. The words were indecipherable to me, but Ravyn's face seemed to tighten a bit. When he finally attacked, I expected the fight to be over quickly, but Ravyn did not move with the grace I had seen before. That was when I noticed the bloodied bandage high up on her leg. Whatever had happened, it had weakened her significantly. The vicious gleam in the soldier's eye meant he was very likely aware of it.

The instant the man put his fist to her face, he sealed his fate. I prowled toward him like a vicious predator. It took every ounce of self-control to keep from charging in like a madman when Ravyn was flung into a tree like a ragdoll. Her head snapped back against the unforgiving wood, probably jarring her senses. She barely uttered a sound on impact and she didn't get back up.

The soldier was completely preoccupied, so I picked up my pace. Ten more feet and I would be within striking distance.

The soldier foolishly left his back exposed when he crouched over her, making it easier to sneak up behind him. The blood-curdling scream that filled the air wrenched through me like a knife in my heart. I heard Ravyn plead with him, call him by his true name, but he taunted her with cruel laughter.

With a roar, I surged out of the ferns and seized the soldier with both hands, yanking him away from Ravyn. It was probably foolish of me not to finish him while his back was turned, but my honor would not allow it.

As he rose to his feet, he inspected me from head to toe and sneered, "So, One has a new champion?"

His disdainful glance shifted to Ravyn, who was still lying on the ground behind me. I did not dare look down at her or my rage would burn out of control.

"Do you really think you can save her?"

"Enough talk." I crooked my finger at him. "Come and kill me, if you can."

I waited with an eerie calm, no weapon in my hands. The man drew a second dagger and did not hesitate to attack. I blocked two thrusts of his blades, twisted one of his wrists until it snapped, and then kicked his feet out from under him. The soldier howled frantically as I shoved him down on his back. The entire skirmish had taken less than five seconds.

He growled, "You can kill me, but he will never stop. He will have her at any cost."

The soldier made one last attempt with his second blade, hoping to take me by surprise. I caught his arm easily and bent his elbow so the blade was angled at his own heart. He groaned and struggled against me for a moment, but his efforts were futile. My weight was enough to force his own knife into his chest. After a high-pitched shriek of distress, he took one final gurgling breath and then relaxed into death.

I left the soldier lying on the ground, his wide eyes staring blankly at the stormy sky, and strode over to see about Ravyn. She was sitting up by the time I reached her side, her palm still resting against her head.

"It's over," I said gently, kneeling down beside her.

With my thumb and forefinger, I tilted her chin to inspect where the swine had hit her. If there had been a bruise or cut on her face, it had already disappeared. Only remnants of blood remained on her chin.

"I've never seen you so angry," she whispered.

"He was hurting you." I reached out for her injured thigh. "You were shot?"

Ravyn untied the bandage and inspected the skin on her thigh. "Through and through. It just took too long to heal."

"Do you need to rest a little longer?"

She shook her head. "The skin's closed over now. I'll get something to eat when we get back to the road. That will help speed the healing on the inside."

"You promised not to be careless," I scolded and then tugged her into my arms. "I will lecture you about it later."

She giggled at the threat, my actions contradicting my words. It did not escape my notice that she held me tightly and dug her fingers into my back.

"Were you able to defeat the rest?" she breathed into my neck.

"Easily," I murmured into her hair. "Are you sure you're alright? You're shaking."

"I'm fine now."

"You sound angry," I said.

Ravyn eased away from me. "I don't like eating my own words, but I guess I was wrong about not needing some help."

Her disgruntled expression had me grinning. I had been eating my words since I met the woman.

"No one does." I brushed the tendrils of hair out of her eyes. "But we are now even."

Our eyes locked again. The silence between us was charged with all the things we needed to say to each other, but now was not the time.

"We should go back. Brock's wound needs tending and this storm is not going to wait."

"What happened to him?"

"Gunter said he took the first bullet."

With a soft curse, Ravyn regained her usual demeanor. Tough on the outside, but definitely softer on the inside. I just had to crack the surface to reach it.

When we reached the dirt road again, Archer and Max had the wagons back on the path and Brock's bleeding body laid carefully beside them. The two cart horses were still hitched, one in front of each wagon. Only two other horses were still alive, tied behind the supply cart. The other two lay dead beside the road. The soldiers had killed them in their ambush.

"Thorne," Ravyn said with a hand on my arm. "Go look after your friend. I'll be right back."

I frowned and seized her hand when she started walking away. "Where do you think you're going now?"

"I'm going to get my bag." Ravyn put her hand on my chest and nodded to reassure me. "I'll be right back. Promise."

After a moment's hesitation, she leaned in and gave me the lightest of kisses on my cheek and then ran off into the trees.

"Well," Gunter said from behind me. "I think she likes you."

I ignored his arrogant grin. "How is he?" I replied, nodding toward Brock.

"The bullet is still inside. Even if we were near Peton, Kemena would have trouble helping him."

Brock was already pale by the time I reached him. He had been shot in his side, the bullet entering his body right beneath his ribcage.

I breathed a sigh of relief when I spotted Ravyn again, making her way back through the undergrowth and onto the road. I knew it was foolish, but I had felt a nagging fear that she would disappear again.

Ravyn sprinted straight toward me and Brock and knelt down with her rucksack.

"Move aside," she commanded.

I was not sure what she thought she could do for Brock. He was going to die no matter what we did. A wound to the gut was always serious because you could never be sure which vital organ on the inside had been injured. Even if we could get the bullet out, too much blood loss, fever, blood poisoning – the complications I had seen Kemena deal with before – were horrible. The chances of Brock surviving this wound were slim.

Ravyn dropped to her knees beside me and rummaged through her bag. She pulled out a bottle of clear liquid and a long, thin pair of tweezers. Her eyes were wide and her mouth was pressed into a grim line. I knew what she was about to do.

"Have you taken a bullet out of someone before?" I whispered so only Ravyn could hear me.

"Only on myself," she murmured. Then, with a more forceful voice, she ordered, "Someone get a fire going."

Archer and Max moved to do just that. Gunter was still kneeling across from Ravyn and me. Pierce approached looking as irritable as ever.

"We are piling up the soldiers' bodies to burn," Pierce reported.

"Did you get all of them?" Ravyn asked him as she prepared for the surgery. She opened a bottle of clear liquid and poured it onto a cloth. She wiped down her tweezers with it and set them on a clean bandage.

"No," he said, raising an eyebrow. "There were two men who ran off after it was clear we were winning the skirmish. One of them was a soldier. He wore the same uniform. He was bigger than the others, with darker skin."

"That was Two," said Ravyn.

I narrowed my eyes at her response to hearing that Two was nearby. Her body had gone rigid and her face was white as a sheet. This soldier named Two must be a force to be reckoned with if Ravyn was so fearful of him. I looked forward to the day that I would face him.

"Two?" asked Pierce, eyeing Ravyn and then me.

"The soldiers call each other by numbers," I explained, giving Ravyn a chance to regain her composure. "It's their rank."

"He's their captain," Ravyn added. "You said there were two of them?"

Pierce nodded. "The other one was the first exile we took captive – the one who escaped."

"The exile?" Gunter asked, frowning in confusion. "Why would he be with these soldiers?"

I gritted my teeth together to keep from swearing. When I glanced over at Ravyn she was staring at me with wide eyes. She'd made the connection as well. The exile that had escaped from our camp was the same man that was tracking her scent. He was travelling with these soldiers, and that meant one of the soldiers – Two most likely – had helped him escape. I gave my head a slight shake so she would not reveal anything to the others. She tightened her lips and continued her work.

Pierce shrugged and said, "They both disappeared shortly after Ravyn pulled that stunt back there. They watched the other soldiers for a minute or two from a distance; I guess to see how they would fare against us. The exile was hiding behind their captain like a whipped puppy. Once the tide turned, he took hold of the exile and high-tailed it out of there."

I watched as Ravyn slid her belt out of her waistband and set it aside. It was made of dark, thick leather and there were deep teeth marks in several places. My stomach churned when I realized what that belt was for. How many times had Ravyn bitten down on that belt to dig bullets out of her own body? How had she withstood so much self-inflicted pain?

Ravyn took the bottle of clear liquid again, poured a small portion of it into her cupped hand, and set the bottle down beside her.

"Why are you soaking your hands in that stuff?" I asked curiously.

Ravyn rubbed her hands together, spreading the liquid over her fingers, palms, and wrists. I snatched up the bottle and took a sniff at the liquid inside. It was alcohol, the kind Kemena used for her healing practice. I had never seen Kemena wash her hands in the alcohol before.

"I'm disinfecting my hands," she explained. "I'm sure your sister would use soap and water. I do my best to be clean, but I don't have soap. This will have to do."

Careful not to contaminate her hands again, Ravyn took her tweezers and marched a few paces away, where Archer and Max were tending the fire. She placed the tips of the tool into the flames for a few minutes. Kemena had done this before with knives she used to sear wounds. I looked down to find Brock watching me. His face was ghostly pale and damp with perspiration.

"It's … not good … is it … Commander?" he groaned.

I wanted to lie to him, to tell him that he would be fine, but I could not get the words to leave my mouth.

"The commander's lady seems to have a plan," Gunter answered. "You just hang in there, kid."

Ravyn marched back over with the tweezers, freshly sanitized, and knelt down again. "Now the belt," she said quietly.

I swallowed back the bile that threatened to rise from my stomach. This was it.

"What … what is the belt for?" Brock glanced warily between Ravyn and me.

Ravyn leaned over him, careful not to touch him and contaminate her hands. "It's for you to bite down on. This is going to hurt badly, but I'm going to do everything in my power to make sure you live. Do you understand?"

Brock nodded and Gunter placed the belt firmly between his teeth. I moved around Ravyn so that I could hold Brock's legs. Gunter took his arms and we prepared to hold him down. With any luck, Brock would pass out during the surgery.

And it began. Ravyn did her best to work quickly but finding the bullet inside him was tricky. Brock kicked and bucked, moaned and screamed through the pain. Max and Archer tried to remain for support, but they could not stomach what we were doing to their friend. I felt Pierce hovering over my shoulder.

Ravyn was as steady as I had ever seen her. She gave Brock words of comfort, encouragement, and apology throughout the gruesome ordeal. After what seemed like hours of torture, Ravyn finally pulled the bullet free of his body. She quickly doused Brock's wound with alcohol, sending him into fresh waves of spasms and screaming. Then she used what little material we could find to bind up the wound. Sweat and tears covered Brock's face.

"You did good, kid," Gunter choked out. He looked like he was on the verge of tears as well.

"Don't …" Brock moaned, breathing heavily. "… don't tell … anyone … back home … that I cried. Okay?"

Ravyn gave him a regretful smile.

I simply said, "Brock, you were braver than any of us would have been."

Gunter chuckled with us. "Yeah, Thorne and I would have both been bawling like babies."

Brock tried to laugh, but it turned into a cough, mixed with groans of pain.

"I need to wash my hands," Ravyn whispered to me. Her hands were covered with Brock's blood.

"Gunter, stay with him?" I asked.

"You got it." He gave me a quick salute, trying to keep things light for Brock's sake. He knew as well as I did that Brock had very little time left. "Now, Brock, you seem to be stuck with me. Let me tell you about the time …"

Gunter went off into storytelling mode and I heard Brock groan and choke with laughter. Gunter's stories were legendary in Peton. They were mostly of his childhood and the mischief he happened to get into as a boy, usually by my side. The stories would keep Brock's mind off his pain.

I followed Ravyn to a small creek trickling through the trees. It could not be more than ankle deep, but it was enough to wash the blood away.

As Ravyn was cleansing her skin, she asked, "How long do you think he has?"

"Twenty-four hours, maybe," I said bluntly. "Kemena always says that bullet-wounds are the worst. It is often a slow and painful way to die."

Ravyn stood, grief etched on her face. "This is my fault," she whispered. "This is why I left in the first place … to keep this from happening."

"What happened to Brock could have happened to any one of us, anytime, anywhere. This was not your fault."

"How can you say that? I bring trouble with me wherever I go!"

"And you never deserved any of that!" I shouted. "If you had not come back, the rest of them might be dead. We were sorely outnumbered."

She stepped away when I reached for her, but I was not letting her back away from me again. I clutched her wrist and drew her into a fierce hug. Finally surrendering to my embrace, Ravyn rested her head on my chest.

"Thorne, he's dying because of me."

"He is dying because of General Wolfe. Do not forget who started all of this."

Her body tensed against me. "What is it?" I asked uncertainly, hoping I had not said the wrong words again.

"I think I may know a way to save him."

25
Ravyn

"I'm not sure what you think you can do for him," said Thorne, shaking his head and shrugging. "He cannot heal the way you can."

Thorne and I stood a distance from the carts talking quietly while Max and Gunter watched over Brock. Pierce and the red-headed Warrior – Archer I believe he was called – were nowhere to be seen.

"I think there may be a way that he could."

"How?" Thorne asked, looking skeptical.

"It's a … medicine," I said, careful not to reveal too much. "The General's scientists concocted it in their labs to imitate what I can do."

"Ravyn, we do not have time to go all the way to that compound to retrieve this medicine. Brock does not have that much time."

"No, but Two will have some with him. And he was here not too long ago. He can't have gotten far."

Thorne eyed me as if he were judging whether my plan was crazy or not.

"Do you want to save him or not?" I challenged. "I will not have him die because of me when I could've done something to save him. We don't have much time, twenty-four hours, right?"

The warmth in Thorne's eyes had disappeared again. "So, you would just run off alone again?"

I gaped at his accusation. "What? No, I -" But he didn't let me finish explaining.

"Do you think I enjoy watching you put yourself in danger?"

I put my hands firmly on my hips. "Thorne, I never -"

"After that last encounter with the soldier that nearly gutted you like a fish, I would have thought you had finally … why did you even come back? Because you needed to be a hero?"

"Because I care about you!" The words flew out of my mouth before I could stop them.

Thorne looked as if I'd just slapped him. Declaring my feelings was not my intention, but there it was. And he just stood there, staring at me. After all that had happened the last few days, I could not believe that he felt nothing. Had I been completely wrong? Was I just another captive to him? No, I could not believe that.

I shifted from one foot to the other. "Thorne, I wasn't planning on going alone. I want … *need* you to help me," I said slowly, silently cursing how vulnerable I sounded. Then I swallowed back the last of my reserve and told him the full truth. “I don’t want to face Two alone.”

I searched his face, waiting for the verdict. Thorne’s messy hair swayed with the breeze and his icy gaze had thawed again. The urge to run my fingers over his scruffy chin and up through his untidy hair was overwhelming, and then my eyes found his mouth. I instinctively licked my lips. That was all the invitation Thorne needed. He moved quickly, pressing his lips to mine in a hard kiss. His hands circled my waist, tugging me nearer. I was disappointed when the moment ended. Thorne evidently had more self-control than I did.

“You are not going to bloody my nose, are you?” he said, teasing me.

I laughed softly and shook my head.

“You’re coming with me?” I asked him.

He rested his forehead on mine. “I have your back, little warrior.”

***

I stared silently into the flames of the bonfire that was slowly burning the bodies of the dead soldiers and the two horses. Thorne stood beside me, his commanding presence a comfort.

When Pierce had said that he’d piled up the soldiers to be burned, I’d been elated, and Thorne hadn’t blinked an eye. Now there was no reason to for me to explain why it was imperative that they do so. Perhaps it was common practice for them. The bodies might attract Sabers or Howlers, like that exile I'd left overnight.

But still, I couldn't keep the truth from Thorne anymore about these soldiers, especially if I was to join him in his homeland. But I couldn't tell him here. Not in front of his men. If what I overheard was true, that there was an informant among them, then I could not trust the information with anyone but Thorne.

I saw him nod out of the corner of my eye, confirming without words that he was ready to go. Together we strode to the supply cart and stocked up on ammunition. I accepted some of their food and water and then checked the supplies in my own bag.

"What are your Warriors going to do while we hunt?"

Thorne took a quick look around. The frown on his face told me he had come to the same conclusion as me: it wasn't safe here on the road.

"Why not send them back to the camp?" I suggested. "Your men can set up the tripwires again. There's water close by, and we can find our way to them easily once we're done."

"I agree," he said quietly. "I thought about sending them on toward Peton, but with Brock in his condition, it would be a difficult journey."

"You tell your men, then. I'm going to find Pierce. He can show me where Two's trail starts."

Before walking away, Thorne stopped me and whispered, "I have not disclosed any information to my Warriors since you have made me aware of an informant among us."

I nodded my head in complete understanding. "I'll be discreet."

"And watch yourself when you are with Pierce. He is the last person in this group that I would trust."

I hesitated a moment but then nodded and turned away to locate Pierce. I was on the verge of asking Thorne how he knew he could trust me over one of his own men. He'd only known me a few days, but I was certain his response would either turn me to mush or make me fuming mad.

Pierce was standing at the edge of the trees with Archer, just off the road. I slowed, not wanting to interrupt what looked to be a very heated conversation, but another part of me wanted to eavesdrop. It could very well reveal what the two of them had been up to. According to Max, they'd disappeared after I'd removed the bullet from Brock's body and then reappeared from the woods together. Could one of them be a traitor? Could both of them be working together? So many questions and no time to dig for the truth. Right now, Brock's life depended on Thorne and me locating Two as quickly as possible.

I was still twenty feet from them when Pierce noticed me and stopped the discussion short. Archer peered over his shoulder at me and then quickly marched away. I watched Archer's retreating form for a second and then turned to find Pierce glaring at me. He was handsome in his own way. His dark brown hair was lengthier than Thorne's but tousled and hanging down over his blue eyes. He had an intimidating stance, much like Two, but his skin was fair instead of dark. I had to remind myself that it wasn't Two that I was dealing with. I had nothing to fear. Unless Thorne was correct in his suspicions and Pierce actually was the traitor.

"You said you saw Two … uh, the dark soldier, this afternoon." His fierce expression was making me nervous. "Can you show me where?"

"I can, indeed," Pierce replied sarcastically. "Can you tell me why?"

I narrowed my eyes at him. He was derisive enough to be the traitor. "Because we're hunting him down."

"So now our commander is running off into the forest … again … because of you."

Then I noticed something about his eyes, his face. It wasn't anger or malice. Was it concern? Was he worried about getting caught, or could he actually be worried about Thorne? I was hoping for the latter for Thorne's sake. He could use a strong ally in this fight.

"He may have some medicine that could help save Brock." I revealed that much to him. It would be no secret once we were back and it might just motivate him to help me. "I can see you don't think much of me, but at least for your fellow Warrior …"

Pierce looked toward the road at his sleeping friend and then nodded. I was alright with him hating me as long as he guided us in the right direction.

Pierce led me down the road in a westward direction. We veered off the road after about fifty feet and strode into the trees. I kept a watchful eye on him and a hand close to my pistol. I was skeptical about Pierce being the informant, but I wouldn't be foolish either. There was something about that quick look he gave me. He may not be the betrayer in this game.

"Here is where I saw him last," Pierce said.

He was right. Two had been just on the edge of the fight, merely watching, but close enough to see the road and the Warriors. His trail was easy to see retreating into the forest. Two sets of footprints moved in the direction of the General's compound.

I was pulled from my thoughts when Pierce gripped my upper arm in a painful hold. My free hand instinctively reached for my pistol, but I hesitated, only to see what he would do.

Pierce drew me close until we were nose to nose. "Our commander is bewitched by you, but I am *not*." He squeezed my arm in an obvious threat. "Do not do anything stupid."

I didn't have a chance to ask Pierce what he meant because Thorne finally caught up with us.

"Pierce!" Thorne bellowed, striding toward us furiously.

Pierce immediately released my arm. Giving me one last fierce scowl, he turned on his heel, bumped shoulders with Thorne, and strode back to the road and the other Warriors. I watched him until he joined Archer by the wagon.

Thorne rubbed my bare arm where there was now a red handprint. "Did he hurt you?" he asked. "I never thought he would harm you."

"He didn't," I said. Then I realized what Pierce's message had truly meant and smiled.

"He threatened you," Thorne said gruffly.

I chuckled and gazed back at Pierce. "Yes, he did."

***

Thorne balked at the idea that Pierce could actually be his – well, not friend, but definitely an ally. I tried to explain that Pierce was merely threatening me out of concern for his commander, but Thorne wouldn't listen.

We made good time following Two's trail. Like the other soldiers, he left his tracks visible for anyone to find. I wouldn't have needed Thorne's help in tracking him. I let him lead though. Having him by my side gave me a confidence I hadn't felt in a while. These last few days made me realize how lonely I had become. I was alone in Terran because I didn't belong. Becoming one of the General's soldiers only isolated me more and made me realize there were far worse things than being on my own. I felt at peace when I was around Thorne, like I was complete again.

Thorne held a steady pace for several hours. I stayed right on his heels as we silently meandered through the towering sequoias. The sun had disappeared long ago even though it was still a few hours until sunset. Dark storm clouds had rolled in and there was a damp chill in the air. Lightning occasionally flashed and the sound of thunder rumbled shortly after. It was not raining yet, but it soon would be. I could smell the moisture on the blustering wind.

Without warning, Thorne pulled me off the trail and into some large ferns.

"Is everything alright?" I whispered, crouching down beside him.

"I figured we should catch our breath before we go charging into his camp."

He passed me his water container and I took a drink without protesting. After handing it back to him, I dug into my satchel for some bread and cheese and started stuffing large pieces of them into my mouth.

Thorne chuckled softly. "You look like a chipmunk with your cheeks so full."

Nearly choking at his remark, I covered my mouth with my hand in embarrassment.

"Promise me, little warrior, that when you meet my family, you will not eat this way." He gave me a boyish grin.

I couldn't say anything with my mouth full, so I narrowed my eyes and punched him lightly on the shoulder. He winked playfully.

Once I'd gulped down my food, I asked, "Did you spot his camp?"

"No, but I feel sure we are close." He packed his food and water away. "I thought I could hear some talking."

"Whatever we do, we need to stay downwind or Two's companion will smell us coming."

Thorne paused in thought. "Maybe we can use that to our benefit. We don't have time for a fight. We'd risk getting injured. I could draw them out away from the camp while …"

"While I find the medicine," I said, finishing his sentence for him.

"Both roles have risks. My scent is unfamiliar to him. Curiosity should bring them both out. Two may insist his companion track me to eliminate me as a threat."

"That's what I'm afraid of," I whispered. "What if they find you?"

"I won't let that happen."

Unfortunately, I didn't share his confidence this time. He cupped my cheek with his hand.

"You know what the medicine looks like. I don't."

I was uncertain about his plan. There were too many things that could go wrong. We were both cunning individuals, but we had never been on a mission together before. This would be a true test of our trust in each other's skills and instincts.

"You are nervous," he pointed out, not quite a question.

"I make a point to avoid Two," I admitted. "He's … unusually brutal with me."

"He will not touch you."

"You can't promise that." Strengthening my resolve, I asked him, "Where do you want to meet after this is over?"

It only took him about ten seconds to decide. "There is a large river that runs east. Blackrock River. It's not far."

“I know the one you mean. We’ll run into it if we run straight south …” I looked around me to determine the direction. “That way?”

Thorne nodded, pleased that I was able to find my way, even in the dark. “Once you have this medicine, go to the river’s edge. You said that this tracker could not make out your scent by the water? Wait there and I will find you when I have lost them.”

He made everything sound simple, but there were too many variables that could change in a second. Taking a deep breath to steady my anxious heart, I forced myself to stop thinking about it all and focus on my job. Get in and out of their camp without being detected.

Night had finally come and the storm clouds were a breath away from spilling their contents down on all of us. The darkness and imminent rain would give us an advantage. This should be easy.

I stiffened my spine and felt the heat of adrenaline flow through me again.

“Let’s do this.”

26
Thorne

Ravyn and I were in perfect position and could see our opponents from a distance. The dark soldier and the exile sat across from one another at a small campfire. Two was busy cleaning and oiling his rifle. The tracker was eating what looked like dried meat.

I pulled Ravyn close and whispered into her ear, "I will see you soon." She kissed my cheek in a silent goodbye.

I prowled through the thick undergrowth like a ghost, keeping the camp in my sights at all times. The sweet smell of rain filled the air. When the wind began to swirl, the tracker's head lifted instantly. He jerked his head back and forth, gesturing toward me, and then in Ravyn's direction. I knew without a doubt that he had scented us both.

A sinister grin formed on Two's face and he began to assemble his weapon. If Ravyn was going to have any chance to accomplish her part of the plan, I would have to do something. I drew my pistol and fired several shots into the camp hoping it would draw them toward me. The tracker hit the ground in fear but it did nothing to faze the dark soldier. Two tossed his companion a rifle, expecting him to defend himself, and then strode off into the forest after Ravyn.

This was not what we intended. From her apprehensive behavior earlier, it was clear that Ravyn had known this might happen, but the goal had not changed. I quickly adjusted the plan. Ravyn would have to deal with Two while I retrieved the medicine.

With my pistol still in my hand, I sprinted through the trees toward the soldiers' campsite. I burst through the last of the brush and into the clearing. The tracker panicked when he spotted me. He backpedaled away when I strode toward him, forgetting all about the weapon in his hand. He tripped over his own feet and both he and his rifle went tumbling into the dirt. Scrambling about, trying to recover, I feared he might actually shoot himself. When he finally got to his feet, I disarmed him easily and knocked him unconscious with the butt of the rifle.

I took a hesitant step toward the edge of the forest and stared into the trees where Two had chased after Ravyn. Part of me longed to run to Ravyn's rescue. There was always fear in her eyes when she spoke of Two. But then I thought about Brock and the reason we had come. Brock would die, and Ravyn would hate me if we did not get the medicine. She would stubbornly tell me to go on, even if I had to leave her.

Two small bags sat by the fire. Opening the first one, I found only food and water. There was no sign of anything that looked like medicine. In the smaller bag, there were rolls of bandages and bottles labeled as alcohol, but there were many things that I had never seen before. Pint-sized pouches of clear liquids, strange looking scissors, and tiny, silver knives. Among them were five glass tubes filled with a pinkish liquid. Their labels read "*Serum—Test Subject 1*."

This *had* to be the medicine that Ravyn needed. I zipped up the bag, slung it over my shoulder and took off after her.

The wind had picked up even more and the rolls of thunder had grown louder overhead. Lightning flashed through the trees, flooding the forest with bursts of blinding light every few seconds. My eyes had to adjust rapidly as the world went dark again.

I stopped to listen. If there was any gunfire it was drowned out by the thunder. When the sky was silent once more, the booming of a rifle echoed through the trees. It was much further away than where I had left Ravyn in the brush. She must have seen Two coming for her and fled. I raced toward the river, eager to catch up with her there.

The sky finally opened up. Large drops of rain splattered down through the branches above, stinging my face as I ran. Knowing that a downpour would hinder my vision, I picked up my pace.

Anxious thoughts began to plague me. What if she had been injured and was alone in the forest? How would I find her? I mentally shook the thoughts from my mind. While there was breath in her body, she would not give up. Ravyn would make it to the river no matter the odds against her.

Rain poured down in heavy sheets, splashing across my face and soaking me through to my skin. The river had to be close. I slowed my gait to make sure I did not plummet into the water. From what I remembered, the embankment of the river formed a small ravine. It was a fifteen-foot drop in some places.

Through the deluge, I finally spotted the riverbank. There was no telling where Ravyn might turn up, so I took a calculated guess and started moving upstream. I kept close to the trees to remain partially hidden.

Through the torrential rain, I saw a dark shadow moving in my direction. I recognized Ravyn's careful, warrior-like movements. Her head was constantly on the swivel, checking her surroundings. There was no chance she had seen me yet, so I moved into the open. She paused for a moment when I emerged, her pistol ready to fire, but then her face broke into a wide smile when she recognized me. Wet, black tendrils of hair framed her pale face. Water streamed down from her nose and onto her soft lips. There was just the two of us in that moment. Nothing else in the world mattered. She was safe.

I stepped forward to close the remaining distance between us and pull her into my arms when the explosive sound of a rifle filled the air. The force of the bullet snapped Ravyn's body back toward the embankment. Her smiling face crumpled into one of pain and anguish. The ground was slick. She was too close to the edge. Ravyn's cry blended with my own as I watched her tumble down the ravine and into the river below.

27
Ravyn

Water swallowed me up as I crashed into the black river. My shoulder was on fire where Two's bullet had ripped through, and now my lungs were burning too. I kicked my heavy, booted feet trying to rise to the surface, but I couldn't make out which way was up. The raging water swirled around me, wrapping me up in its deadly grasp.

When I hit something solid, I pushed with all my might against the swift current. My head finally broke the surface and I was able to inhale new air into my starving lungs. I did my best to keep my head above water but my left arm was useless. I kicked and paddled furiously, desperate to get to the bank. This was the same deep river that I had bathed in just this morning, only further upstream. There were rapids throughout, which meant I would crash into rocks if I was carried too far.

The powerful current pulled me under again, the water dragging me down by my boots. I pushed against the bottom again and came up gasping for breath. My shoulder continued to bleed freely and my energy waned. Swimming toward the bank seemed impossible, but it was all I could do. When I was nearly at the point of giving up, I felt a muscled arm wrap around my waist.

"I've got you!" Thorne shouted against the roaring of water and thunder.

The relief that coursed through me made my eyes prick with tears. His powerful body was next to mine, helping me fight the fast-moving current. How he had ever found me was beyond my comprehension, but I didn't care.

Thorne finally grabbed hold of the bank. With my good arm, I helped him drag my aching body until I was completely out of the current. Lying face down on the muddy bank, I panted and coughed the remaining water out of my lungs while my shoulder throbbed and continued to bleed.

Thorne rummaged around behind me but I made no move to see what he was doing. I closed my eyes and tried to ignore the pain, just like I always did at the compound when General Wolfe was done working me over.

What are you doing? I thought, a wave of panic coursing through me. *We need to get out of here.*

When I started struggling to get up, Thorne placed his hand on my back and held me in place. "Don't move, Ravyn. You'll get dirt in your wound."

I went still immediately, but his commands didn't alleviate my anxiety. Thorne seemed to be fine, but I was facing the river to keep my weight on my good shoulder so I couldn't see if he'd been shot.

"Where's Two?" I asked. "Did he hurt you? Did he follow us?" *Please don't let him find us.*

"I'm not sure where Two is," Thorne admitted. "Right now, you need to lie still and let me tend to that wound."

"But he could be tracking us -"

Thorne interrupted me. "The river carried us at least a quarter of a mile. I doubt he'll be able to find where we came out of the water in this downpour. Our trail will be washed away."

Thorne touched my shoulder and pain surged through my body like an electric current.

"No!" I cried, quickly turning onto my back and grasping his hand. He had bandages ready to wrap up my shoulder.

"Ravyn, I have to stop the bleeding," he insisted.

"The bullet … it's still inside," I gasped through the pain. "There's no exit wound, is there?"

Thorne checked the back of my bare shoulder and then muttered a curse.

"Thorne …"

"No, I can't do this," he said, running his hand through his wet hair in frustration.

"You have to." I squeezed his hand and quickly reassured him. "If you don't, the skin will close over and my shoulder will never be the same."

Thorne's brows pinched together. "I won't be able to see it," he warned me.

"Use your fingers. Feel for it." I unbuckled my belt with my good hand and slid it out of my waistband. "Remember, I'll heal. Whatever damage you think you'll do … it will heal. Do it now," I pleaded, "before my skin closes over."

Thorne turned his face away and swore again. I could see the dread in his eyes. He didn't want to hurt me. I had felt the same way when I was digging for the bullet inside Brock earlier.

I swallowed my own fear and spoke more confidently. "Thorne, do it now. Don't wait." He turned his gaze back to me. I gave him an encouraging nod and said, "You can do this."

His eyes hardened with determination as I bit down on my belt. I clasped my left arm to my chest to keep it from twitching and closed my eyes.

I nearly blacked out when Thorne's fingers began to probe my wound. My moans of pain were muffled by my belt. He mumbled an apology but thankfully didn't stop. He pressed down on my torso with his forearm to keep me from writhing and flinching away. The tears running down my face blended with the rain that continued to fall down on us.

I was ready to admit that I'd had enough when he finally pulled the mangled bullet free from my shoulder. There was instant relief inside the wound. The pain and throbbing continued, but it wasn't quite as sharp as before. Thorne took the damp gauze and wrapped my shoulder to staunch the flow of blood.

"You didn't answer my question before," I said, my voice still trembling. I took a deep breath to keep from breaking down into sobs, then asked, "Did Two hurt you? Were you shot?"

Thorne was frowning and his eyes were tight. From a quick glance I didn't see any bullet wounds. The expression on his face was due to the surgery I had just forced him to do.

"I'm not injured," he said, reassuring me. "When you went over the edge, I jumped in the water after you. If Two did fire at me, I didn't hear it over the rain and the river." He slowly lifted me into a sitting position. "Do you think you can walk? I'm confident we lost Two, but maybe we shouldn't wait around and make it easier for him to locate us."

I nodded. "As long as it's not too far." I reached up to feel my shoulder and noticed that he had used real gauze to wrap the wound. "Where did you get this?"

Helping me to my feet, Thorne kept an arm around my waist for support. "After I saw Two go after you, I raided his camp and stole the medicine bag. The bandage was inside. Luckily, the bag is waterproof." He pointed out the small bag slung over his shoulder. Then he said, "I know a place we can rest. I don't think it's far."

Allowing me to lean heavily on him, Thorne led us further west, away from Blackrock River and away from where I'd last seen Two in the forest.

Our plan to raid Two's camp had gone wrong, just as I had feared it would. Once Thorne had left my side to circle around to the far side of their camp, the wind had changed. The tracker had scented me immediately. Two shots rang out – I assumed that had been Thorne drawing them out – and then Two charged into the forest to hunt for me.

I had to run. It was foolish and cowardly. I should have hidden and waited for an opportunity to kill him, but once Two had entered the dark shadows of the forest, I'd lost sight of him. My only plan at that point had been to lose him and somehow make it to the river.

I veered through the trees as fast as I could. The cold rain poured down on me in waves, making it nearly impossible to know which direction I was going at times. Shots fired behind me, so I dove into the brush. I crawled away on my hands and knees until I was hidden beneath some thick ferns at the base of a sequoia. My heart raced as I waited, wondering if he would find me huddled there. In mere minutes I heard his boot steps drawing closer to my hiding place. I pulled my knees up to my chest and gripped my pistol tightly in my trembling hands. The pounding of his boots had grown louder between the cracks of thunder and splattering rain. The branches of the undergrowth slapped against his legs.

Then I saw his boots. They were just a few feet from me. I held my breath, waiting for him to turn and spot me through the branches of the fern I was hiding beneath. He paused for a moment, then kept on marching.

It had been a close call. I waited a few more minutes, frozen in place, to make sure he was gone and then started for the river again.

That was the last time I'd seen Two. I wasn't even certain he was the one who had shot me by the river's edge. Finding Thorne had distracted me.

After twenty minutes of staggering through the forest, Thorne and I finally made it to the place that he had mentioned. It was a good thing, because I was beginning to feel chilled with fever.

"There is a cave just up here on this hill," Thorne reassured me.

My body was protesting greatly, but I didn't argue. Thorne nearly had to carry me up the rocky slope. He never complained and his feet never faltered.

When we reached the top, I still couldn't see the cave that he was talking about, but he continued forward until we were standing in front of a fern that was taller than Thorne. He pushed the leaves and branches to the side, revealing a dark opening. It was the perfect place to hide. He held the branches aside while assisting me the rest of the way into the cave. Only when we were both safely inside did he let the fern fall back into its original position, muffling the sound of the storm.

"Aren't you worried about Sabers?" I whispered.

I felt Thorne turn his head. "I don't see anything," he said confidently.

"You can see? Even in here?" I tightened my grasp on his waist and he squeezed me in turn to ease my fears.

"I have always had excellent night vision. Wait here a minute."

He left me leaning against the damp wall and began rummaging around again. I couldn't see what he was doing, but I hoped that he was starting a fire. The warmth would be wonderful and the ability to see would help me rest easier while we were here.

Standing motionless, my body began to shiver violently because of my wet clothes and boots. My continuous movements and Thorne's warm body had kept it at bay until now. I gave in to my exhaustion and slumped to the ground.

"Hang on, Ravyn," he said. "I almost have it."

I heard clicking and saw tiny sparks shooting out in the dark. Then the room lit up almost blindingly with a brilliant flame. I gasped at the sight, certain that we were both going up in smoke with a fire so great, but it immediately died down into a low campfire in front of Thorne's crouched position.

He chuckled. "Sorry. I put some alcohol on the flint to get it to catch faster."

The corners of my mouth lifted in as much of a smile as I could muster. "Where did you get wood, and wood that is dry, no less?"

He grinned like a mischievous boy, making my heart race. "Wood has been stashed here for a long time." Striding over to me, he effortlessly picked me up and carried me to sit by the fire. "The former commander, Hawke, brought me out here and made me as familiar with the Valley as possible. There are five or six different places out here where I could live for days if I had to. There is plenty of firewood, blankets, and even extra clothes here. The forest provides water and food, but we have that in our packs for now."

After setting me down, he sat behind me, much like he did the other night by the stream. This time I was not shy of his touch.

He unwound my bandage as gently as possible. "How does it feel?" he asked, inspecting my shoulder to see the damage.

I mustered the courage to finally look down at my wound. The skin was very close to closing over.

"The pain is subsiding," I replied wearily. I glanced back over my shoulder to see that his expression had turned dark. "What is it, Thorne?"

His eyes had a haunted look about them. "I thought I was going to lose you." His voice was gruff with emotion.

I turned and wrapped my good arm around his neck. "I thought I was going to die, too," I said, teeth chattering from the chill. I let him pull me closer to his warmth and rested my cheek on his shoulder. "But I didn't. You saved me."

"I don't ever want to take a bullet out of you again."

"I'm so sorry," I whispered.

He stroked my hair tenderly and kissed my forehead. He was careful not to agitate my shoulder as he soothed me with his touch.

"You need to eat," he suggested when I finally stopped shivering.

He pulled out a few packages of dried meat, cheese, and bread. I reached for a piece of the meat first and tried to eat slowly without stuffing too much food into my mouth at once. My shoulder began to tingle with increased momentum as it healed. Now it was only a mild throb beneath the skin.

"I never did ask you before," I said, lowering my eyes and picking at the piece of bread in my hands. "How is it that you can accept my healing ability so easily?"

Thorne tilted his head and gave me a curious stare. "How is it that you can accept my scars so easily?"

I scoffed and shook my head at the comparison. "It's not the same thing."

Thorne shrugged and tugged on my braid playfully. "Why not? There are plenty of people within Peton that have known me all my life, and they cannot look me full in the face anymore. They are afraid of staring and yet, they don't see me at all."

"That explains why you hid your face from me at first."

"They see my position, or they see me as my father's son," he said bitterly.

I gazed at his scars for a moment, then lifted my eyes to his. "Even your Warriors stare? I would think they'd have just as many scars. And what about your family?"

Thorne shook his head. "Just civilians. Sometimes the Elders."

I snorted. "The people who don't matter as much?"

He stared into the fire, considering my remark. "I suppose you're right."

We chewed our food in silence for a few minutes, then Thorne changed the subject. "Do you believe that there could be others in Peton who have gifts? Or maybe even in other clans? They are just … less obvious. Like my night vision."

"Maybe," I said thoughtfully. "One of the brothers from that village, Kaelem, could be gifted as well. He seemed to read my thoughts before I spoke them aloud. It was strange. I hope I don't run into him, or any of them, ever again."

Thorne skimmed his hand up my back and rested it on the nape of my neck, making me forget all about Kaelem. His silver-blue eyes sparkled in the flickering firelight. They pierced right through me into my soul.

"You didn't answer my question," I said softly, my voice trembling. "How can you accept my gift so easily?"

"I saw you before I knew of your gift," he murmured.

Bringing his other hand to my face, he brushed his finger along my hairline, my jaw, and then my lips. Slowly lifting my hand to his face as well, I traced the claw marks along his cheek with three of my fingers, as I'd longed to do.

"I saw you before you hid your face," I whispered in return, astonished that I could do more than stutter like an idiot.

I expected him to lean in, and he did, but only to rest his forehead on mine. My disappointment came out in a deep sigh.

"I *do* want to kiss you, little warrior," he explained. "But if I start to kiss you right now, I may not stop there. This is no place for that, and you are not yet seventeen. Too young to join, at least in our clan. I will respect this."

I was relieved that his eyes were closed because I felt my face heating up. It wasn't as if the thought of being with Thorne hadn't crossed my mind, and here we were, alone. In Terran, sixteen was old enough if one were married. Apparently, this was not the standard with each clan.

Much of my relief had to do with his restraint as well. If he were anything like Two or Six, he wouldn't have even asked my permission. It was a miracle I was still untouched with all the attempts they had made to corner me at the compound. I shivered again but for very different reasons.

"You are still cold," Thorne said, feeling me tremble. "We should shed our wet clothes and wrap up in the blankets."

"Shed our clothes? Don't you think that's going to make the temptation worse?" I asked, grinning.

He gave me a lopsided smirk and ducked his head. "Probably, but I promise to be a gentleman tonight."

"Shouldn't we get back to Brock now that I'm healed?"

"It has only been a few hours," he said. "Some rest will do us both good. We will return while it is still dark."

Turning our backs on each other, we stripped out of our clothes and I spread them out in front of the fire to dry while we rested. They would still be damp when we returned to them, but it was better than nothing. My cheeks heated as I wrapped up in the blanket that Thorne had offered me and settled down near the warmth of the fire. My heartrate picked up and I couldn't stop fidgeting after I'd tucked the edges of the blanket around my legs and feet. Thorne sat beside me looking as calm as ever.

"Why is your face so red?" Thorne asked with a grin.

I wanted to smack him. He knew I was embarrassed and was making fun of me. I had only ever felt this vulnerable in front of General Wolfe and his scientists, but that was not by choice. They had always knocked me out with a sleeping gas before they brought me in for their experiments. I'd never told Thorne about any of this though, so it wasn't fair to scold him for it.

"Being … you know … it makes me nervous," I stuttered. I couldn't even say the word 'naked' without blushing.

"You have nothing to fear from me," he said. The grin on his face disappeared into a frown again. "I'm not like those soldiers."

"I know, Thorne," I assured him. "And you were right. I'm already feeling warmer."

It occurred to me that I hadn't asked about the serum, so I put the question to Thorne.

"I believe it is here." He grabbed the black bag he had picked up from Two's camp. The bag wasn't large but it was filled to the brim. I dug in with both hands until I found them – the syringes filled with serum. There were five of them.

"Lucky they didn't break when you dove into the river after me."

“What is this stuff?” His eyes narrowed slightly, full of questions. “It does not look like any kind of medicine I have ever seen.”

I took a deep breath and carefully placed the vials back into the bag. The time had come to come clean. I’d made the decision yesterday that I was going to trust him. He’d protected my secrets this far.

“Tell me, little warrior,” he pleaded. “Your eyes have been full of secrets from the moment I saw you.”

My hands began to sweat and my heart raced. “You already know a lot of my story. I told you about much of my life in Terran.”

“But after you ran away, what happened to you?” he inquired. “If you truly care for me, then trust me with the truth.”

Pulling the blanket tighter around my shoulders, I stared into the flames.

“General Wolfe’s soldiers found me about a week after I left Terran. It was the middle of the night and I was surrounded by Sabers when they came along and scared them away. They told me all about their life at the compound and how great it was. They had plenty to eat and great jobs. They had nothing to worry about. They made it sound wonderful. I went with them.

“The compound was everything they said it would be. There were lots of people there, of all ages. I was most interested in becoming a soldier. They had saved me, and I wanted to do the same for others. And even if they decided to banish me like the

Terran Elders did, I would have the skills to stay alive in the Valley."

"How old were you then?" Thorne asked.

"I was only nine years old when they found me."

Thorne's eyes widened. "They let you begin training at the age of nine?"

I shook my head. "The first year I lived in the compound I worked other chores with the kids: cleaning, doing dishes, that sort of thing," I said, rolling my eyes. "It was annoying at first because I hated doing those things in Terran."

"So you were ten when you began training? That's still young," Thorne pointed out. "Our female Warriors do not begin until they turn thirteen."

I shrugged. "It was mostly body conditioning and strengthening."

"How did you keep your healing gift a secret from them? Didn't you get injured?"

"In the first three years, I was able to hide it. But people started getting suspicious once I began learning how to fight. I was thirteen when that phase of training began and the boys my age were all bigger than me so they were always bullying me."

"And you never showed bruises because you healed so quickly," he muttered to himself.

"I didn't know it at the time, but the older soldiers had been watching my progress since I was one of the only girls training. They reported everything to General Wolfe, including the fact that

I never seemed to be injured. But he let me be for two more years. I did nothing but train, every day, all day. To be the best, I had to work harder than everyone else. When the boys were napping or messing around during free time, I trained, and soon enough I was beating them more and more."

I shuddered when I thought back on the next part. That was when the nightmares truly began. "By the time I turned fifteen, I was at the top of my group. There was only one who was better than me. I had caught up to the rest of them in height. I wasn't as strong as they were, but I was quicker." That was the year the General had found out for certain. I had worked hard to avoid being cut or scraped, but working with knives and guns – it was inevitable.

"How did he finally find out?"

"He paired me up with more experienced men who were older than me and my group of trainees. Usually when we trained, we didn't use real blades, but that day he ordered us to. I knew then."

"He did it purposefully to injure you," Thorne said. He ran his hand through his hair in frustration, making it stick up in all directions.

"One of the men slashed me right across the cheek." I ran my finger across my cheek to show Thorne. "They took me straight to the General after they witnessed my skin closing up. The General didn't even look surprised."

Thorne furrowed his brows. "You believe he already knew?"

"There was one person who knew my secret."

“Who was it?” he growled. “One of the soldiers who’s been hunting you? Was it Two?”

I glanced over at Thorne. His eyes seemed to be blazing in the orange glow of the fire. “His name was Kieron,” I said reluctantly. “We had been friends for years. He was my only friend and I foolishly trusted him.”

I gave Thorne a sharp look, letting him know I was done speaking about Kieron.

“And then Wolfe started torturing you?” he asked. “Why? What did it achieve?”

“He was testing my healing capabilities. He wanted to know if there were limits. He started with minor injuries, slowly working his way up to broken bones, and -” My voice caught in my throat.

“And stab wounds? That was how you had been stabbed before? By him?”

When I nodded, Thorne surprised me by pulling me onto his lap. He hugged me tightly against his warm skin.

“He will never touch you again,” he promised.

I tightened my hold and hoped that he was right.

28
Thorne

Holding Ravyn was a soothing balm for my anger after hearing more of what Wolfe had done to her at the compound. I stroked her hair to keep my hands from clenching into fists. It was a miracle she was here, trusting me with her secrets after everything she had gone through. My protective instincts screamed at me to make her mine; to claim her so that I could protect her the rest of our days.

I knew I would not like the answers, but I kept asking my questions.

"When did he begin making this army of mind-slaves?"

"He's been training kids for years, but these soldiers are more recent," she said. "I wasn't quite sixteen yet. About a year ago."

"He allowed you to keep training?" I asked. "Why would he do that?"

She murmured against my neck, "He was confident that he would finally succeed. He didn't want me to fall behind. I thought about refusing, but he would have punished me. Besides, I knew that if I had any chance to escape and survive in the Valley, I needed to be at my best."

"And then he started his methods – his experiments – on you."

"In between workouts," she confirmed. "I'm not sure the General ever understood why I never broke. There were times he would get so out of control that his scientists would have to intervene to keep me alive. They risked a lot to help me."

"They did not do enough," I growled.

"They were afraid of him."

When I felt her shiver again, I squeezed her shoulders and whispered, "And you too? I can feel your fear when you speak of him, as with that dark one. Two."

Ravyn eased out of my embrace to look me in the face.

"Everyone is afraid of something," she admitted with a sorrowful frown on her lovely face.

The typical grunt I used to shut down a conversation was on the tip of my tongue, but I quickly reconsidered. Ravyn was not just one of the Warriors, or even Gunter who knew me better than anyone. I did not want to shut her out. Perhaps if I led the way, she would let me in.

"That is true," I agreed.

"And what does the commander fear?" Her tone was teasing, but it was obvious she truly wanted to know.

"Mostly I fear losing my sisters, as they lost their mothers. And the Warriors ..." My voice sounded gravelly and thick in my own ears. I cleared my throat and continued. "… I am always afraid of failing them." Pausing again, I knew I was delving into some of my deepest secrets and it frightened me. "Letting my father down, and also – and I know this may seem foolish – but losing my position as commander."

"Not at all," she said. "None of that is foolish."

"And what of you, little warrior?" I trailed my finger down the side of her face.

"You're always touching me," she whispered, but this time she leaned into my hand instead of flinching.

"I like touching you, now don't change the subject."

Straightening her spine, she confessed, "I'm afraid I'll never stop being hunted, that I'll never experience a true home of my own. The dark frightens me. I'm terrified of dying alone in the dark. Worse yet, I'm scared that I'll go on living forever with no end in sight." Ravyn's eyes grew glassy with unshed tears, though she never turned away. "And I'm most afraid of loving anyone again … because the General will take them away from me."

My heart seemed to swell and drop all at once. Could I have heard her properly? Ravyn was afraid of loving *again*? I could not understand why she had fled last night until this moment. She was terrified of loving me. At the same time, it was painfully clear that I was not the first male that she had cared for.

Keeping my face neutral, I asked, "You loved someone at the compound? The one you trusted? Kieron?"

Ravyn nodded. The grief on her face tore at my heart. I hated the idea that she was loved by someone else. What else would I expect? She was beautiful and clever. Anyone could see that she was a rare gem. But knowing that she had loved him in return filled me with self-doubt again.

"As I said before, Kieron was my only friend. As we grew older, we grew closer. But he's dead now, so there's no need for you to worry."

The jealousy that had sprung to life died just as quickly as it had come. I felt ashamed and selfish. Ravyn was here. She had chosen to come back and admitted she cared for me. Perhaps that was not quite love, but her love for this Kieron had developed over many years. Ravyn and I had only known each other for a few days. Surely these things took time, and her words gave me hope that someday she would love me.

"My jealous pride aside," I said, grinning in return, "it is nice to finally know you, but where does this serum come into the story?"

Ravyn visibly swallowed, nervous about the topic. I shifted my hand to the curve of her neck beneath her thick braid to gently knead her tight muscles and hopefully help her relax, when I noticed the tattoo. TS1. The tiny characters were inked onto the back of her neck like a brand. Grazing my fingers over it, I suddenly recalled a different tattoo on a different neck. TS39. From the very first time I had spoken to Ravyn. The soldier she'd killed had that same type of marking. And there was a woman called Twelve. I would bet she had the same brand: TS12.

Ravyn was TS1.

Test Subject One?

"I can see that you've figured things out," Ravyn said, picking up on my stillness. She covered her neck with her hand, hiding the tattoo in shame. "They put me to sleep so I couldn't stop them from marking me."

"Are those things filled with your blood?" I pulled a vial from the bag and inspected it again.

"No," she answered. "It is a serum that's supposed to replicate how fast I heal. It is more than just blood. The General's scientists had been working on it for over a year before I was able to escape."

I recalled another strange bit of information. The same day Ravyn and I met outside the village, I remembered being shocked when she had cut the throat of that soldier. *They can never be too dead to suit me*, she had said. Could it be possible?

"Why did you cut the throat of that soldier that day? I believe I know the reason, but I want you to say it." My jaw was clenched and my hands tightened into fists again.

With a shaky voice, Ravyn answered, "He wants his mind-slaves to be invincible. That's how he sees me."

"So the soldiers are all like you?"

"No, not all of them," Ravyn said, relief evident in her voice. "When the General's scientists first started their experiments, they just injected my blood straight into the bodies of the soldiers. Many of them had terrible reactions; some even died; something about our blood not being able to mix together in its purest form, or something. I was mostly drugged when they would talk around me so I didn't hear everything."

"But some of them were fine? Their blood was able to mix with yours?"

"Yes, but the bad news is, I don't know which ones. He's had so many men and women join since my own recruiting class that there's no way to know who can heal and who can't. I just make sure that they are so dead that they can't come back. Bullets to the head, bleeding out completely, burning the bodies, beheading. Those are the surest ways."

I now understood why Ravyn could not let herself fall back into General Wolfe's hands. With her blood and his technology and team of scientists, he could bring devastation to all of our clans. Not to mention that Ravyn would suffer for the rest of her life.

"The good news is, I believe those that have taken my blood eventually go back to normal," she added.

"It would not be a permanent change?"

"Their bodies can't produce my blood, so …"

"So, the General needs you as their personal blood donor?"

She nodded.

Leaning in close, I brushed my lips over her cheek, then the tattoo on her neck, and finally the smooth skin of her bare left shoulder where her wound had disappeared completely.

"I promise you, little warrior," I murmured into her ear, "I will keep you safe."

Ravyn turned to face me, fighting to keep her blanket over her body. Her struggle to maintain her modesty was amusing to watch. I had to pinch my lips together to keep from laughing at her predicament.

"You keep making promises that I'm afraid you won't be able to keep."

"There may be a way to keep you safe and hidden from the General without anyone knowing about your gift."

Ravyn blinked in confusion. "I'm listening."

"I want your word that you will not interrupt or argue with me until I have said what I need to say." When she nodded her assent, I continued, "Gunter and I discussed you coming home with us to Peton, but there may be some … opposition to you staying since you are an outsider."

"But you take outsiders in as captives all the time," she pointed out.

"They are captives, and there are certain rules that go along with their station in Peton for a while after they join us. I was under the impression that you did not want that title."

"Of course not," she agreed.

"There is an old tradition in Peton; one that Gunter reminded me of two days ago."

"Two days ago?" she interrupted. "We hadn't even met yet!"

I pressed a finger to her lips, halting her arguments. "You promised."

She narrowed her eyes, but merely pinched her lips together when I removed my finger.

"I was not certain of you," I reassured her. "Gunter mentioned it because … well … all he can think about is women most of the time. If I claimed you as my own woman, no one would argue, and you would have as many rights as I chose for you."

Ravyn was frowning, her eyes wide at my pathetic explanation. I was positive that I was making a mess of my words, but I carried on, hoping she would hear every bit.

"I have never claimed anyone before. Essentially, claiming another, in everyone's eyes, would make you my … others would think …" I stammered like an idiot.

"Thorne, just spit it out."

I nodded and choked out, "These couples tend to become life-mates."

"Your life-mate?" she said, gaping at me. "As in … your *wife*?"

"It would be at our own discretion," I added hesitantly. "Ravyn, you would be safe behind our walls. My home lies up in the mountains, isolated and far from the village. The only person in Peton you would answer to is me. No one else would have that right. You would have freedom there, to run, to hunt, to train. You would have every provision you needed. It is only a stone's throw from the Fairuza Sea as well."

"You live next to the sea?" she whispered.

I shrugged, but I knew she had always longed to see it. "I realize this sounds crazy. You are young and we have not known each other that long. And you have loved another. Perhaps you even still love him. I accept that. The claiming is merely a formality. It might be the best way to get you into Peton without question."

Ravyn glanced away, but I could see her working things through in her mind.

"Do not answer tonight," I told her. "Think on it. We should get some sleep in the meantime. We will make our way back to Brock in a couple of hours."

We shifted to lie down, side by side, cocooned in our blankets. Ravyn's back was to me so I could not see her expression. Her silence was worrisome. I hoped against hope that she would accept my offer. The thought of her wandering the Valley forever, or dying alone, was unacceptable to me.

29
Ravyn

My eyes were open. I could see, hear, and feel everything. My body was paralyzed. I couldn't even blink. There was nothing I could do but stare at the blank wall to my right.

I was in one of the scientists' testing rooms. Of that much, I was sure. The room was stark white and the fluorescent lights were blinding. The table I was strapped down on was a slick, silver metal. It was cold against my skin through the thin paper gown I was dressed in.

As the door opened, I felt a cold wave of air brush across my body. My neck tingled, sending a feeling of pure terror through my soul. It must have been General Wolfe coming to boast of his power over me.

As always, I willed my body to move, but it was hopeless. Whatever was in the gas that they used, it disconnected my brain from my muscle-movements. I could only lie here, listening to his footsteps getting closer and closer.

The General leaned down so that I could see only his face staring back at me. His gray eyes were gleaming with the evil he had in store for me today.

"Hello again, my dear," he sneered.

Instinctively, I wanted to respond with an insolent remark, but my tongue was frozen in my mouth. He deliberately taunted me, because he knew that it was not in my nature to be brought low by anyone. He would always take pleasure in knowing how powerless I was in this state. He could do whatever he wanted, and I could not do anything about it.

"You know, I do this for the good of all," General Wolfe said. "You of all people should understand, having been tossed out of your own clan. Even that decision was for your puny village's own good."

How did he know about that?

"Yes, I know all about your miserable past. Your Elders and I had an agreement that I would take you off their hands as soon as you turned nine, but in your rebelliousness, you ran away before they could deliver you to me."

What was he talking about? He knew the Elders? Had he spoken to my family?

"They were instructed to watch you and your pretty sister very closely when you were born to see which of you was going to have

a special ability. I've been collecting them for a long time, trying to find the ones that can benefit the cause."

Collected people with special abilities? I strained my mind against the drugs that were paralyzing me, but my body remained motionless. I was just a slab of meat for the General to cut to pieces on this table.

"You are my prize," he gloated, still just inches from my face.

He tilted his head this way and that, using my glassy eyes like a mirror. He ran his fingers through his salt and pepper hair, making sure it was all laying perfectly in place. "And now, my dear, it is time to get on with it."

He moved out of my line of sight and I was stunned by what I saw behind him. It was the most wonderful sight I had ever seen. But he should not be here. Thorne should not be standing here in this room. His blonde hair was almost as light as the walls behind him and as messy as ever. He was dressed in his usual black sleeveless shirt and black pants that tucked into his boots. He looked every bit the commander that he was. His usual icy blue eyes were filled with a deep sadness. Why did I feel as if I'd somehow put it there?

"Thorne," I tried to utter, but the room remained silent around me.

"I am here for you Ravyn." I heard his deep, gruff voice, but his mouth never moved.

My unmoving eyes filled with tears. They dripped down the bridge of my nose and onto the table beneath me. "Thorne, help me!" I tried to speak again, but I could only hear the words in my mind.

Thorne tilted his head to one side. Again, his mouth was motionless, though I heard his voice clearly. "I want to save you, little warrior. That is what I offered you."

He could hear me! But he made no move to kill the General. He didn't cut me free. "Thorne, I need you! Please!" More tears fell down the side of my face.

"I know that you need me."

"I'll never be free from this if you don't save me!" I silently screamed.

"You have to choose, Ravyn. What is more important? Being with me, loving me, or living out in the forest alone with your freedom?"

Why didn't he do anything?

"I care for you, little warrior. Do you trust me?"

"I don't know," I admitted. "I want to."

Thorne's figure began to fade away and I could only lie here in agony as he left me to the General's tortures. "Don't leave me, Thorne! I don't want to be alone!"

"You must decide."

Thorne's arrogant figure disappeared completely from my sight, leaving me alone with General Wolfe. My tears continued to drip onto the table from my ever-open eyes.

Suddenly, General Wolfe was back in my line of sight.

"Awww. Is someone scared?" He mocked my helplessness again. Chuckling cruelly, he raised a scalpel, one of his many tools of torture, and inspected the blade with his finger. "There is no one here to save you, my dear. No one."

***

Warm, gentle hands stroking my bare back roused me. My eyes were still closed from my restless slumber and I could feel wetness on my eyelashes and cheeks. When I opened my eyes, Thorne's face was barely an inch from mine and he was watching me warily. The same sadness I saw in my dream was still there in his eyes. We were squeezed together, skin to skin, except for the blanket wrapped around his lower extremities. Thorne's muscled arms were wrapped around me protectively, and somehow my blanket had shifted to cover us both. My face heated again at our position but I was thankful I wasn't waking up alone.

"Another nightmare?" Thorne asked softly in the dark.

I bit my lip to keep from breaking out in fresh sobs and nodded my head. The dream was still fresh in my mind. I vaguely recalled General Wolfe boasting of his knowledge of my past. The drugs he used on me must have made my memories foggy after I woke from being paralyzed. It had surprised me that he would reveal those secrets to me. He must have been very confident that I would never break free from his clutches. This was one of the many reasons he wanted me back so desperately.

"Do you want to talk about it?"

I started to say no, but I hesitated. This dream was different from the others. Usually the events of my nightmares were identical to what had actually happened in reality, but not this time.

"It started the same way they always do," I whispered. Thorne's body immediately relaxed against mine, as if he was preparing for my rejection again. "Some event from my past comes back to haunt me whenever I shut my eyes. But this time you were there, in my dream, talking to me. I'm not sure what to make of it. My dreams have never deviated from reality before."

"Maybe it was because you sensed me near you," he suggested.

"It could be." But I felt like it could be more.

Only a few minutes had passed since I'd awoken and I wasn't sure what to say to Thorne about his offer. I was ashamed that I hadn't said anything to him before we'd lain down to sleep.

Placing my palm flat on his chest, I said, "Thorne, I … I'm sorry. I …"

Thorne brought his calloused fingertips to my lips once again. "There is nothing to forgive. It is difficult for you to trust people. The soldiers promised you sanctuary and instead you lived in hell. I did not expect you to jump for joy at joining me behind a new set of walls."

He ran his fingers idly over my face and hair, memorizing my every feature. Warmth spread through me again at his touch.

"So … why are we wrapped up in our blankets like this?" I muttered, very aware of my nakedness.

"When you began tossing and turning, I did not want you to roll into the fire." He winked and grinned at my obvious embarrassment.

"I hate that you have seen me at my weakest," I grumbled.

"Every person has a weakness," he stated. "Just as every person has fears."

"Really?" I said sarcastically. "And what is your weakness, warrior?"

Thorne leaned in and gave me a feather-light kiss on the end of my nose. "You are, little warrior. It does not seem to matter how far you run. I will come for you. I will be here for you."

Thorne's words from my dream came back to me all at once. *"I have been trying to save you. You have to choose."*

In my heart, I knew he was right. As much as I had cherished my life since I'd been free of Terran and General Wolfe, it would all be for nothing if I didn't have anyone to share it with. I could not go on like this, running around like a wild thing in the Valley with the soldiers on my heels at every turn. Didn't I tell myself a few days ago that my luck would eventually run out?

From what Thorne had told me of Peton, it sounded like I could not do better. Joining any clan would come with a set of rules that the people lived by. I would be naïve to believe otherwise.

"Tell me more about what this 'claiming' means, then."

Thorne gave me a squeeze of approval. "First, it is not a way to turn you into a captive. Captives work at any number of jobs within the city, depending on what is needed and what skills the captives have. There are Warriors assigned to oversee their work."

"Am I going to have a job?" The thought of maybe helping to train Warriors put a smile on my face. That was the only true skill I'd ever enjoyed.

"Maybe." He grinned at my enthusiasm. "I will be honest. Most claimed women are taken for one purpose only."

"One purpose?" He raised his eyebrow at me and waited. "Oh, I see," I realized, blushing and painfully aware that we were still naked and pressed against each other.

"You must live with me in my home," he said. Then he added, "How our relationship develops … I will leave that up to you. I promised you before that I would not touch you without invitation. I would, of course, hold to that."

"Thank you," I whispered. My cheeks were still hot with color.

Thorne chuckled and ran a finger down the side of my face making my skin tingle and my stomach flip over again. "Most importantly, as I said before, the claiming is merely a formality."

"What does that mean?"

"Well, with most, a claimed woman is under the authority of the man who claimed her. He is her only master, taking only his orders. Captives brought to Peton take orders from any number of Warriors or Elders. I do not want things to be this way between us. I have no need for another person to order about. I have two women assigned to my household to do chores and the like."

"You have two women living with you already?" I asked, disgruntled to hear this.

"They are exiles rescued from the Valley. They requested to stay in my home because they enjoyed working away from the village," he explained. "Also, they are at least twice our age. More like mothers. They tend to boss me around more than anything."

I giggled at this image. "I can't imagine anyone trying to boss you around!"

Giving me a lopsided grin, he said, "For us, I would like things to remain the same, as they have been out here."

"You mean as equals?"

"Yes." But then his brows furrowed. "The Elders would not accept this type of relationship between us at first, thus the need for claiming. It is for appearance's sake. Do you understand?"

"I think so," I replied.

"We can go on as we have when we are in private. My family would accept you as my equal. The Elders … well …"

"Yes, Elders always seem to think they know what's best for everyone, don't they?" I said without thinking and then gasped at my foolishness. "Forgive me! I meant no disrespect to your father. I'm always saying things like that … it gets me into trouble."

Thorne just chuckled again. "Just keep those kinds of things to yourself in Peton and you will be fine. It may come as a surprise to you, but I like you just as you are. I enjoy your honesty. It's rare."

I scoffed at his remark. "You may live to regret those words."

“I am also counting on you helping me uncover the connection between General Wolfe and our clan.”

“You know I will,” I reassured him.

After a few minutes, he grew solemn and gazed deeply into my eyes. “Do you accept me as your partner? Your Warrior?”

There was no hesitation in my reply. “Yes.”

“Do you accept my protection?”

“When it’s needed, yes.”

Thorne was so close, his lips brushed against mine when he murmured, “And will you trust me in all things, little warrior?”

“Yes. Of course, I do.”

As soon as I’d uttered the words, Thorne captured my mouth in a possessive kiss. It seemed so desperate, as if he was terrified I’d take the words back if he gave me the chance. I was too caught up in the kiss to care.

He pulled away abruptly, leaving me dazed. “It is time to leave this place now. We must get back to Brock.”

“Of course,” I agreed, feeling like a horrible person for actually forgetting about him.

As we dressed and packed our belongings, I thought on the words that Thorne had said to me. I hadn’t realized that a claiming ritual would require such formal questions. Thorne had never hinted that words needed to be shared for the claiming. In Terran, couples said vows for courtship and then more elaborate vows for marriage. Thorne had mentioned that a claiming usually led to marriage in Peton.

I snorted. He was probably feeling insecure and wanted to be certain I was serious about him. Either way, I wasn't about to take back what I'd said. Though I was sad to be putting aside my memory of Kieron, I was pleased to be moving forward in life. This was my destiny, my future. Thorne was meant for me. I could feel it.

Outside the cave, the rain had stopped, but it was still dark. Stars and black sky peeked through the sequoias above us and the air was clean and refreshing. I smiled up at the heavens, feeling like a new person. Thorne grabbed my hand, linking our fingers together, and grinned at my happiness. I leaned in to give him one last kiss before we made our way back to his Warriors' camp. This kiss was soft as a whisper and filled with a new hope; a promise of what could be. Suddenly, Thorne's words from my dream filled my head in a resounding echo: *What is more important? Being with me, loving me ...*

I jerked away and lowered my head to hide my expression. The darkness should've been able to conceal me, but Thorne's gift for night vision kept me uncomfortably exposed. *It was just a dream*, I thought to myself.

"Are you alright?"

He sounded as if he'd done something wrong so I quickly reassured him. "Yes. I was just ..." I placed my hand on my forehead, wondering what on earth to tell him. "... just thinking about my nightmare." Wolfe's secret confessions came back to me again. *That was it!* "I remembered some things that the General revealed to me that I meant to tell you, but we'll have time to discuss them later."

There was relief written all over his face, as there probably was on mine. I had been jolted out of my moment of bliss by the revelation that I might love Thorne. But that was crazy. Love didn't work that way. It was too sudden. The claiming I'd allowed was enough for now. There was no way I was telling him that I loved him.

30
Thorne

We had no difficulty finding the tripwire on our way back into camp. In fact, the camp itself was giving off enough light to be seen all the way from Peton. I was not sure if they were attempting to light the way for us or trying to appear larger in number than we actually were. Every Warrior was armed and manning a section of the camp for any kind of threat. Everyone was on watch except Brock and Gunter. *Gunter had better be in Brock's tent and not the only Warrior sleeping,* I thought. He owed me an explanation for allowing all of the Warriors to keep watch instead of taking shifts.

I marched into Brock's tent, Ravyn just a few paces behind me.

"Gunter," I said in quiet greeting. "Why is no one resting?"

A disheveled Gunter was bent over Brock, wiping the sheen of sweat from his face. Brock was so pale, if he had not been perspiring, I would have thought him dead.

Gunter took my irritation in stride, as he had always done. “I suggested that we should take shifts, but none of them would agree to it.”

“Then, in my place, you should have ordered them to.”

Ravyn placed her hand on my arm to ease my ire. “Thorne,” she whispered. “They are only worried about their friend.”

“But now none of us will have had any sleep tonight.”

Gunter’s brow furrowed. “We will sleep now that you have returned with the medicine.”

“No,” I argued. “We should leave here as soon as Brock is well.” I turned to Ravyn for her take on the situation. “We should get back to the safety of Peton before the soldiers have a chance to regroup and ambush us again.”

Ravyn nodded her agreement. “If we leave immediately, we can put some distance between us and the soldiers.”

Ravyn knelt down at Brock’s side and began removing her supplies from the small bag we’d stolen from Two. Gunter joined me by the tent-flap.

“You got the medicine then?” he asked. “No trouble?”

“We would have been back sooner, but Ravyn was injured again.”

“She looks well now,” he remarked, giving her a once-over. “You think we will be able to leave soon?”

“He’ll be ready to ride with us in less than an hour,” Ravyn explained without looking up from her work.

Gunter's jaw dropped in astonishment. Mine might have fallen open as well. "Tell the men to pack up the camp as quickly as possible. We will leave in one hour."

He nodded and then turned to exit the tent.

Ravyn set out one vial of the pinkish liquid that I now knew contained some of her blood. She also removed one of the pouches filled with clear liquid with which I was unfamiliar.

"What is that?"

"Fluids," she clarified. "They always gave them to me after … it never hurt me, so I figure it can't hurt him."

"What if your blood does not mix with his blood?"

"The serum was created to mix with anyone's blood. It was only my blood in its purest form that couldn't mix with certain people."

Ravyn's movements were smooth, confident. Her hands never once shook. She bit her lip as she worked, completely focused and calm, the opposite of how I was feeling. Not only was I a wreck over Brock's condition, but I was on edge about what I had done back in the cave.

"Give me a task," I commanded, hoping that it would take my mind off both of my failings.

She handed me the pouch of liquid. "Find something we can hang this from."

The only thing we could use was the tent itself. I strode out of the tent to the supply cart and rummaged around until I found what I was looking for. Archer had constructed metal hooks for us to hang out our clothes to dry. The hooks attached to the poles that held our tents in place. We rarely used them, but it would work perfectly for this fluid pouch.

Brock was beginning to stir when I returned. A needle had been inserted into the inside of his elbow, just under the skin.

"Don't worry," she said, noticing my stare. "The liquid runs from the pouch into his bloodstream directly."

After I looped the hook around the supporting pole of the tent, Ravyn passed me the pouch.

"That works great!" Ravyn beamed at me for a second and then went back to work on Brock. The longer she worked on him, the more he stirred. I moved to the opposite side to calm him as he awoke from her ministrations.

"Brock," I murmured, as if to sooth my jittery stallion. "Just hang on. You are going to feel better soon. You are not going to die. Do you hear me?" His body seemed to relax even though he was still mostly unconscious.

"Good," Ravyn approved. "Keep talking. He can hear you. Your presence is surely comforting to him."

Ravyn attached another needle to the vial of pink serum and tapped it systematically. Then she squirted the excess air out of the tip of the needle. I didn't bother asking her to explain. She knew what she was doing so I left her to it.

"Hold him still for me," she ordered, lowering the needle to his hip.

I held Brock steady and watched as Ravyn slowly injected the serum into the thick muscle of his buttocks. Just as she had asked, I spoke reassuring words to him.

Once she had removed the needle and empty syringe, she looked up at me with an exhausted smile. "All we can do now is wait."

I knelt beside her and wrapped my arms around her, allowing her to lean into me.

"Everything will work out as it should," I whispered into her hair.

"Why don't you go help your Warriors?" Ravyn said, her face still hidden in the crook of my neck. "There's nothing more for you to do here." She pulled away and cupped my face with her hand. "I'll keep watch and let you know if anything changes."

But there was more that needed to be said. I opened my mouth to confess what I had done back at the cave, but no words came out.

"Thorne, what is it?" Ravyn asked, waiting expectantly for me to say something.

"Ravyn, I …" But I hesitated. I could not tell her here. Not now. It would be better to wait until we were in Peton. Yes, that was it. I would wait until we were home at my cabin.

I gave her a quick kiss and departed.

***

For the next twenty minutes, I oversaw the packing. We could not afford to lose a single minute, and the other Warriors appeared to think the same as they hurried about the camp. Even Pierce had not questioned my order or taken time to give me any belligerent looks.

Every one of the Warriors was armed to the teeth now. They were not going to be caught by surprise again. I had a mind to go a different route back to Peton, but the path we had been taking for years was the most direct and the quickest.

"Commander? Any word on Brock?"

Archer had spoken, and Max approached with him. I was uncertain how much to reveal. The secret would soon be out, but they did not have to know that information just yet.

"He should be fine," I told them. It was not an outright lie, but I did not tell the full truth either. I seemed to be doing that a lot lately.

"Gunter said something about a medicine?" Max inquired. "Do you think it will work?" His eyes looked haunted, though he put on a brave front for his friend.

"Ravyn is confident. As am I." I gave Max a brotherly pat on the shoulder to reassure him. "Continue packing. We will be leaving soon."

As they walked away, I studied my Warriors from a distance. Archer got back to working furiously, making sure every cart and horse had extra weapons and ammunition handy. Every weapon was meticulously checked to be certain they would fire properly and accurately. Pierce helped Max inspect the horse's hooves, bits, and harnesses to make sure they would last the swift pace we would be setting.

Was I crazy to think that any of these Warriors could be my enemy? My suspicious nature began to twist what I was seeing into the worst possible scenarios. Could Pierce be plotting to be rid of me and take over as commander? He did challenge me at the beginning and his attitude had never been more than just tolerant. He and Archer had disappeared at the same time after the first attack on the road and I still had not uncovered where they went. They could be working together to betray me and Ravyn to General Wolfe. It would have been a perfect opportunity to meet up with one of the General's soldiers to update him on our actions.

Archer could be working alone. He was more intelligent than anyone knew. His ideas for gadgets and explosives could be coming straight from General Wolfe and his scientists. Archer had been teaching Max how to prepare and set those same explosives and tripwires. Max was a quiet one, but just as clever. No one would ever suspect him when he was so young and inexperienced. There had been just as many opportunities for him, setting up those wires, to meet with any number of soldiers while our backs were turned.

And Gunter … how could I even think to suspect my best friend? Could he betray me after the two of us had grown up together like brothers?

No one was beyond at least some suspicion, even Brock. When I sent him with Pierce to spy on the village, he could have made contact with a soldier there. Being shot could have been a strategy on his part to dispel any uncertainties we had about his loyalty. Two would have known that Ravyn would come after him for the serum to save Brock's life.

One thing was certain; we needed to get back to Peton quickly. I was anxious for our safety and for the chance to uncover the truth.

Only minutes had passed since talking to Archer and Max before Gunter tracked me down.

"Thorne," he greeted me.

Ignoring the doubts in the back of my mind for now, I got right to the point. "Have the captives been able to stretch their legs and take care of their private business?"

"Of course," he answered swiftly.

"Do they understand how rough the ride is probably going to be on the road this time?"

"They sense the tension. They were a bit fretful about the last attack so they have been very cooperative," he said with a grin. "I think you'll find they are going to be very compliant workers once we reach the safety of Peton."

"Good."

Gunter chuckled and said, "This has been quite a trip, hasn't it?"

"Humph," I replied. I felt Gunter's eyes on me.

"Alright, what did you do, Thorne?"

"I don't know what you mean."

"You look almost jittery," he remarked. "What's going on? Is it about Brock?"

"No, he'll be fine, like I said."

Gunter gave me an exaggerated sigh. "Spit it out, Thorne. I'll find out anyway. You're a terrible liar, you know."

"You really are a pain. Do you know that?"

He folded his arms over his chest and waited for me to come clean.

Taking a deep breath, I told him of all that had happened tonight, up until Ravyn awoke from her nightmare. I did not go into details about the serum or Ravyn's involvement with the making of it. I was still leery about divulging too much about her past to anyone, even Gunter – the Warrior I had trusted more than any other.

"So, she accepted the claim?"

"Yes, she did. You were right all along." I peered at him out of the corner of my eye. "Don't gloat."

"I wasn't planning on it. So what's wrong with you? I thought this was what you wanted?"

"I did more than claim her, my friend," I uttered in shame. I still could not believe that I had deceived her in such a way.

"Well, that would be expected -"

"No!" I said sharply. "We did not get intimate in any way."

Gunter frowned. "Then what are you talking about? What did you do?"

I sighed and ran my hand through my hair. “I said the Binding Words and made her my life-mate.”

Gunter gaped at me. “You did what?” he shouted.

I shushed him and hissed, “I said the Binding Words. Sort of. It was a loose interpretation.” The true Binding Words spoken in front of the Elders were formal and often said in front of other witnesses. The Elders knew the exact words. I had not needed to say these words in order to claim Ravyn. A mutual understanding was all that was needed to claim a partner.

He leaned in close. “I seem to recall you never wanting a wife. What were you thinking?”

“I did not plan it.”

“Well ... that certainly is ... something,” he sputtered.

“Humph. What is wrong with your voice? You do not approve?”

Gunter appeared to be lost in thought. Then he shook his head and said, “Oh ... no ... it’s nothing.” He punched my shoulder playfully. “Hey, congratulations, Thorne. I told you that you would find the right woman, and I really think that this one is a good fit for you. She is a warrior like you, intelligent and loyal … she’s risked her life for us on several occasions now. If you find you don’t want her then I’ll take her.”

Gunter’s comment made me want to pound him into the ground again. I glared at him fiercely.

“Hey, I was only joking. Take it easy.” He held up his hands in forfeit. “I’ve never seen you this territorial.”

"I am not worried about her being my wife, though she is young. She would have already been courted had she stayed in her own clan," I pointed out. "I believe it was the right thing to do. I stand by what I did, especially when it comes to the Elders."

"You mean your father?" Gunter crossed his arms over his chest, pondering the situation in my shoes. He knew that my relationship with my father had always been strained.

"He will not be able to break this bond. Why are you worried?"

"I did not tell her what my words meant for us," I confessed. "She doesn't know that we are bonded now. All she is aware of is my claim to her."

Gunter raised his eyebrows. "How is that possible? You both have to say the Binding Words."

"I said my part. She has yet to say hers."

Gunter rubbed his chin thoughtfully. "That's not as bad as I was thinking. She could still bow out of the union then."

Placing my fists on my hips, I glowered at him again. "There will be no talk of breaking the bond. All I kept thinking in that cave was that my father would not stop until he ended our relationship. Like you said, he cannot do that if she's my wife."

Gunter just took it all in stride, yet again. "She'll come around. You need to allow her space to decide for herself if she wants to complete the bond with you. You've just given her that time."

"And what if she doesn't want that?" My chest ached, thinking about not having her by my side.

Gunter slapped his hand on my shoulder and said, "Thorne, you don't give yourself enough credit. She allowed you to claim her. Just be your charming self and she will begin to care for you."

"I'm not charming," I muttered. "I am surprised that she chose me with you strutting around here."

Gunter grinned at my dower mood. "She thinks you're plenty charming. I see the way she looks at you. You are more than fancy words and a pretty face, Thorne."

We both snickered over our long-standing joke. It was Gunter that had the pretty face and fancy words. Even before that Howler had sunk his claws into me, I was not the male that women fawned over. Perhaps it was because I was too serious, as Gunter had suggested a few days ago. None of this seemed to bother Ravyn in the least; yet another reason I had reached for her.

As I stood there, joking with my friend, I could not imagine that he could be the one to betray us. Clearly I was overreacting. If there was an informant, it was not Gunter. I was sure of it.

"Enough of this talk," I said. "I am going to check on Brock. We should be ready to leave soon."

31
Ravyn

It didn't take long for color to return to Brock's face. His fever left him soon after I administered the serum. I sat beside him, watching him closely for signs of any side-effects. Within thirty minutes, he'd started opening his eyes.

Brock's eyes blinked rapidly, trying to focus on his surroundings, but he was still dazed from his weakness. Finally resting his gaze on me, he stared for a long moment and then asked with a scratchy voice, "Am I dead then?"

"No," I said. "Here, drink this." I helped him to rise and handed him my water canister.

He took the bottle, but still stared at me with confusion in his warm, brown eyes. "I remember you taking out the bullet." He paused to clear his parched throat and ran his tongue over his cracked lips. After taking a quick sip of the cool water, he asked, "Why don't I feel any pain?"

I pinched my lips together, wondering if there was any way to get around the real explanation, but there probably wasn't. Until it was absolutely necessary, I decided to leave out the part about my own gift.

"I gave you medicine that helped you heal faster."

"How long was I out?" Brock inquired.

"About eight hours."

"What is all this?" He reached for the unfamiliar needle in his arm, but I gently caught his wrist.

"That's just to give your body some water and nutrients."

Groaning from the effort, Brock ran his hand over his side where the gunshot wound used to be. It reminded me of how Thorne had reacted to watching my wound disappear right in front of him. It was difficult for him to believe at first, too.

"That's *some* medicine." He was surprisingly calm. Running his fingers over his skin once more, he added, "There's not even a scar. I was expecting some stitches, but this ..." After inspecting his side, he raised suspicious eyes to me. "There is more to this than you're telling me," he murmured.

I swallowed nervously and had to fight the urge to fidget under his scrutiny. Brock seemed younger than Thorne, more around my age or younger, but I knew I could not underestimate his intelligence. Thorne wouldn't have him out here with his team of Warriors if he were not one of the best in the village. Instead of answering, I began taking out the needle, careful not to hurt him.

He continued despite my silence. "I thought it was strange that you were able to take off on your own so soon after you'd been stabbed, but the commander didn't say anything against you, so I let it go."

He paused to give me a chance to explain, but I still refused to answer. Brock's words were not angry or accusing. He was simply curious. He watched as I continued sorting through the supplies and repacking. There were still four other syringes of serum and a couple of pouches of fluids left. I hoped we wouldn't need them again.

"I convinced Commander Thorne to go after you when you ran away."

I turned to him with wide eyes. "You did? Why would you do that?"

"Because the commander likes having you around," he replied. "He's different when you're near. He trusts you."

I stopped packing up the medical instruments for a moment and knelt beside him. "Do *you* trust me?"

"I don't know yet," he said with an appraising look. "But I trust Commander Thorne."

I thought it would be difficult for me to believe Brock's words of loyalty. He could be lying, but I didn't think he was. I searched his face for signs of deceit, but all I could see was concern and respect for Thorne.

"Where is the commander?" he asked, raising up on his elbows.

"He's packing with the other Warriors." I heard his sigh of relief and giggled. "Did you think I would leave him out there?"

The muscles in Brock's jaw clenched as he raised himself up from his elbows to a sitting position. I thought he might be experiencing some pain from his wound. Before I could ask him about it or react at all, he gripped my arm and pulled me closer until we were almost nose to nose.

"It's not a joke," he said fiercely. "I would kill anyone who tried to harm him."

I bit my lip to keep from grinning. His words were not funny. In fact, he was deadly serious. My joy came from having just discovered another ally. Thorne didn't think it possible for Pierce to be his supporter. Brock's loyalty would be easier to accept.

"I believe you, Brock," I told him. "He will need your loyalty in the days ahead."

"What do you mean?"

I patted Brock's hand and then gently removed it from my arm. "I will leave it to Thorne to explain what's going on. It's not my place to tell you."

"He can count on me," he said matter-of-factly.

I nodded my head in approval. I liked this kid already.

"Let's go let Thorne know that you are well and that we can go home."

When I exited the tent and motioned to Thorne, he was busy talking with Gunter, who grinned at me and then walked away. I hadn't had much interaction with Gunter, but he seemed to be a close confidante of Thorne's. I needed to spend more time with him to know if I could trust him. It would not go well for Gunter if he turned out to be our spy.

"How is he?" Thorne murmured once he reached my side. Before I had a chance to even answer Thorne, Brock stepped out of the tent behind me to answer his question.

"I'm good as new," he announced, his eyes gleaming.

Thorne eyed me warily and asked under his breath, "What did you tell him?"

"I left it for you to decide," I whispered. "He knows there's a connection between me and that serum, though."

Thorne nodded and then turned back to Brock. "It is good to see you looking so well. We were all concerned."

"Thank you, Commander," Brock said, half bowing out of respect. "I, uh, hope you will trust me enough to tell me what's going on."

Thorne nodded. "We will talk later. I swear it."

"Yes, Commander."

Brock walked away from us to help with the packing but was bombarded by the other Warriors. Thorne and I stood silently, side by side, observing them as they interacted with the quickly-healed Brock.

"Are you watching their reactions?" Thorne whispered in my ear, sending chills down my spine.

Of course, he had to stand closer to me to speak privately, but it was distracting. "Yes, aren't you?"

"What do you see?" he asked.

I watched closely for the exchange between the Warriors. "Those two that have just approached -"

"Archer and Max. Archer is the one with red hair," he clarified. "Archer has been teaching Max about his tripwires and explosives. Max and Brock were ranked in the same Warrior class together and Archer was only a year ahead. I think they are good friends with Brock."

"You *think* they are friends?"

Thorne huffed. "I am not familiar with what they do outside of Warrior business. I am their commander only."

I jabbed my finger into his chest. "Don't take that high-and-mighty tone with me, *Commander*. Why don't you know more about these men? Aren't they your friends?"

"Gunter is my friend," he replied.

"But not the rest of them?"

He merely shrugged. "We work and train together. There's not time for much else."

I pinched my lips together to keep from pushing him about his lack of companions. Just from my observations during my short time with him, I could see that Thorne was in desperate need of trustworthy friends. If not for Gunter, he would be just as alone as I was.

I thought of Laelynn and her village. If things had been different, if I hadn't been on the run, would I have stayed? In my heart I believed I would have. She was a kind, honest soul and there were so few of them in the world.

Then the images of her lying brothers coursed through my mind. One of them attacked me for reasons I couldn't fathom. Regardless, I wouldn't believe Laelynn was a minion of the General, especially when she had warned me of the danger coming and helped me escape.

Thorne's words of caution in placing my trust in her helped me focus on the task at hand.

"Archer is the one who went missing with Pierce for a while," I recalled. "He's asking a lot of questions, isn't he?"

"Yes, he is, but I would be too in his position," Thorne reasoned. "They are not going to understand the serum because they do not know about you. Only Gunter knows."

"Gunter knows?" I didn't recall Thorne mentioning that. That was interesting. "How?"

"He was there when I brought you into the camp. As far as I know, he has told no one. No one has approached me about it."

The fact that Gunter knew about my gift but had not badgered me with questions was odd, but he was Thorne's friend of many years. Thorne could be keeping him informed.

"It looks as if Brock is trying to explain what he knows about the medicine, but I didn't tell him much," I said. "The other one, Max; he's staying pretty quiet."

"He's always been a quiet one. I would not be surprised if either of those two are in league with the General," Thorne stated. "Only …"

"Only what?" I urged him to reveal his thoughts to me.

"I would think they are too young to be tainted against Peton," he admitted. "I do not want to believe it is one of them."

"Have they had opportunities to slip away?"

"He set up the perimeter wires with Archer," he replied. "They do not always stay together to do this, and they are out of sight of the camp. But Pierce and Brock have both been away from the camp as well. I had them spy on the village."

I folded my arms over my chest. "Before we started tracking Two, I saw Archer and Pierce arguing about something after they returned to the camp. I didn't hear what was said, but they stopped suddenly when they saw me coming."

"I thought you were adamant that Pierce was my ally," said Thorne, quirking his eyebrow.

"Well, I've been wrong about people before," I confessed, glancing up at Thorne. "Maybe he's just not a friendly person. We don't know what he and Archer were talking about."

"I still don't trust him."

I shrugged. Thorne had known Pierce longer than I had. The history between them was still a mystery to me and, until I was able to get to know each of the Warriors, I wouldn't be able to make a clear judgement. My opinions were based on their actions over the course of the last three days.

I turned my gaze back to the other Warriors and found Pierce glaring at the two of us with his arms crossed. The anger in his expression made me think he'd overheard us talking about him. But that was impossible. We were thirty feet away and speaking in whispers.

"He does not look very pleased with Brock's recovery," Thorne remarked.

"You don't know what he may be thinking, Thorne," I said, still hoping that we were wrong about Pierce, though he did seem to be the most likely informant.

"The expression on his face makes me think that he wants to kill the two of us."

I sighed in frustration. "I'm not completely convinced, but I will keep my guard up." I tried to put the question of Pierce's innocence out of my mind for the time being and turned my eyes to the young Warrior I'd just healed with the serum. "What about Brock? I feel confident he is on your side."

Thorne snorted. "Since you opened my eyes to this betrayal and trade between Peton and Wolfe, I have been suspecting everyone … including Gunter!"

I turned to him and placed my hand on his arm. "We don't know anything for sure. All Two said was that there was an informant. Maybe the informant doesn't know that the General is an enemy? Perhaps the true traitor is the person who's been in charge of Peton's trade with other clans?"

Thorne scoffed and tousled his hair again. "That would be me and the Elders."

"Okay … well, are you the traitor?" He snorted at my attempt to tease him. "No? Well, I'm not the traitor either, so that's two people that are not on the list of suspects."

Thorne's lips twitched in amusement and I found myself smiling up at him. He cupped my face in his hands, and his blue eyes glittered from the fire that was still blazing in the middle of the camp.

"You are a barrel of laughs, woman. I would like to believe that none of these Warriors would put another's life in jeopardy."

"So you're not convinced it's Pierce, either?"

Thorne pinched his lips together, then said, "I don't *want* to believe it's him."

After all of our discussions about Pierce's possible guilt, his response astonished me. "Why not?"

"Hawke raised him as his son," he explained quietly. "And I trust Hawke more than my own father."

"A person's upbringing doesn't always account for how they turn out."

"Yes, I'm a prime example of that," Thorne muttered to himself. "I truly hope it isn't any of these men."

"Me too." I ran my hands up his arms, trailing my fingers over the thorn tattoos.

"We need to get going. You will ride with me." He dropped his hands as abruptly as he spoke and turned for his mount.

I stared after him, anxious and excited about moving on to Peton; to my future. And I was even more excited about riding my first horse. In Terran, we learned in our history classes about people who used to ride horses during wartime, to travel to different clans, and even for recreation at times. That was before the fences were constructed for our protection. Our teachers had said most of the horses were killed by raiding clans and the rest were killed for food. Since leaving Terran, I wasn't sure what to believe, but it didn't matter now. Where I was going, there would be horses! Maybe Thorne would even teach me to ride one on my own. The thought of it made my heart quicken.

The familiar tingle on the back of my neck interrupted my thoughts. Instinctively, I reached for my pistol, forgetting that I'd lost it in the river when I'd fallen in earlier. I searched the soon-to-be-empty camp but saw nothing in the darkness.

Someone was watching me. I scanned the woods again, looking for signs of anything that could be a danger. The bustle of packing behind me was the only noise I heard. Turning back to the Warriors, I caught Pierce staring at me again. His glare was unnerving, especially considering that I'd been sensing a threat. Was it the soldiers I was sensing or was Pierce the danger now? I was quickly losing all confidence in my first reaction to Pierce. Could I have misunderstood his warning yesterday afternoon? Maybe he *was* Thorne's betrayer, because at this moment Pierce looked ready to kill me.

Before making my way over to Thorne, I sought out Archer who was crouched down, cleaning some rifles by the supply wagon. According to Thorne, he was the man I needed to talk to about weapons.

"Archer?" I asked tentatively.

He looked up from his work, but his hands continued. "That's me," he grinned. "It seems we owe you some thanks for helping our friend."

His friendly manner made me nervous. I wasn't expecting it.

I waved my hand in dismissal and replied, "You don't owe me anything."

"Well, I think we were all a little troubled by Thorne's attachment to you, but -"

"I would have done it anyway," I interrupted.

Once Archer had packed the weapons away in the cart, he turned and gave me the once-over. His intelligent eyes probably didn't miss much.

"What can I help you with?" he finally asked. "I assume you came to talk to me for a reason?"

"I lost my pistol," I said. "I wondered if I could get a replacement."

I expected to see a smug look in his eyes. It would be just like a man to lord his superiority over a woman, but surprisingly his eyes lit up and turned to the cart. He rummaged through the supplies and then pulled out three pistols.

He grinned like a mischievous boy. "Which one would you like?"

Archer convinced me to take two of the pistols and gave me a rifle, too. Now that I was armed, I strode over to the horses to find Thorne. The tingle in my neck was a constant reminder of some unknown danger. Whether it was a threat from one of the Warriors or from the General remained to be seen.

Thorne glanced at the rifle slung over my shoulder. "Packing some heat, are we?"

"We need to leave," I whispered, glancing back over my shoulder. Pierce was working with Archer, packing the rest of the supplies onto the wagon and loading weapons with ammunition. He wasn't staring at me but it didn't lessen my doubts about him. "I feel like we're in danger," I whispered.

"We are leaving now," he said, taking the rifle from my shoulder and strapping it to his stallion's saddle. It would be easy to access if we needed it.

"Thorne, will you have someone watching behind us?"

"Pierce is riding with Archer in the wagon and Gunter will ride behind them," he assured me. "Gunter will watch our backs."

He grabbed his horse's reigns and mounted in one fluid motion. The horse danced in place for a moment, but Thorne quickly gained control. He held out his hand to me. Having never been on a horse, I hesitated.

"Take my hand. I'll pull you up to sit in front of me," he instructed.

I bit my lip and stared apprehensively at his mount. He wasn't the meek and playful animal I had met two days ago. His front hoof dug into the ground impatiently and his powerful neck bobbed up and down, as if he understood the urgency as well.

"I don't know how to ride," I admitted.

"I know. Do you trust me?"

They were the same words he'd said to me in my dream last night. I smiled and took the hand he'd extended to me. Without any effort at all, he lifted me up into the saddle. He took the reins in one hand and wrapped his other arm around my waist, pulling me snug against his chest. Was it just a day ago that I was afraid to be this close to another person?

"Relax," he murmured, his lips brushing the back of my neck.

I was beginning to think he did that to me on purpose, just to make me shiver.

"That's going to be difficult," I said, mentally scolding myself. I shouldn't feel nervous when sitting close to him.

"Because of my horse or because of me?"

"Both," I admitted.

He chuckled softly in my ear and placed a feather-light kiss on my exposed neck, sending even more chills down my spine. The strong body of his horse began moving at a steady gait. "Do not worry, little warrior. We will be home soon."

Thorne led the way. With two of their horses killed in the fight, Brock was riding shotgun with Max on the captive's cart, while Pierce and Archer followed in the supply cart. Gunter rode the other horse, trailing behind everyone.

If the danger was someone or something other than Pierce, I had no idea what it could be. More soldiers? It seemed unlikely that Two could have had time to gather more men from the compound. I glanced around once more, looking for signs of any danger; the glint of moonlight on a rifle or the yellow eyes of a Saber. But there was nothing in the darkness.

It seemed difficult to believe that it could be Sabers. I hadn't seen any in weeks and their den was far from here, closer to the compound. My blood could have attracted them to us, but the rain should have washed all traces of the scent away. Night Howlers were always a threat as well, but there were no cries filling the skies tonight.

Whatever was out there, it wasn't good. My neck was still tingling and that meant something was coming.

32
Thorne

I had been traveling this road for many years and I had never had such an ominous feeling. Usually the trip back to Peton was more lively and victorious. The last hunt, the Warriors fell into singing crude songs that they had learned from Peton's taverns. Now, the ever-present threat of General Wolfe seemed to taint the air around us, choking us.

Ravyn had been tense in my arms ever since we had left the campsite hours ago. Every now and then I caught her rubbing her tattoo and then peering through the tangle of shrubs and trees that had grown wild around the dirt path we were following.

"I have been watching our surroundings," I murmured. "I see nothing in the shadows."

"You're sure?"

I gave her a reassuring squeeze. "What has you worried, little warrior?"

"I just … have a feeling," she mumbled slowly. "Like someone or something is out there."

"Why do you think that?"

She nervously cleared her throat. "My neck tingled."

She glanced at me out of the corner of her eye, as if she were waiting for me to ridicule her. Knowing she was already extraordinary made the strange comment easier to swallow. Ravyn never rambled about ridiculous things like other women, and she would not reveal something so odd if it were not important.

"And?"

"My neck always tingles when there's danger coming." She took a deep breath and covered her tattoo again. "Ever since General Wolfe branded me, it's like the ink in my skin is warning me that he's close. I felt it back at the camp."

"Do you feel it now?"

"No."

Her answer surprised me. "Do you think the danger has passed then?"

"I don't know," she said as an apology, covering her face with her hand. "I'm just useless. The General has a habit of being full of surprises, none of them good. There's no telling what he'll do next."

She placed a hand on top of mine and I laced our fingers together at her waist. I welcomed the touch but it concerned me that Ravyn was so anxious.

"You're usually calm and collected when danger is lurking about," I remarked.

"I worry about more than just myself now," she said, squeezing my fingers.

"Whatever is out there, we will face it together."

For the first time in my life, I was not looking forward to the excitement of a battle. I wished that we were at my mountain home, out of danger instead of waiting for it to catch us. Keeping Ravyn safe had become the most important thing to me. Was it possible that merely a week ago I had scoffed at the notion of having a wife? Or of anything being more important than my position as commander?

After silently signaling the Warriors to have their weapons at the ready, I gave my stallion a nudge to quicken his pace. Unfortunately, we would never make it to Peton at a gallop. The wagons would fall apart on the road and the noise would alert whoever was hunting us. It was better to remain quiet and vigilant.

"Tell me something about your life, Thorne," Ravyn said, interrupting my thoughts. She was resting her head against my chest, her fingers still entwined with mine, and staring out into the dark forest.

"What about my life?" I asked quietly.

"Anything," she said. "I could use a distraction." She peered over her shoulder at me, turquoise eyes twinkling every time a hint of moonlight peeked through the foliage.

"I am not a good story-teller," I confessed.

"I don't mind." Then she suggested, "Tell me how you and Gunter became friends."

"Gunter and I grew up together as boys. We're the same age. Our families lived next door to each other before my father took his place as an Elder."

"Were your families close friends?"

"I thought so when we were younger, but now that I'm older I do not think so," I recalled. "My father was always at the Council Hall. Gunter's father was a wood-worker and always around so he looked out for me and my sisters. He died a few years ago."

I thought back to my life with my family, trying to picture my father at home, but I could only remember his absence. My step-mother and Kemena were the ones who had stayed at home, making sure that my sisters were brought up properly. I was at the Warriors' barracks and the training grounds, trailing after Commander Hawke.

"Father was busy even before he became an Elder of the clan. My step-mother mostly took care of my sisters … until Lenna was born."

"How old were you when she died?"

"Kemena and I were children when *our* mother died," I explained. "Father remarried and Tallon was born soon after. Several years later, my step-mother died giving birth to Lenna. Kemena was fifteen years of age at that time, I was eleven, and Tallon seven."

"What happened to your sisters after your step-mother died? Who took care of them?"

"Kemena, since she was the oldest. Gunter and I had already begun our training to become Warriors. With our step-mother gone, and father off at the Council building most of the time, I immersed myself in my training. Commander Hawke told me once that he'd never seen anyone advance so quickly at such a young age. He and Gunter's father became my biggest supporters during that time. I was determined to make something of myself even though my father didn't approve."

"Why wouldn't he approve?" Ravyn asked. "Being a Warrior is a prestigious position, isn't it?"

I shrugged. "He wanted me to be a politician, like him. He hates that I don't want to follow in his footsteps. Gunter is the ambitious one."

"I see," she said with a quiet giggle. "You're not ambitious at all, challenging for commander at eighteen years old."

I chuckled at her teasing. Maybe it was ambitious, but it would never be good enough in my father's eyes.

"You said Kemena is a healer in your village?" Ravyn inquired, quickly changing the topic. "How did she manage it while taking care of your sisters?"

"Healers begin studying at the age of sixteen usually, but Kemena decided to wait. She was only fifteen when our step-mother died and had too much responsibility with Lenna. I'll be forever grateful to her. Once Lenna turned four, Kemena was able to begin her training. Lenna was a little more independent and Tallon was older, better able to help out with our youngest sister."

"I wish I knew more of healing, other than what my own body can do," Ravyn remarked. "Perhaps she could teach me?"

"She would enjoy passing on her wisdom. She's the best in Peton along with her husband, Aaron."

I pinched my lips together and felt my face and neck heating up. I had never been one to chatter on or share things except with Gunter. He had been my only friend for a long time. For some reason, Ravyn brought out this new side of me. I wanted her to know me and my family. Hopefully, she would come to care for them as much as she seemed to care for me.

"Please don't stop," Ravyn said, interrupting my thoughts. "I like hearing about your family. It's helping me relax."

I peered through the trees for any sign of soldiers, then continued on.

"Kemena has always been the responsible one. She is not a Warrior, but she is tenacious when it comes to protecting the people she cares about. She honors our family well. Lenna will be much like her." I let out a frustrated sigh. "And then there is Tallon. She is fifteen now, and I do not know what to do with her most of the time."

Ravyn chuckled softly. "What do you mean? She's a Warrior, you said. What's wrong with her?"

"She is headstrong, argumentative, and stubborn … completely undisciplined. She's skilled, I will admit that. But she is willful and constantly trying my patience."

Ravyn giggled softly. "Sounds familiar."

I shook my head. "You and Tallon are nothing alike."

She glared at me over her shoulder. "I was talking about you."

"Humph."

"Headstrong, argumentative, *and* stubborn?"

"Perhaps," I reasoned. "But I am not undisciplined."

"With you and Kemena as her older siblings, I doubt she's as undisciplined as you think."

"You have not met her. When you do, you will understand."

"Maybe you're right but, having had a sister, I know how easy it can be to compare the strengths and weaknesses of siblings. That was one of the things that had made me feel so alone in Terran. People were constantly talking about how beautiful and well-mannered Camellia was. Even my own father would brag about her right in front of me. He acted as if I wasn't there."

The way her family had treated her had my teeth grinding again. My own father was not around but at least he did not criticize me or disparage my achievements to other citizens. If anything, he encouraged my efforts because it made him look good.

"You are her older brother, Thorne. You are a strong Warrior and commander. That has to be complicated for you both," she said perceptively. "I'm betting she feels like she has a lot to live up to with a legacy like that. She has much to prove, to you and to the clan."

"I never thought of it this way," I admitted.

"And I didn't have that obstacle when I was training. I had nothing to prove to anyone – only myself. I also started training at an earlier age. How old was she when you allowed her to begin?"

"Females cannot begin training until they are thirteen," he explained.

"You see?" Ravyn pointed out. "I had a three-year head start. She probably still has a lot to learn. She's lucky to have such a gifted and dependable person to teach her."

She turned her face up to me and kissed me softly. "I have full confidence she will be a better Warrior because she has you."

I was struck speechless by her perspective. I had never looked at Tallon in that light. She was very skilled for her age and training level. Perhaps she should be given more opportunities to prove herself. Commander Hawke had done the same for me, Gunter, and Pierce. Once we returned, I decided I would work on remedying the situation.

"What about your tattoos?" she inquired, brushing her fingers along my forearms.

"What about them?"

"Does every Warrior have tattoos that represent their own name?"

"No," I said, grinning. "I got them as an act of rebellion. Hawke, the commander before me, has one; a huge hawk spread across his back and shoulder blades. My father disapproved of them. I got mine just to defy him."

"Oh, Thorne, you didn't," Ravyn teased.

"I wanted to be like him. Hawke, that is. Father didn't speak to me for weeks when he discovered what I had done."

"I'm not condoning your rebellion, but I'm glad that you got them. They suit you."

After a few minutes of silence, I suggested that Ravyn get some sleep. I was accustomed to just a few hours of sleep at night, but I was not sure if she was. She seemed to be keeping up with me, but I did not want her strength to wane if we encountered more soldiers.

Ravyn shifted in my arms and rested her head back on my shoulder. "I don't like to sleep," she whispered, staring up at the night sky. "If I close my eyes, I'll have nightmares."

I wanted to insist that she try to rest, but it was Ravyn I was dealing with. I could not make her do anything she did not want to do. I bit my tongue for once and continued to lead the caravan toward Peton.

Dawn was finally approaching. With every step my horse took, I had expected to hear Ravyn raise an alarm, but she remained silent and watchful. I could not speak for the other Warriors, but I was certainly breathing easier. The ride out of the Old Sequoia Valley had everyone on edge. There had been no sign of the soldiers or any other threats, and we had been moving so quietly, I felt positive we would have heard something approaching. I scanned the trees for danger countless times, even upon arriving into the outer rim of the Old Sequoia Valley. There had been nothing. The Warriors from decades before had deemed this outer rim of the Valley a safe zone because they had never spotted Sabers or barbarians so far out. The forest was thinner, the trees smaller, leaving fewer places to hide or stalk prey. In the grassy fields that led to Peton, one could only crouch down in the tall grass. It was not ideal for an attack. Surely, whatever Ravyn had felt, whatever was out there, would have attacked by now.

Rays of light streamed through the trees around us from the rising sun, giving the forest a friendlier feel. The trees here were not giant sequoias like those in the deepest parts of the forest. These had leaves that had turned beautiful shades of yellows, reds, and oranges, showing the change in the seasons. The path was lined with them, their branches hanging low, creating an archway for us. We were halfway through autumn and it would only be a few more weeks before the first snow fell on Mount Asa.

"These trees are lovely," Ravyn said with an admiring gaze.

"They are," I agreed. "Many are fruit trees. Apples, peaches, and cherries, mostly." I pointed out a few of them as we passed by.

"I've never seen leaves this brightly colored before," she said in wonder. Her eyes were wide, taking in the incredible array of colors.

"It is my favorite time of year. The fruits are harvested, which means I do not have to eat as much seaweed."

Ravyn giggled and then reached out with both hands to graze her fingers through the leaves hanging over us. The birch trees were dazzling shades of pure sunshine, and the maples were clothed with scarlet flames. Her excitement and the smile on her upturned face thrilled me.

"They are so beautiful, Thorne."

It was not the trees I found beautiful. She was even more stunning now that she was in the light of day. The black tendrils around her face had dried into corkscrew curls framing her high cheekbones. Her eyes sparkled brightly, like the choppy waves of the Fairuza Sea in the early morning sunrise. The urge to stare at her was overwhelming.

The path wound its way through the last of the trees. The prairie spread for miles with green grass and clover, waving carelessly with the breeze. Looming before us was Peton's rocky mountain range. Only a small hill obstructed our view of Peton, so I gave my stallion a kick and trotted ahead of the other Warriors. We reached the top of the rise, just past the line of trees into the plain, and there in the distance was our grand city.

The moment was lost when Ravyn stiffened against me and gasped. My stomach dropped as she slapped her hand to her neck.

Instinctively, I turned my stallion to look back at the trailing Warriors, who had just left the shelter of the woods, and I knew from Ravyn's expression that we were all about to be ambushed.

33
Ravyn

The second I felt it, I jumped from the saddle and snatched up one of the rifles from where Thorne had tied it down.

"Wait!" Thorne snapped at me. He hopped down and grabbed his weapons as well. Then he slapped the rump of his horse, sending him running toward Peton.

"What did you do that for?" I asked.

"The Warriors waiting for our return will see it as a signal for help."

Thorne shouted warnings to his men as we moved toward them. They were sitting ducks now that they were out in the open, just beyond the trees. There was nowhere for them to take cover, no safe place to go.

"Can you sense what is coming?" he asked as we ran.

"It's only ever been soldiers," I said. "But we've killed so many. I wouldn't think …"

And then I saw it.

"Stop!" I grabbed Thorne's arm and skidded to a halt in the grass.

A lone Yellow-Eyed Saber prowled out from behind a line of fruit trees. Its gray and black fur was sleek along its muscled, feline body. Sharp claws extended from each paw and the deadly canines that hung down well below its lower jaw glimmered with the cat's saliva. It was ready to taste its prey.

The beast stalked us low to the ground, taking slow measuring steps and sniffing, searching. The fur on its back bristled as it drew closer.

"I need to leave," I whispered to Thorne, keeping my eyes locked on the Saber. A feeling of dread swept through me. "That beast is hunting me."

"You don't know that," Thorne argued, gripping my arm, forcing me to stay. "Sabers could have been hunting us all along."

Before I could answer, the Saber's feral eyes shifted to us. It had completely dismissed the other Warriors who were a much closer target. The yellow, hypnotizing eyes stared at me for another heartbeat, then it snarled and sprung out of the grass.

The Warriors fired their rifles as the giant cat continued charging us at full speed, growling fiercely. Taking careful aim, I joined the others, squeezing out round after round. The beast's eyes gleamed and its teeth flashed a deadly grin. Peering down the barrel of the rifle, I took a deep breath and fired one last shot. With an ear-splitting howl, the Saber slid to the ground not five feet from us. There was no telling how many bullets it had taken to bring it down.

Before my knees could buckle from the close call, Thorne seized my arm and dragged me back to the supply cart where the other Warriors were waiting. The other cart was gone.

Looking around at each of the men, Thorne shouted, "*Where is Gunter?*"

Brock approached us, looking disgruntled. "He took the cart of captives back to Peton."

"We tried to tell him that the exiles would be safe inside the bars," said Max, shaking his head. "But he wouldn't listen, and neither of us wanted to leave you."

I jerked my arm out of Thorne's grasp. "You all have to get out of here!" Everyone fell silent at my outburst. My voice trembled a bit when I added, "You should go, and I need to stay."

Thorne stepped closer. "How could that Saber be from the General?"

"He has my blood, Thorne." I lowered my eyes so he wouldn't see my shame. "He could have used it to lead them here."

"That doesn't mean …"

I cut my hand through the air to halt his words. "You have to trust me. He knows how terrified I am of those things. He's taunting me." I looked at each of the Warriors in turn. "Didn't you see it look at the wagons and then shift its gaze to us? To me? It was hunting me. Sabers don't usually differentiate between targets, unless they've tasted blood. You know that. It's the same -" My jaw dropped open and cold chills raced up and down my spine as I recalled how the Sabers had stalked me relentlessly for days when I was a child. That was not normal hunting behavior. Carnivores gave up and stalked other prey if they were truly hungry.

"The same as what?" Thorne asked.

I swallowed the lump in my throat and said, "It's the same way the Sabers hunted me when I first ran away from Terran. He sent them after me then, too."

The anguish on Thorne's face was like a knife through my heart. "If what you say is true – and I'm not convinced – do you really believe you could overcome them alone?"

"Better for me to die than all of us," I said, biting the inside of my lip to keep it from trembling.

"She's right about the Saber," Archer agreed, stepping forward into the charged silence. "They don't favor one target over another if they're hunting for food, but it won't matter now."

"What do you mean?" I asked him, another wave of nausea coursing through me.

Pierce, irritated as usual, spoke up. "That one was probably an Alpha. Whether it was after the woman or not, the rest of the pack won't be far behind. They'll be after us just for spilling the blood of their pack-leader."

"Right," Archer nodded. "We need to prepare, and quickly."

"No, you should get to Peton," I argued again, but no one listened.

Brock's eyes shifted from Thorne to me. "We aren't letting you stay out here alone. None of us would do that."

I heard Pierce mutter, "I might." He was immediately knocked to the ground.

Like that Saber, Thorne had pounced on him, punching him square in the jaw before anyone could stop him. With a bloody lip, Pierce rose up from the grass and the two fierce Warriors stood nose to nose, fists clenched and looking ready to kill each other.

Thankfully, Archer intervened, the voice of reason. "We don't have time for this, Pierce! Thorne!"

But Thorne's eyes were ice-cold, filled with pure hatred, and his voice was just as menacing. "You do what you like, but I will not be leaving her out here to die, Pierce. I will stand with her."

Pierce didn't back down. "So that's the way of things? You would risk your life for her. Someone you've only known a week."

"I would risk everything."

I glanced back and forth between Thorne and Pierce, hating that I had caused more friction between the two Warriors; hating the whole situation. Gunter had run back to Peton, a potential coward and Pierce was challenging his commander while we were in the midst of danger. However, Thorne was saying things to make my heart melt.

I shook my head at them. "Stop it right now! Thorne?" I pleaded with him to back down.

Finally letting the argument go, Thorne bumped Pierce's shoulder as he passed by to take his place at my side. The other

Warriors spread out on either side of Thorne and me. Then we waited. Watched.

The soft rumbling of growls began soon after, like a low hum of bees at first. Then I spotted a set of eerie yellow eyes watching us from the tree line.

"Whatever happens," Thorne whispered softly. "We will finish this together."

He cupped the nape of my neck and pressed his lips to my forehead. My throat too thick with emotion, I simply nodded and gripped my rifle a little tighter.

Then they charged. Their hind claws dug into the ground, kicking up dirt behind them. The Sabers were about a hundred feet away. There were only six of them, but that was plenty. These beasts were tough and not easily taken down if they were anything like their Alpha.

We opened fired on them. The two Sabers in the front of the pack went down first, just thirty feet past the tree line. That still left four ferocious cats, each one nearly as tall as my chest. Their sharp teeth glittered in the morning sunlight, anticipating the feeling of sinking them into our skin.

I froze in place, unable to even squeeze the trigger on my rifle. My heart raced inside my chest and my breathing quickened with dread. I was a child again, alone in the Valley, hiding from the pack of Sabers. Hungry yellow eyes searched for me as I hid inside the trunk of a tree. Their breath smelled of raw meat. Only a small boulder kept them back.

A cry from Max drew my gaze. He was one of the youngest Warriors on the hunt and had probably never faced a Saber. He'd been closest to the tree line, to my right, shooting the Sabers as they sprinted toward us. My stomach dropped as one of the beasts charged right through the bullets and pounced, sinking its deadly teeth into Max's shoulder. The rifle hit the ground and then snapped in half under the weight of the Saber's paw. I stared, horrified, as Max was pushed to the ground, screaming in agony. The young Warrior had both hands on the cat's mouth, trying to pry open its jaws.

Archer, who had been standing next to Max, turned to fire upon the beast. He kept shooting until his magazine was empty, then tossed aside the rifle and drew his dagger. While the Saber was occupied grappling with Max in the dirt, Archer jumped on his back and plunged his blade into the beast's neck from behind.

In just a few minutes, three Sabers had fallen.

I let out the breath I'd been holding, praying that Max would live.

"*Ravyn!*" Thorne shouted from over my left shoulder, startling me out of my stupor. I'd been standing paralyzed, frozen with fear while he was busy shooting the Sabers. The bullets didn't seem to be causing much damage. General Wolfe had told me these animals were about six hundred pounds of pure muscle.

A Saber was closing in on me with extraordinary speed. Lowering my body into a defensive stance, I dropped my rifle and sidestepped its lunge for my throat. The beast flew past and skidded to a halt, tearing up the grass under its claws. While it struggled to change directions and pounce again, I drew my pistol and filled the Saber with bullets until I'd emptied my magazine. The beast howled as it tumbled to the ground.

It was chaos all around me, knives and claws flashing in the sunlight. Warriors circling and sidestepping the Sabers that stalked them, like a dance.

Thorne had moved away from my side while I'd fought off the Saber. I whipped my head around to find him in the melee.

Please let him be alive, I thought desperately.

I breathed a sigh of relief when I spotted him standing with Brock against one of the two remaining Sabers. Pierce was facing the other about ten feet away from Brock and Thorne.

The cat was bleeding from several wounds already but didn't look hindered by the blood-loss or the pain. Thorne and Brock lunged and twisted, staying just out of reach of the Saber's jaws and sharp claws. The cat growled and jumped at Thorne, but he was already rolling to the side through the grass, avoiding the Saber's bite. The Saber dug its claws into the dirt and grass, churning it up as it scrambled back around to attack again.

While Thorne was rising to his feet, his back to the forest, I glimpsed movement over his shoulder. Another Yellow-eyed Saber – slightly smaller, but just as deadly – had lagged behind the pack and was padding stealthily through the grass toward Thorne, who was the closest prey. Its golden eyes sparkled in the morning light and it's tongue flicked up around its canines, as if it could taste Thorne's flesh already.

I tried to call out to him, but only a whimper got past the lump in my throat. None of the other Warriors were aware of the lone beast prowling closer to their commander. Brock and Thorne were focused on the Saber they fought with. Archer was too far away, busy tending to Max's wounds by the wagon. Pierce was a few feet away, but he was facing another of the beasts on his own.

Quickly reloading my pistol, I started sprinting toward the lone Saber. Once I was certain I wouldn't hit Thorne, I fired at the beast. My bullets seemed to do nothing but singe its hide. The cat roared and flinched from the wounds, but my efforts merely turned its attention, and not toward me. The Saber's eyes had turned to Pierce.

I raced toward the gray beast, squeezing the trigger over and over in hopes that one of the bullets would kill it, but my magazine emptied too soon. Pierce was focused on the Saber he faced, dodging swipes from vicious claws and slashing back with his daggers. He had no idea he was about to be slain. The prowling cat bristled up and flew out of the grass. With red-hot adrenaline coursing through me, I ran faster. I ditched my pistol and threw myself in its path, hoping to at least knock it off course. The collision with the Saber knocked the breath out of me. We rolled to the ground in a wild heap, the beast snarling and slashing at me. Its claws raked through my clothes even as I held back its powerful jaws with my hands. The Saber snapped at me again and again, going for my throat.

On my back, I kicked out with both feet against the cat's torso. With a growl, it was sent flailing through the air, but not far. I had only seconds to recover. I reached for the dagger still in my boot; my last hope before I was mauled to death. That was when I felt the second pistol that I'd forgotten about, holstered at my thigh.

As I lay bleeding on the ground, I watched the Saber roll smoothly to its feet and flash its fangs at me. I drew my pistol and fired until the Saber was a dead heap beside me on the grass.

Blood seeped from my body as I lay there, gasping for breath, but frozen with fear at who I'd lost in the fray. There were no sounds around me except for those blasted cicadas. They seemed to know that the danger had passed and had started their singing again. The grass tickled my face and the clouds in the sky looked like wisps of pink and purple cotton from the morning sunrise.

Suddenly Pierce was there, standing over me with only a few scratches on his arms and chest, with a befuddled expression on his face. I'd only ever seen him glare at me, so I didn't know what to make of it.

Silently, he crouched to inspect my wounds, lifting the shreds of my shirt to expose the worst of them. There was no avoiding discovery as he watched the deep gash across my ribs tightened up and close. His eyes, full of wonder, met mine, but his response was completely unexpected.

"So you're the one."

I didn't have a chance to question him. When Brock cried out Thorne's name, my heart stopped. Pierce helped me to my feet, and we ran to join the other Warriors. Archer was still crouched over Max by the supply wagon. He was bandaging up Max's shoulder and what must have been a deep gash to the leg. Thirty feet away from the wagon, Brock was on his knees in the grass, a dead Saber lying motionless behind him. And Thorne was before him bleeding from several places on his lifeless body.

"Brock, what happened?" I wailed, my voice thick with fear. I had to remain calm. I could fix him. No matter what had happened, I could heal him.

Brock's fist was pressed against his mouth as if to keep his pain locked inside him. Blood was pooling at Thorne's belly. I reached for his neck, feeling for a pulse, and then leaned down to feel his breath on my cheek.

"Is he dead?" There was concern in Pierce's voice for once. He knelt down at my side.

The very slow thumping of blood could still be heard. Tears filled my eyes and spilled down my cheeks at the sight of him so hurt. I took a slow breath, willing myself not to fall apart.

My voice shook when I replied, "No, he's alive, but his pulse is weak."

Archer joined us. "Max should live. His shoulder is a bit mangled and he took a claw to the leg, but I've stopped the bleeding."

I swallowed my fears and cut away Thorne's ragged shirt to see the damage. When I saw the gaping wound across the soft part of his belly, my hands began to tremble. Muscle and intestines were exposed and blood was leaving his body at a rapid pace.

"He saved me," Brock explained to no one in particular as we stared at the horrible sight. "We had him. It should have been easy. But I was careless." He peered up at me, his eyes full of grief. "When you started shooting at that last Saber that snuck out of the forest, I got distracted. I took my eyes off the Saber we were fighting. It was just for a second, but … the Saber … he lunged at me and Thorne blocked him. He saved me, and now he's dying."

"No!" I yelled tenaciously. "He will not die! Where is my bag, the one with the medicine?" I jumped up immediately to go and get it, but I hit my knees again and the blood drained from my face when I realized what had been done.

"He tied it to his horse, didn't he?" Archer said sorrowfully. "I saw him send his mount away to Peton. It's long gone."

I was going to fail him. If I didn't do something, Thorne was going to die.

"What do I do? What do I do?" I whispered over and over again to myself.

I felt a hand on my shoulder. "Ravyn," Pierce said sadly. "There's nothing you can do. You have to let him go."

I shook my head, my eyes still on Thorne. "There's one thing I can try."

Leaning down over my warrior, I cradled his face in my hands and placed my forehead on his.

"Thorne," I whispered so only he could hear. "I don't know if this will work, but I have to try. I can't let you die." I ran my fingers through his blonde curls and down his cheek. "Please … please forgive me." My body trembled from the sobs that I couldn't keep inside anymore. "Please, Thorne," I begged. "Please just live."

I kissed him gently and then wiped the tears from my face with the back of my hand. The men's eyes grew wide when I drew my blade and I sliced my own skin at the wrist.

"What are you doing?" Archer shouted in disbelief.

Pierce stopped him from interfering with a hand to his shoulder. "She's trying to save his life."

In that moment, I didn't care that Pierce knew about me. Maybe he *was* the General's informant, but at least he was allowing me this last gift. A chance to save Thorne.

"Have you ever done it like this before?" Brock asked me quietly.

"No," I whispered to them through trembling lips. "He could still die."

The men hovered over me as I raised my arm and held my wrist steady over his open belly. I closed my eyes and let my blood trickle out of my body and fall into his. None of us, not even Pierce, knew what this might do to Thorne. The General had tried this method on many soldiers. There were very few positive outcomes from those experiments, but Thorne would die if I did nothing. The cut on my wrist soon closed over again and the flow of blood stopped. That was all that could be done.

"We must bandage him up to stop the rest of the bleeding," I ordered. Brock jumped up and ran to the wagon at my request. I turned back to Pierce. "We'll know very soon if it doesn't work, but ... but it'll be quicker than the alternative."

Suddenly, Pierce raised his head, turning his eyes toward Peton.

Archer was the first to notice Pierce's sudden movement. "What is it?"

"They're coming." Pierce watched the meadow intently, then he turned to the other Warriors and shouted, "Get Max and Thorne into the wagon. Quickly!"

Then I heard it too; the sound of hooves thundering across the plain. Either they had seen Thorne's horse or Gunter must have warned them. They would be here in minutes and still would have been too late to aid us and spare Thorne his injury.

Archer and Brock reacted to Pierce's command immediately. When Brock had finished wrapping Thorne's abdomen, the two Warriors lifted their commander gently from the ground and carried him to the wagon. They started toward Max next.

Pierce gripped my upper arm, pulled me to my feet and hissed, "You need to flee."

"What?" I gaped at him, tears still brimming in my eyes. The urgency in his tone startled me.

"Gunter has likely sent those Warriors back and probably told them about you." Pierce narrowed his eyes at me. "Did he know about your gift?"

My stomach clenched in fear as I peered over my shoulder, toward Peton.

"Those men will take you into custody, if not for your gift, then for what has been done here. You *cannot* be seen. The Elders must not capture you."

I stared back at Pierce's intense blue eyes and then nodded in understanding. Their Elders must be in league with General Wolfe and he somehow knew about it. It was clear that Pierce didn't trust the Elders or Gunter. If I stayed, I would put myself and these Warriors in even more danger than before.

I wiped my nose and eyes to clear away the remaining tears. "Then I will go."

Pierce guided me to the wagon. "Archer!" he shouted. "She needs food and ammunition."

While Brock was making Thorne comfortable, Archer started rummaging through the supplies in the wagon.

"What will you tell them?" I asked Archer.

"We will come up with something," Archer said with a grim smile, handing me a bag stuffed full with food, water and weapons. "We'll make sure that Thorne is taken care of by his sister, Kemena. She is our clan's finest healer."

Pierce took hold of my wrist and started dragging me toward the forest but I twisted my arm out of his grasp. I rushed back to the wagon, brushing past Archer on the way. Brock stepped down out of the cart to give me room to see Thorne one last time. I climbed up into the cart and crawled on hands and knees to Thorne's side. Careful of his wounds, I leaned over and kissed his soft lips.

"You must hurry," Pierce called out to me.

I jumped down from the wagon and, clutching the bag to my chest, turned and marched back to the forest.

"Where will you go?" I heard Archer ask from behind me.

I pivoted around to face the Warriors and shook my head. "I don't know yet, but I swear to you, I won't stop until the General and all his soldiers are dead." I gave each of the three men stern looks in turn, Pierce last of all. "Now *you* swear that you'll do everything in your power to see that Thorne lives."

Pierce placed a fist over his heart in pledge. "If what you have done works, then I swear it."

"You must find that bag of syringes," I added, taking a few steps back toward the Valley. "The Elders must not get their hands on that medicine. They cannot even know that you have it. Keep it hidden and safe."

"We will get it back," he agreed. Brock and Archer both nodded, though they didn't seem to understand the importance as Pierce and I did.

Once I'd turned my back on them to flee into the forest again, Brock called out to me. "And what do we tell the commander … when he wakes up?"

I froze in place, my eyes fixed on the trees. My heart ached inside my chest. What could I say? That I would come back or that he should wait for me?

No, I couldn't tell him those things.

I glanced over my shoulder at each of the Warriors, then toward the wagon where Thorne rested. My lips trembled and I felt warm tears slip down my cheeks again. Without a word, I turned away again and sprinted back into the Old Sequoia Valley. My heart had shattered to pieces again and my eyes were blinded by my own tears. Even when I felt someone following me, I flew through the brush and trees until I had rid myself of the desperate need to return to the man I loved.

34
Thorne

All sense of time was lost in the dark place. I felt as if my body had been pulled into a great abyss, dragged there by hundreds of icy fingers gripping my flesh. For a moment, I almost gave in to them.

Then the most beautiful voice whispered in my ear. It was the sound of an angel, driving away the fear. Her voice was sad as she spoke to me, begging me sweetly to live. How could I refuse an angel?

Though I struggled, I could not free my body from the cold bindings that held me prisoner. The angel saw my hopeless fight and poured life from her own radiant spirit into mine. Warmth began to fill my belly and, from there, it spread life to all parts of my body.

The icy fingers began to fall away from me one by one …

35
Ravyn

I'd felt someone following me for a while. It was probably Two, tracking me with that noser of his. I veered through the forest, confusing my tracks until I found a suitable tree to hide in and wait for him. He was not the boy I once knew. Avoiding him forever was not the answer, either. It was time to face him and end things. Then I could finally make my way to the coast as I'd been longing to do since my escape. I'd build a home overlooking the great expanse of blue that I'd only ever heard about. It didn't even have to be as grand as the few homes I'd glimpsed when we overlooked Peton. Nothing elaborate, but it would be mine. Maybe I would be happy. Maybe I could finally put all the pieces of my heart back together.

I had done it after Kieron. I could do it again with Thorne.

Smacking myself in the forehead, I heaved a sigh of frustration. "Four days," I silently mouthed. "You only knew him four days."

The familiar stomping of boots drew me back to the present. They were getting closer. Squatting on the limb, not fifteen feet in the air, I pressed the rifle to my shoulder. One quick shot was all I would get.

The boot-steps halted. I held my breath, waiting for him to reveal his position.

"Don't shoot, Ravyn."

That voice. I wasn't expecting to hear it again. "Kaelem," I whispered to myself.

"That's right," he announced.

I frowned, narrowing my eyes. Either his hearing was extraordinary or I was right in thinking …

"Yes, you guessed what I could do back in Linwood. It was how I tracked you. You have very loud thoughts … about cottages on the beach."

"Come into the open, where I can see you," I demanded, keeping my finger on the trigger. If he stepped out with that crossbow firing, I would be ready.

Kaelem edged around the trunk of a tree, hands lifted in a gesture of peace, his crossbow slung over his back.

"Was it you that stabbed me?"

"No. It was Hagan. He … look, I'll not make excuses for him. He did what he thought was best under the circumstances. Things have gotten complicated."

"Where are your brothers then? Waiting to ambush me? Turn me into the General?" Knowing that he could read my thoughts, I reflected on every gruesome encounter I had ever had with the General so that Kaelem would see for himself.

Kaelem squeezed his eyes shut and gritted his teeth at the horrifying memories I revealed. "Stop! I saw enough the night you stayed with us." The earthy eyes I had thought so warm a few days ago now seemed troubled.

"Was it also Hagan who told the soldiers that I was in Linwood?"

Kaelem lowered his eyes, his mouth pinched in shame.

"It was you," I whispered. So Thorne had been correct. I should never have trusted them. But what of Laelynn?

"That is why I have come."

Lowering my rifle, I snorted. "Tell your brothers to come out where I can see them as well."

With his empty hands still raised, he glanced over his shoulder and signaled them with his fingers. Silently they stepped out from their respective hiding places, hands raised in surrender, like Kaelem.

"One of you is missing."

One of the twins spoke up. "Raimond."

Their miserable expressions told me everything I needed to know. He was dead.

A small part of me thought they deserved it, but no. No one deserved to have their sibling taken from them that way.

"No, you're right." Kaelem answered my thoughts again. "When we sent for the soldiers, we didn't know that Laelynn would help you escape. She was innocent. But the soldiers were angry, so one of them … a dark one …"

"Two," I whispered, a sense of dread nearly choking me.

"He took Laelynn and said we could have her back with a trade."

The lump in my throat was too much to swallow. They were going to trade me to the General. But then how did Raimond …?

"Raimond tried to stop them and was killed in the struggle."

Laelynn. The General had my friend.

"So you want me to go willingly?" I glowered down at them. "Trade my life for Laelynn's?"

"We came to beg for your help."

After throwing the rifle's strap over my shoulder, I swung down from the tree, landing lightly on my feet.

"If you knew the General, you would know he has no intention of giving her back to you alive. Even if you overpowered me and handed me over."

Kaelem paled but didn't give in to the panic I saw in his eyes. "We know. That's why we came in good faith, for your help to break her out of that place."

Fear rose up in me when I recalled the endless white halls and fluorescent lights. The place was a maze. I only knew it because I had been a prisoner there for so long.

"That's why we need your help."

I pursed my lips. His constant read on my thoughts was going to get irritating.

"I'll help you." When their shoulders sagged in relief, I stopped them. "No, I'm helping *only* because of Laelynn. She was my friend." I glared at each of them in turn. "If any of you try to double-cross me, I'll kill you."

Without waiting for a reply, I marched past them and headed west and the brothers, now only four, silently followed. This was the worst idea in the history of ideas, but I wouldn't leave my only friend to the mercies of the General. And Kaelem was right. I did know my way around the compound, but it was so risky what they were asking me to do. We'd have to plan it carefully.

And that wasn't the only danger waiting. Sabers. Howlers. Two.

I mentally closed the door on my plans for journeying to the coast. Those would have to wait. I stiffened my spine and headed deeper into the Valley to face my demons again.

ACKNOWLEDGEMENTS

First, I want to thank my mom, who has read every book I've ever written. Don't ever forget that it was you who helped me use my wild imagination to make up stories as a child. That is where all this began. Many thanks to my amazing editor, Maddy Glenn. Without you, this project would still be sitting on the shelf in hiding. My cover artist, Christian Bentulan, did a beautiful job and brought my Saber to life! My husband, Bobby Pugh, has been wonderful throughout this entire journey, never letting me give up. I am so grateful to have your unconditional love and support. I cannot forget my best friend, Michelle Armstrong, who read through this book before it went to my editor and still thought it was something special. Finally, thank you to all of you readers who took a chance on this book. I hope you enjoyed it as much as I enjoyed writing it.

ABOUT THE AUTHOR

C.R. Pugh lives with her husband and daughter just outside of Dallas, Texas. Though she has always been an avid reader with a wild imagination, she never imagined she would become a writer. Mrs. Pugh is a former teacher who enjoys long-distance running, watching crime-fighting shows on television, and playing with her daughter. Hunted in the Valley is her first novel.

Made in the USA
San Bernardino, CA
22 August 2018